SILENT DEATH

Nolan rogered up and started to move from the water, then froze. Between Sonny and him was a small wooden platform stilted a few inches above the waterline. It was too small to be a dock but would serve as a small-boat tie-off and loading pier. The big SEAL and his chief were still shoulder deep in the dark water on either side of the structure. As they waited motionless, a sentry stepped from behind a tree and out onto the platform. It was always the one you didn't see. As Engel, Nolan, and Sonny held their breath, Weimy sighted in. "I have him," Weimy whispered over the tac net, and he did.

The shot took him just over the heart on his left side, spinning him to his left and over backward toward Nolan. Nolan reached up and caught him before his body splashed the water, and eased him below the surface. Not yet dead, the guard jerked involuntarily as he inhaled water, but it did not last long. When he stopped moving, the chief released him and pushed him under the wooden pier.

Tom Clancy Presents

ACT OF VALOR

SCREENPLAY WRITTEN BY
KURT JOHNSTAD

NOVELIZATION WRITTEN BY
DICK COUCH AND
GEORGE GALDORISI

BERKLEY BOOKS, NEW YORK

THE BERKLEY PUBLISHING GROUP
Published by the Penguin Group
Penguin Group (USA) Inc.
375 Hudson Street, New York, New York 10014, USA

Penguin Group (Canada), 90 Eglinton Avenue East, Suite 700, Toronto, Ontario M4P 2Y3, Canada
(a division of Pearson Penguin Canada Inc.) • Penguin Books Ltd., 80 Strand, London WC2R 0RL,
England • Penguin Group Ireland, 25 St. Stephen's Green, Dublin 2, Ireland (a division of Penguin
Books Ltd.) • Penguin Group (Australia), 250 Camberwell Road, Camberwell, Victoria 3124, Australia
(a division of Pearson Australia Group Pty. Ltd.) • Penguin Books India Pvt. Ltd., 11 Community
Centre, Panchsheel Park, New Delhi—110 017, India • Penguin Group (NZ), 67 Apollo Drive,
Rosedale, Auckland 0632, New Zealand (a division of Pearson New Zealand Ltd.) • Penguin Books
(South Africa) (Pty.) Ltd., 24 Sturdee Avenue, Rosebank, Johannesburg 2196, South Africa

Penguin Books Ltd., Registered Offices: 80 Strand, London WC2R 0RL, England

This is a work of fiction. Names, characters, places, and incidents either are the product of the authors'
imagination or are used fictitiously, and any resemblance to actual persons, living or dead, business
establishments, events, or locales is entirely coincidental. The publisher does not have any control over
and does not assume any responsibility for author or third-party websites or their content.

TOM CLANCY PRESENTS ACT OF VALOR

A Berkley Book / published by arrangement with the authors

PUBLISHING HISTORY
Berkley premium edition / January 2012

ISBN: 978-0-425-25935-1

BERKLEY®
Berkley Books are published by The Berkley Publishing Group,
a division of Penguin Group (USA) Inc.,
375 Hudson Street, New York, New York 10014.
BERKLEY® is a registered trademark of Penguin Group (USA) Inc.
The "B" design is a trademark of Penguin Group (USA) Inc.

PRINTED IN THE UNITED STATES OF AMERICA

10 9 8 7 6 5 4 3 2 1

ALWAYS LEARNING   PEARSON

This book is dedicated to the men and women of the United States Special Operations Command, who for the last ten years, and counting, have been on continuous deployment in harm's way. Their service and their sacrifice, together with that of their sister armed services, have kept our nation safe and free from a recurrence of the events of 9/11.

The authors would like to thank their agent, John Silbersack of the Trident Media Group, who in true Navy SEAL fashion—and against heavy odds—hung in there and completed his mission to make this book a reality.

FOREWORD
by Tom Clancy

Navy SEALs are Olympic athletes that kill people for a living. But they never get to stand up on a podium at the end of the race, heads bowed in anticipation of a gold medal, while the national anthem plays overhead. They are the most special breed of Americans. They typically pass unnoticed to civilians, but are almost instantly recognizable to one another—even if they have never met before. They don't stand out, spin webs out of their wrists, or wear capes when they work. They breathe and bleed like the rest of us, but they live life differently and that's what distinguishes them.

BUD/S (Basic Underwater Demolition/SEAL) Training is perhaps the most challenging training program known to man. The dropout rate is almost 80 percent of those invited to participate, and if you're part of that roughly 20 percent who graduate, you've earned yourself a place atop my list of most respected individuals on the planet. The SEALs risk their lives protecting the freedoms and privileges too many of us take for granted. They are most deserving of our deepest and most sincere respect and thanks, yet it goes against their nature to seek appreciation or recognition. We rarely hear or read about their successes (with some rather notable exceptions), but their real or imaginary failures make front page news. The modest amount we pay these guys is most certainly not enough.

Most people are generally aware that SEALs are gifted athletes, but they are not just fighters, they are thinkers as well. I have had the privilege of getting to know several SEALs and one of the first things I noticed about them is that they're really smart. And they're really brave. They consider it a privilege to be an American citizen and are willing to put their lives on the line and do whatever is asked of them when duty calls, at any time or place. It takes a special type of individual indeed to jump out of a cargo plane, let alone into pitch black darkness in a dangerous foreign land, carrying one hundred pounds of gear while temperatures hover below zero. Fortunately their survival rate is incredibly high— and but for two incredibly disheartening helicopter crashes, this rate would be even higher.

When I first learned about the plans the SEALs had to make the *Act of Valor* movie and accompanying novelization, I immediately wanted to support the project in any and every possible way. The events in this book and movie may not always be easy to read about or watch, but it is important for us to get a glimpse into the lives of these courageous Americans, and to gain a deeper appreciation for the sacrifices they make for us.

We have an obligation to honor the SEALs and their families—not just in the event that we are fortunate enough to meet any of them one day, but by living our lives to the fullest, enjoying and preserving the liberties afforded to us because of their work.

And the next time you see one of our nation's young champions bowing for a medal at the Olympic games, while his or her tearful and joyous family looks on, perhaps you might take a moment to consider a similarly talented but entirely different set of champions, working anonymously in darkness overseas. Champions whose families go to sleep each night wondering when, or if, they will see them again.

Read the book. See the movie. If you are inspired by what you read and see, please consider joining me in making a donation to the Navy SEAL Foundation at: nswfoundation.org.

Thank you.

ONE

Lieutenant Roark Engel stood with his hands on the back of his head while Chief Dave Nolan moved around behind him, systematically running hands over his body, checking each fastening, pulling here and tugging there. Nolan finished with the main chute and stepped again to Engel's front, lifting the reserve with a jerk to check that it was securely attached to the torso harness. He cinched up the crotch straps with a violent jerk. Engel winced and staggered a bit to keep his balance but kept his hands on his head.

"Feeling a little aggressive this morning, are we, Chief?"

"Hey, Boss, just trying to keep your personal equipment intact in case you have a bad opening. You know," he continued with a grin, "I did tell Jackie that I'd look out for you. That means having your back in a firefight as well as protecting your cods in case you're upside down when your chute opens. You just may need them in the future."

Engel started to say something, then refrained. Nolan slapped him on the helmet, stepped back, and put his hands to his own helmet. Engel returned the grin, then began a jumpmaster inspection of Nolan. Engel was methodical and thorough, but not all that gentle. It was a game between them, but in the process of the game, they inspected each other thoroughly.

Once finished with Nolan, Engel then began to work down one stick of seven parachutists, Nolan the other. There were other jumpmaster-qualified SEALs in the platoon, but both Engel and Nolan liked the ritual of inspecting their men. Today was one of the rare times when the platoon would jump Hollywood, meaning they would do so without equipment, and they would jump in the daytime. This evolution was a bonus jump with no training objective or requirement. The serious airborne portion of the deployment workup, which included the night-equipment jumps and the water jumps that led into full-mission profile training, were now behind them. Indeed, all of the pre-deployment work was behind them. Their bags were packed, so to speak, which meant that their operational equipment—weapons, dive gear, parachutes, mission-support equipment, and all the rest of the necessary combat support gear that keeps a SEAL platoon in the fight while deployed—was palletized and ready for loading onto the transport aircraft. The Bandito Platoon was ready for war.

Roark Engel was the platoon officer and Dave Nolan was the platoon chief, or senior enlisted SEAL. They were the leaders for Delta Platoon, SEAL Team Seven.

The *Bandito* nickname had come about years ago during one of the platoon's trips to Baja California for off-road motorcycling in the desert. There was a cantina where they often stopped for a beer after a ride. During one of those stops, the proprietress called them the Yankee Banditos, and the name had stuck.

After the head-to-toe jumpmaster inspections were completed, Engel and Nolan led both sticks of SEALs up the ramp of the big C-130H Hercules transport. As stick or squad leaders for this jump, Engel and Nolan would be the last out. The jump and the timing of it had been carefully planned. The platoon SEALs had just reported back from their pre-deployment leave, so they had scheduled this non-equipment, daylight, low-altitude jump—a hop and pop. They all wore basic military HALO rigs, but they would not be jumping from any great height. After close to a year of training and preparation, it was time to refocus the platoon on deployment. The simplicity of a Hollywood jump would serve to ease the platoon SEALs back into their routine, with none of the stress and logistics of a night combat equipment jump, which was their norm. Most of their night combat jumps were at the front end of a three-to-five-day training mission, in which they humped for long distances with a hundred pounds of gear and slept for only an hour or two a night. This jump was just for the fun of it—for the brotherhood.

The big Hercules spun up its four Allison T-56-A-16 turboprop engines, neatly pirouetted upon the tarmac, and headed for the downwind threshold of the main runway at Naval Air Station North Island. The Air Force pilot brought the power up to takeoff power, and they rumbled down the concrete toward the Pacific Ocean. The bird needed just a third of the runway before it rotated and lifted gently into the air. They gained altitude, turned south then east, crossing Coronado and heading for the SEAL drop zone at Otay Mesa.

Engel ran his gaze slowly over the SEALs seated across the sterile metal canyon that was the bay of the 130. Each was equal measure friend, brother, and responsibility. It caused him a flashing moment of guilt to realize that he knew each of these men and the intimacies of their personal and professional lives in far more detail than that of his own biological brothers. Yet he was quick to remind himself that these men were brothers by choice; they shared a passion for their SEAL calling and for going into harm's way in the service of their nation. As his gaze continued to pass man to man, his mind flashed back on their time together, like some sort of sports highlight film—from the recurring, lighthearted moments during the long training periods, which were a way of life with Navy SEALs, to the life-and-death episodes of previous deployments. There was no question that Engel loved each of these men. SEALs have a saying for this: brothers by different mothers. At the end of the stick across from him was his platoon chief. Nolan winked, and both of them broke into broad smiles of understanding. This was what it was all about. It was not about the jump or the training or the enemies of their nation they would soon engage—those insurgents and terrorists who were certainly worthy of their attention. This was about the brotherhood and what they all knew was the privilege of going to war as a team.

We few, we blessed few, Engel thought as he unclipped his seat belt and made his way up to the flight deck. Without consultation, Nolan also rose and headed aft.

The pilot and copilot were mirror images in flight suits, squadron patches, ball caps, headphones, and aviator sunglasses. "Thanks for coming out on a Saturday for a lift to the DZ, guys," Engel shouted over the roar of the engines.

It was only when the pilot, a major, turned around that Engel realized that he was a she. "Not a problem, Lieutenant. Saturday's as fine a day as any to jump out of a perfectly good airplane. Understand that you're going overseas soon."

"That's right, ma'am. We deploy to WESTPAC a week from today."

"Good luck on the drop and the deployment."

Engel tossed her a salute and headed back to the cluster of jumpers seated in the middle of the aircraft. He did not buckle in because they would soon be at altitude near the Otay drop zone. They'd jump at 12,500 feet— the legal limit for a free-fall parachute jump without oxygen. Even in training, most of their jumps were well above 20,000 feet. Chief Nolan was back talking to the aircraft loadmaster and another SEAL who would serve as jumpmaster for the drop. Nolan thanked them both for spending part of their Saturday to support the jump. He returned to his seat and, once again, looked across at his platoon officer. Engel now had his head tipped back against the canvas webbing that served as a backrest for the bench seating along the fuselage. His eyes were closed, and his features were a mask of serenity. This deployment would mark Nolan's ninth rotation and his third as the Bandito Platoon chief. It was Roark Engel's third with the platoon, and probably his last. He was a senior lieutenant and in the zone for lieutenant commander. Time for him to move on to a more senior position. Roark Engel was, in Nolan's opinion, the best officer he'd encountered in the Teams, and he'd known a few good ones.

What word, Nolan thought, *best describes this lieutenant?* Understatement—*that's it; he's understated. He doesn't look all that big at six feet and 190 pounds. And that round baby face makes him seem soft or even sedentary. He looks like an attorney or a financial consultant. But when it comes to SEAL work, he's a bull. He can carry his load and part of someone else's farther and faster than anyone in the platoon. And he's quick, as the rest of us learned during a pickup soccer game when he was new to the platoon. He could go around any of them and score at will. Once that was established, he defended skillfully and passed the ball so that others on his team could score. His SEAL professional skill set is unmatched; he can move, shoot, and communicate with the best—especially the shooting. Once he shoots a top score, he easily reverts to the role of teacher and mentor, helping the others to bring up their scores. And on training operations, he's good about calling periodic halts to the training to talk things over so that everyone understands the mission flow and the role of each member of the patrol. I guess that's what's really special about him,* Nolan concluded. *Lieutenant Engel makes us all just a little bit better. He leads well and, since we want to live up to his standard, we follow well.*

Chief Petty Officer Dave Nolan was a New Yorker, and even the Navy SEAL Teams could not dilute that part of him. Actually, the same values found in most guys who came from a blue-collar, New York hood—tenacity, toughness, self-reliance, with a generous dose of community and ethnic pride—only seemed to complement his service in the Teams. His platoon and the men in his platoon were family, and that counted for a great deal with Dave Nolan. One afternoon during his second semester at City College, he quietly rose from the back of the room in an economics class and slipped out the door. Forty minutes later he had been standing in front of a Navy recruiter.

"What's the hardest, most difficult program you have?" he asked the man behind the desk.

"Well, son," the recruiter told him, "that'd be the SEALs, but they aren't really a part of the Navy. An' most of 'em who put in for SEALs don't make it through."

"I'll make it through," Nolan replied. "Where do I sign?"

Dave Nolan returned from his first SEAL deployment, a series of training exercises with Pacific Rim allies, in early September of 2001. He had been back in Coronado for only a few days when the two airliners slammed into the twin towers of the World Trade Center. The Nolan family was well represented in both the NYPD and the FDNY, and more than a few Nolan women kept an anxious vigil during that terrible day and well into the night. But the burden of 9/11 fell heaviest on Dave's immediate family. Nolan's father was a cop, as was one of his bothers; two other brothers were firemen.

By the following day, there was no escaping the terrible reckoning: Two of his brothers, a policeman and a firefighter, had perished in the attack. After attending the wakes and funerals of his two siblings, he headed back to Coronado to prepare grimly for his second deployment. He'd been at war ever since.

Like many in the Teams, Nolan did not fit the image many civilians had of a Navy SEAL. He appeared too average. With dark hair, dark eyes, and sharp features, Nolan at five feet eight, was smaller than most SEALs. He was not the best shot, not the best runner, and not the best swimmer in the platoon. Nor was he particularly athletic, as many SEALs were. There seemed to be no hard edges to Nolan, and he had a wry sense of humor that he liked to direct at himself. Yet when it came to the execution of their duties, there was a palpable intensity about him that no one missed or ever questioned. He never gave orders, only suggestions, after which platoon SEALs moved with a sense of urgency. In the purest sense of the word, he was a warrior and more than that— a *serious* warrior. And he was a winner. He had always done whatever it took to win—to win the fight, to win the day. Furthermore, he expected nothing less of the SEALs with whom he served. Nolan was respected by his teammates and everyone up and down the chain of command. A term coined by their fellow warriors, the United States Marine Corps: "No better friend, no worse enemy," was most applicable to Chief Dave Nolan.

Roark Engel was the picture of relaxation as he waited for the jump. He savored moments like this, much as an experienced wine connoisseur would savor a delicate pinot noir. The roar and turbulence of the aircraft, the prospect of jumping into a 130-knot slipstream, the falling to Earth as a human projectile—he enjoyed all of it. Yet what he savored the most was the Team. These were his SEALs, his Team. This jump had little training value, but as a team-building evolution, it would be a great jump. This one wasn't for proficiency; it was for each other, and that made it special. Engel was not naive. He was a combat leader, and he knew that, as such, he would always be balancing the importance of the mission against the safety of his SEALs. Get the job done, get everyone home alive; that's what combat leadership was all about. But not today. Today, they would defy gravity, if not death, for the pure enjoyment of doing so in the company of their own.

Roark Engel was born in Grand Rapids, Michigan, and was an all-state running back in high school. He was the ideal picture of a high school hero—tall, sandy-haired, handsome in a boyish kind of way, and a student-athlete. He was heavily recruited by a number of Division I schools but elected an NROTC scholarship at Notre Dame and the opportunity to not play football. He could not articulate it at the time, but football simply did not seem like a team game to him. It bothered him that he got the attention while those who blocked for him received little or none. It violated his sense of fairness. He'd never played soccer but tried out for the varsity team as a walk-on. He was good, but he never became a starter. Yet the brutal practice sessions hardened him and refined his sense of team play. And on occasion, when an opposing midfielder became a little too physical with one of their side's forwards, Roark was sent in to even things up a bit.

But it was in Basic Underwater Demolition/SEAL training, with its cold water, punishing physical regime, and Hell Week, that he came to know what it was to be a member of an elite team and a leader among equals. Combat only served to put a premium on team play and the bonds that can form only when you routinely risk your life with others. He knew he was doubly blessed—to be a SEAL and to lead a SEAL platoon. Lieutenant Roark Engel often felt this was what he was born to do. His brief reverie was broken by a hand on his shoulder.

"You wanna jump, Boss, or do you want to ride this crate back to North Island?" It was Nolan. "I mean, if you don't wanna jump, I can have the duty driver pick you up and take you back to the Team area."

"In your dreams, Chief."

The two sticks of SEALs filed to the rear of the aircraft in preparation for the jump.

"Check equipment!" yelled the jumpmaster. Behind him, the ramp and top door of the 130 yawned open. "CHECK EQUIPMENT!" the platoon echoed as each man checked the equipment of the man in front of him. Engel checked Nolan's and Nolan checked Engel's. The SEALs then crowded on the ramp butt to belly. The unspoken game was to see just how fast the sixteen jumpers could cross the ramp and exit the aircraft.

"Get ready!"

"GET READY!"

"Green light. Go! Go! Go!"

The drop zone crew on the floor of the Otay Desert watched as what seemed to be a dense black mass of insects mushroomed from the rear of the aircraft and dispersed. Most were lost from view as the sixteen SEALs plummeted to the earth. Each stick or squad had a designated lead jumper, identified by a square of iridescent tape on his helmet. The others in his squad formed up on him in a loose V-formation, like a ragged gaggle of geese. It was not a long flight, just under sixty seconds. The lead jumpers pulled first. The other jumpers turned outward from their leader and quickly followed. Parachutes blossomed above the DZ.

On the way down, Lieutenant Engel and Chief Nolan flew as the tail-end charlies in their respective squad Vs. Nolan carefully watched his jumpers, noting with satisfaction that they held good formation. Engel watched his SEALs as well, a contented smile wind-pasted to his face.

The next day, and half a world away, in Jakarta, Indonesia, an ice cream truck rumbled through a crowded section of town. Small cars and scooters zipped past it in the narrow, dusty street, a street squeezed between dilapidated two-story buildings. Shoppers looked over the wares merchants hawked in their ground-floor stores and stalls, while those living in the second-story apartments above leaned out of their windows, trying to get some relief from the torpid heat on that oppressively hot afternoon. The collective mood was hurried and busy.

The ice cream truck pulled up to the security gate of the Jakarta International School. Established in 1951 for expatriate students living in Jakarta, it was the largest international primary and secondary school in Indonesia. The school had students from sixty nationalities and was where the international elite were educated. The ice cream truck was a routine fixture at the school in the mid-afternoon. Even elite children loved ice cream, and the vehicle was allowed on school grounds as a reward to those who had to sit for a full day in the air-conditioned classrooms with the very high instructor-to-student ratios.

The woman driving the truck—the same one who drove it every day—gave a casual wave to the guard at the gate as another guard opened the gate. The ice cream truck pulled into the school's large asphalt courtyard right on schedule. With bells tinkling, she guided the truck to the three-story low-slung building with enormous tiled overhangs on every story, a colonial design intended to shield the school's 2,500 students from the blistering equatorial heat. It was the school's main building, with the name displayed in letters a foot high on its second story. Primary school had just let out, and a cluster of first- through fifth-graders began to scamper toward the ice cream truck.

A large limousine, a Mercedes 600 flying the American flag on a stanchion attached to the right front of its hood, approached the gate and was waved through. The car came to a stop just inside the courtyard, and American ambassador Antonio Marguilles stepped out, donning his straw hat in deference to the mid-afternoon sun.

Abu Shabal stepped from the ice cream truck. At six feet two and 220 pounds he towered over the children, and his bulk gave him a presence that caused the children to immediately look at him.

"Come, children, line up, line up," Shabal called jovially as he waved the children toward the truck's open side door. "Graciela will take your orders."

"Come, come," Shabal continued as he herded the children toward the truck. He moved among the young-sters, yet his head was on a swivel. The welcoming smile was there, but his eyes were those of a predator. The children did what Shabal asked them to do because he was an adult and because he spoke in a commanding but disarmingly friendly tone. They also obeyed because of the horrible, disfiguring, crescent-shaped scar that cov-ered the left side of his face. Instinctively, the children knew he was not to be trifled with.

"Now, children, line up, please," Graciela enjoined them. "No pushing, no shoving, be patient," she contin-ued. "There is plenty of ice cream for everyone."

The scores of milling children pushed and shoved their way forward holding out their coins for Graciela as she began to dispense ice cream. The crowd swelled as more primary schoolers converged on the truck. It was joyful chaos. One of the students who was off to the side of the swelling queue was fourth-grader Nicolas Mar-guilles, the ambassador's only son. He saw his father approaching and bolted toward him.

"Papa, Papa," shouted Nicolas as he continued toward the ambassador, holding the straps of his backpack to keep it firm on his tiny back.

"Nicolas," replied Marguilles as he took his hat off and waved it at his son. Soon Nicolas was at his side. The boy grasped his father's legs as he hugged him.

"Papa, can we get some ice cream?" the boy entreated as he looked up at the tall ambassador.

"No, son, we have to go," he said solemnly, but there was a twinkle in his eye.

"You always say no, Papa. Please."

"Well, Nicolas, are you going to buy?" Marguilles teased.

"No, Papa, you buy!" replied Nicolas as he dragged Marguilles toward the ice cream truck.

"Well then, what are we getting today?"

"Passion fruit, Papa."

"Okay, passion fruit it is," replied Marguilles as he let Nicolas continue to drag him toward the ice cream truck.

Shabal noticed the ambassador approaching the ice cream truck. He smoothly detached himself from the crowd of children and began to walk calmly but deliberately away from the truck. Without looking back, he made his way to the school's gate, which was now wide open as several other cars entered the school grounds— more parents picking up their kids at the end of the school day.

As Shabal crossed the street and turned the corner he slipped his right hand into his pocket, finding the remote transmitter. He did not need to remove the device. His fingers found the on/off rocker switch, then the activation button.

A low, buckling explosion shattered the calm day as a monstrous fireball engulfed the ice cream truck and a huge column of black smoke rolled upward. Moments later, ice cream bars mixed with small torsos and limbs rained down on the scene in a wide circle around what used to be the ice cream truck. Dozens were killed instantly, followed immediately by the piercing cries of wounded children. Ambassador Marguilles and Nicolas were nowhere to be seen; what was left of their bodies was part of the collective burning mass of flesh and twisted metal.

Shabal felt the pressure wave and heard the explosion. Yet he never looked back as he disappeared into the crowded city. It was not the first time he'd left burning and lacerated bodies in his wake.

TWO

As he surveyed the vast Pacific Ocean from his palatial mansion near the city of Puntarenas, Costa Rica, Christo had the world in the palm of his hand—for the moment. Perched on a mountaintop on more than twenty acres of pristine forest, the twelve-thousand-square-foot manse was far more than he needed for his small family—his wife, Dominga, and four-year-old daughter, Solana—but he had worked hard to get where he was, and he felt entitled to enjoy the fruits of his labor. There were, of course, close to a dozen servants and caretakers that Christo considered an extended part of his family. It was a part of his patron image.

"Daddy, jump in the pool and play with me," Solana squealed as she frolicked in the 80-degree water of their Olympic-size, zero-level pool.

"In a moment," he replied, holding the satellite phone away from his mouth. Then back to the caller, "So you are telling me that the ambassador is no longer with us . . . I see . . . and it was the work of our associate . . . Quite right, my friend. Well then, I guess that's how it is . . . Yes, thank you for the call, good-bye."

"Please, Daddy, please," Solana pleaded.

"You'd better jump in soon," Dominga encouraged him. "I'm almost finished preparing lunch, and I want you to eat it while it's hot."

"As you say, my love," Christo replied.

He stood up and stripped off his shirt. He was vain enough to admire his own body—if only for a moment. At just under six feet and a well-muscled 185 pounds, Christo cut an imposing, athletic figure. He had jet-black hair that he allowed to grow to shoulder length, deep-set blue eyes, and dazzlingly white capped teeth. Only a narrow, prominent hawklike nose saved him from movie-star good looks. The hair and the nose gave him something of an academic bearing, on which he was quick to capitalize. Before entering the water, he took a moment to look around. He saw all that was his and realized, not for the first time, that he, in fact, did live the life as *capo* in this part of his adopted country. He dove into the pool, coming up directly underneath his daughter and giving Solana's leg a gentle tug, bobbing her in the water.

"Daddy, Daddy, let me ride on your shoulders," Solana shouted.

Christo obliged, taking big, monsterlike steps in the shallow end of the pool, giving Solana a ride up and down in and out of the water. Dominga looked on, seeing the genuine love he had for their daughter.

Christo reflected as he bobbed up and down, carrying

the squealing Solana all around the shallow end of the pool. Yes, he had untold riches, close to a billion U.S. dollars, gained in part from narco-trafficking and later in the even-more-lucrative arms-for-drug trade. But hadn't he lavished his largesse on a range of worthy causes in his adopted country of Costa Rica? Were not the Catholic Church, medical clinics, schools, and other worthy undertakings he funded for the still-poor inhabitants of this coastal section of Costa Rica all the better because of his generosity?

He had certainly lined the pockets of local politicians, and they had, in turn, protected his estate and turned a blind eye to his illegal activities. But that was just how business was done in Central America—and everywhere else, for that matter. For the Wharton-trained Christo, it was, in fact, all business—nothing more. Whatever damage his dealings did, and he wasn't convinced any of it really did any damage, he more than made up for it in the millions of dollars he gave back to the people— his people. In many ways, Christo saw himself as a modern-day Robin Hood. He took from the wealthy, drug-addicted Europeans and *Norte Americanos*, and gave back to the *campesinos* who lived at the subsistence level.

Yes, life was good, but good by his own initiative. But now they were closing in on him, and it was getting too risky—for him and for the fanatical elements with whom he now dealt. All he needed was one final score, and he would leave this life behind and escape with his small family. He had put the wheels in motion. Now he just needed it to play out. He had made it happen in the past; he would do it again—one more time. Let someone else take care of the less fortunate for a change, he told himself. It was time for him to take care of those closest to him. In the final analysis, they were his world.

It was Sunday, just before noon, when Dave Nolan arrived at Danny's—Home of the Slamburger. Danny's was one of the older, and some would say shabbier, burger joints on Coronado's Orange Avenue, and yet it was a favorite among Team guys. The slamburger was indeed impressive—a third of a pound of very lean beef that came in a variety of configurations. Lieutenant Engel had asked Nolan to meet him for lunch, which in itself was strange. Engel and his wife were both avid surfers and could usually be found at the break in La Jolla on Sunday mornings. Nolan was there ahead of his platoon officer. He worked his way down the long bar, exchanging hellos with a few of the SEALs seated on barstools. Everyone knew Dave Nolan. In decades past, SEALs would be there to nurse hangovers. Now, after ten years of war, most of them were there for a late breakfast after a morning workout. Nolan found a booth in the rear. As he swung into the booth, the waitress set a mug of coffee in front of him. On the wall-mounted TV, CNN was replaying the graphic footage of a terror attack in Indonesia. "Ain't it just awful what those bastards did to those kids," the waitress said. "How can someone go out and blow up a bunch of kids?"

Nolan glanced at the wall-mounted TV. He'd seen the coverage of the school bombing in Jakarta earlier that morning. At first, the act itself made his blood run cold, then it began to boil as he considered the animals who would commit such a thing. For Dave Nolan, things like this were black-and-white; there was good and bad, us and them. He didn't like the bad, and he didn't like people who did bad things. So he drew no small measure of comfort from the fact that it was his sworn duty to find these bad people and deal with them. A duty and a privilege.

"That's why they call them terrorists, Cindy, and that's why we chase 'em. Don't look for it to get better anytime soon. But point taken: They are a bunch of assholes."

"You'd think that things might get better since you guys got Osama."

Nolan smiled to himself. It was an East Coast SEAL element that led the raid on Bin Laden's compound in Pakistan, but all SEALs seemed to get credit for what they had done. Dave had just finished dinner that day and was in the front yard playing with Gretchen, his oldest daughter, when a neighbor came over to congratulate him—as if he'd personally shot the guy. As with nearly all SEALs who were not directly involved with the operation, he'd learned of the raid like any other American, at home on a Sunday evening. And that, thought Nolan, was as it should be. If he and the Banditos were ever lucky enough to go in on a super-high-value target, he could only hope that few people, SEALs or otherwise, would know about it. Mission success depended on absolute security.

"Osama was just one big turd in the sewer. It seems there are a lot more floating along behind him." Sometimes, Nolan thought to himself, the world was awash in a sea of assholes.

Cindy shook her head in disgust and took a pencil from behind her ear. "Still. What kind of animals kill kids, for Christ's sake? Bacon slam?"

"Not just yet. I'm meeting Roark, so I'll wait for him."

She moved back to the bar, and Nolan sipped tentatively at the mug of coffee. He used to take his coffee with cream and sugar, but since he made chief, he drank it black. He might be a SEAL chief, but he was still a Navy chief, and that's how Navy chiefs drank their coffee. It was interesting, he mused, referring to his officer as "Roark" with Cindy. He and Engel had known each other for nearly four years, and in that period of time, they had become tight—more than tight. They were perhaps closer to one another than to anyone else but their wives. Yet even when they were alone, just the two of them and well away from the teams, the platoon, or the Navy, he would always address Engel as "Boss"— and Engel would never call him anything but "Chief." Cindy, or just about anyone else outside the military, would call him *Dave* and Engel, *Roark*, but between the two of them it would always be *Boss* and *Chief.* Nolan had seen Vietnam-era SEALs meet and embrace each other as brothers in the same way. One would say, "Good to see you, Boss," and the other would reply, "Good to see you, too, Chief." That was just the way it was, and it was good.

Engel came in the back door to Danny's and slid onto the seat across from Nolan. He had two books with him that he set on the table, out of the way. Engel was a voracious reader and was seldom without a book. They exchanged greetings and ordered, Nolan his bacon slam and Engel a garden burger.

"Thought you and Jackie would be up in La Jolla this morning," Nolan offered.

"It's pretty flat out there today," Engel replied. It always amazed him that his chief seemed to never be aware of the ocean—like today it was almost a dead calm with no chance of finding a wave to ride. But if they were on an over-the-beach operation or parachuting into the ocean for an over-the-horizon penetration, Nolan would know everything about the conditions. For Engel, the ocean was a thing of beauty to be enjoyed and appreciated all the time; for Nolan, it was just part of the commute to the job site.

"And besides, I got a call from the skipper late last night and had to go into the Team area this morning." This piqued Nolan's attention, yet he said nothing. Something was going down, probably something that would impact their deployment, but he knew from experience that Engel would tell him in his own good time.

Cindy arrived with their burgers, and they ate in companionable silence, both drinking large glasses of water. SEALs were like camels; they stayed ahead of their hydration needs. They knew your performance today depended on what you drank yesterday, so you always remained topped off. Engel finished ahead of Nolan, in part because his chief ate two of his fries for every one that Nolan ate. Not for the first time, he regarded Nolan across the table.

Dave Nolan, Engel thought, *is a study in what is both good and noble.* At home, he lived for his family. He'd tell anyone who would listen what a wonderful woman he'd married—how lucky he was to have found such a fine lady. He worshipped her. He and Julia had five kids; he doted on them, and they idolized him. They were a wild bunch and uninhibited around him, yet he had power over them. If they were fussy or throwing a tantrum or out of line, he had only to speak. No baby talk—he simply dropped to one knee and asked them to take a breath and talk to him. Then father and child decided on a course of action, and the issue was resolved. He had the same effect on the men in the platoon. Like his kids, the Bandito SEALs seemed to want to please him. It was as if his kids and his platoon SEALs somehow knew that if what they were doing would meet *his* approval, then all was okay. On deployment, he was totally focused on the mission and the men and seldom spoke about his family. At home, he was all about family.

Nolan finished his slam and fries, then inspected Engel's plate for any alibis. It was then that he noticed the books on the table.

"So what does Oprah have you reading this month?" Nolan asked as he picked one up. He was trying for levity, as he already knew the answer. "*Churchill: A Biography*," he read from the spine. "Something new and different." It was a serious book—well over nine hundred pages. Last week it was *Winston Churchill* by John Keegan. "How much do you have to know about a guy who's been dead for a century?"

"He died in January of 1965."

"Okay, a half century."

Engel smiled. "You can never know too much about a great man. He stood against the dark forces of tyranny, just like you and me, Chief."

"Yeah, right," Nolan replied. "What else we got here?" Engel reached for the other book, but Nolan was too quick for him. He again read from the spine, "*How to Be a Dad*? This for real? You and Jackie going to launch one?"

Engel leaned forward. "Yeah, it's for real, but we're not telling anyone just yet."

Stunned, Nolan just sat there a moment staring at Engel. For Nolan, children were happiness—the more kids, the more happiness. Though he would never have voiced it, he had long wished this for his friend and lieutenant. There were tears forming in his eyes.

"Aw, man, I'm so happy for you." He bolted from his seat and leaned across the table to execute an awkward hug. He pressed his forehead against Engel's. "You're gonna be a great dad, and you and Jackie are going to be so happy. And I'm happy for you. Wait'll I tell Julia. She's going to flip."

"Okay," Engel said, his palms hovering above the table in a hold-it-down motion. "Just Julia. We want to keep this quiet for a while."

"Ab-so-lute-ly," Nolan said in a whisper. "I get it. No problemo; mum's the word."

"Can I get you guys anything else?" Cindy said as she refilled their water glasses.

"You sure can," Nolan replied. Then in a louder voice, "We'll have two shooters of Bushmills, and I'll buy the bar. My lieutenant is going to be a father!"

"Oh my God, Roark!" Cindy blurted. "That's wonderful. Congratulations." The sentiment rippled along the bar.

"Aw right!"

"Well done, El Tee."

"Good on you, sir."

"To the new little girl. Frogmen always have little girls."

"Here's to you, sir."

Engel simply lowered his head in mock surrender. This was typical Nolan and, with but a moment's reflection, it was just fine. Had their situations been reversed, his reaction would have been much the same as his chief's. It was simply the joy of one SEAL brother for another.

"Here you go," Cindy said as she placed two shots on the table. "These are on the house. Dave, I'll let you get the bar. Congrats again, Roark, and my love to Jackie. This is so exciting."

Nolan handed her a credit card. "Put the chow on here as well." After she left, he placed a hand on Engel's shoulder. "Seriously, Boss, this is terrific. You were born for this. Trust me, I know about these things. How far along is she?"

"About nine weeks."

"Great, and your timing couldn't be better. We'll get this deployment under our belt and get you back in time for the birth of your firstborn." He took up his glass. "Here's to you, Jackie, and the first of many."

Nolan knocked back the shot, and Engel followed suit. Both winced. Nolan drank only beer and that sparingly; Engel was seldom good for more than a glass of red wine at dinner. They talked for a while about kids, kids' names, and the inevitable changes that they brought about when they arrived—all good, Nolan resolutely claimed. Then Engel got around to the real reason he'd wanted to meet for lunch, just as Nolan knew he would.

SEALs deployed in squadrons composed of a full

SEAL Team along with an expanded intelligence collection and combat-support package. Once deployed, SEAL Team Seven became SEAL Squadron Seven. The squadron was further broken down into three task units, with two SEAL platoons per task unit—each TU with a stand-alone intelligence collection and operational capability. As needed, the two TU platoons could operate independently or together as a two-platoon troop. The Bandito Platoon was currently assigned to a squadron task unit that would be operating out of the Philippines. But, as Engel was about to explain, that had just changed.

"I went in this morning for a meeting with the squadron skipper and an intel update," he said, lowering his voice. "It seems that al-Qaeda has put out some kind of a fatwa on all Americans. They're calling for all related AQ splinter groups to strike hard and strike now. The good news is that this leaves little time for a well-planned attack like 9/11. The bad news is that there will probably be a lot of smaller attacks, and given the fanatical nature of the remaining al-Qaeda cells, they may be vicious attacks. And it may not just be al-Qaeda. They have allies in the criminal world as well. So while the task unit will still be headed for the Philippines, the squadron has been asked to spread out to cover more territory. And we've been asked to send one of our squads with an intelligence-support package to a fleet unit off Central America. They are to join an amphibious ready group in the Pacific that's cruising off Colombia."

"So we have to send one squad with the TU to the Philippines and another squad to an afloat unit—probably a big-deck amphib?"

"That's about it, Chief. How do you want to play it?"

Nolan paused to give this some thought. "Boss, where do you think the action will be?"

"Who knows," Engel replied. "But they wouldn't split a platoon and put a squad down there without some indication of terrorist activity. If something goes down in the Philippines or Indonesia, our one squad there will be just one of the SEAL squads that might be tasked. And if it's a full platoon operation, we'll see none of it. But if something happens in Central or western South America, that afloat squad will get the call."

Again, Nolan paused to think. "It seems like the best bet for a mission tasking is with the amphibious ready group. And since it's independent duty away from the rest of the task unit, let's you and I take the Bandito squad afloat."

It took them another fifteen minutes to make personnel assignments and decide who would go west with the task unit and who would go south. Engel, Nolan, and five other SEALs would go south to rendezvous with the afloat units; and the rest of the platoon, with the other platoon officer and the platoon leading petty officer, would stay with the task unit main body and head for the Philippines. This would require a re-palletization of equipment, but nothing more than that. The Bandito Platoon had trained to operate independently in squad units. The only thing that was on each of their minds was the issue of where the action might be. If they had chosen unwisely and the key mission tasking went to the other squad, neither would be there to help. Yet the platoon was deep in talent; there were plenty of veterans to carry the load. Bottom line: All of them wanted to get their guns into the fight. On balance, those who went south seemed to have a better chance. In addition, Roark Engel and Dave Nolan had a responsibility to place the platoon's two most experience leaders—in this case the two of them—in harm's way and where they thought the action would be the most intense.

"When do we tell them?" Engel asked. "Tonight?" The platoon was having a family barbeque at Gator Beach, just north of the SEAL Team Seven complex and only a few hundred yards south of the Hotel del Coronado. It was the last platoon social before deployment.

"The guys will want to know as soon as possible—give them some time to get their heads around the change. Besides, dad-to-be, tonight's family night. So let's do what we can to concentrate on the families. I'll initiate a call-down this afternoon and let everyone know about the change." They were silent a moment before Nolan continued. "Not that it changes much." As they both knew, most SEAL operations outside of Iraq and Afghanistan, the ones you never hear about, were squad operations. "We're nothing if not versatile. If there were no last-minute changes, the guys would get suspicious."

Engel grinned and nodded. "One thing I did do. I asked the skipper if he would assign Senior Chief Miller to our detached squad. I figured we would need him if we have to launch a mission with a short time fuse, which is probably how it will go down."

Nolan sat back and regarded his platoon officer. Engel was not only looking ahead but also looking out for the mission and the men. And it was a smart call. Senior

Chief Miller was the best operational planner at Team Seven. This was yet another reason Nolan respected Engel as well as liked him. He was always thinking about the mission as well as the men. He was also a little sneaky.

"But, Boss, how did you know *we* would be going with the detached squad—before *we* had even discussed it."

Engel gave him a Cheshire-cat grin. "I've got a sharp platoon chief. I knew that's the way he would want to do it. Why don't you give the senior chief a call and have him join us tonight?"

Nolan nodded. Another smart call. "Consider it done, Boss."

The two rose and bear-hugged. Engel scooped up his books and headed out the back. Nolan went to the bar to settle up with Cindy.

Lisa Morales was an internist and had been with Doctors Without Borders for the past six years. She was Mexican born and U.S. trained. At thirty-four, she was single, attractive, and passionate about helping those who were less fortunate, which is why she found herself working for DWB and was not in private practice. Her current assignment was in Costa Rica. She was tending to a patient in a Spartan medical clinic in the small town of Barranca, about eight kilometers east of Puntarenas near the intersection of highways 17 and 23. Unknown to her colleagues at DWB, she also worked for the CIA.

Had it been known that she worked for American intelligence, her colleagues would have shunned her, and

Doctors Without Borders would have fired her. The fact that she would serve as a covert agent was a testament to her commitment to the poor of Central and South America. She knew that much of the poverty in the countries where she worked was a product of corruption promoted by the drug trade. So she was both healer and spy—the former role was her profession, the latter a personal obligation. Lisa Morales felt she simply had to do more than just fight malnutrition and disease. As she worked, she watched a gaggle of small children play soccer on a dusty, makeshift field adjacent to the clinic.

Without warning, an SUV pulled up and Christo got out accompanied by his enforcer, Tommy. The two men were a study in contrast. Tommy was clearly a thug, a blunt object alongside the slim, urbane Christo. Pandemonium broke out as the children rushed Christo.

"Christo! Christo!" they shouted almost in unison.

He patted them on their heads, picked them up two at a time, clearly basking in this sea of adulation. In truth, he loved these children as much as they idolized him.

Christo and Morales made eye contact for an instant. He nodded and moved on. He made a quick tour of the clinic, which his financial assistance made possible, but he was not there to see his pesos at work. He was there for the affection and near worship of the kids. For all his education and sophistication, Christo seemed to need the attention. After passing out coins and candy, he was back in his SUV. With Tommy behind the wheel, the vehicle swerved in a circle and accelerated sharply away, covering the children and the clinic in a fine layer of dust. Still, the children cheered wildly until he was out of sight.

Later that day, as Lisa Morales made her way into the small city after another fourteen-hour day at the clinic, a man on a motorcycle skillfully weaved his way through the afternoon traffic. He was riding a 1961 Triumph split-case TT dirt-racing bike. The rider traveled at breakneck speed, causing pedestrians to scatter and bicycle riders to turn sharply to avoid getting hit. The bike eventually disappeared into the disorder of the crowded streets. That evening, as Lisa Morales was putting a bottle of water in the refrigerator, she heard a motorcycle outside and headed to the balcony.

The biker, Walter Ross, took off his helmet. Ross was a CIA contract case officer. He was an experienced Latin America division handler and had been running agents in Central America long before Morales entered medical school. He was basically an expat who had not been north in quite a while. He was good at his job and trusted by his own CIA handlers in Mexico City and at Langley.

"Hey, I'll be right down, all right?"

"Whatever you say, Doctor," Ross replied.

Morales ran down the single flight of stairs and joined Ross on the dusty street below. After exchanging greetings, they walked toward Barranca's main plaza.

"How was the ride?"

"Left Colombia this morning," Ross replied.

"Colombia to here in one day?"

"Piece of cake," he replied, a tinge of pride in his voice.

"Look, about Christo," Morales began, getting to the reason for Ross's visit, "we now estimate he's worth close to a billion."

"Was that with a *B*?" Ross replied, the surprise registering on his face.

"That's an estimate from Doctors Without Borders. They know a lot about him because he's one of our primary backers in this area. He gives back a lot to the local people here with medical clinics, schools, and assistance to the elderly. But he's no fool. He also lines the pockets of the politicians and police. So they're extremely loyal to him. But why all of the Agency interest in him? I thought this would be a DEA matter."

Ross smiled and lowered his voice. "We became interested when a 707 leased by him and filled with Soviet weapons was intercepted in Lagos."

Morales and Ross continued to walk, passing through the plaza and down a sheltered path.

"Langley says the boys over at NSA have picked up some interesting intercepts connecting Christo to a jihadist network out of Southeast Asia," Ross continued. "It seems that Christo and one of the guys running the network were childhood friends."

"So what's going to happen to this animal? We know he deals drugs, and now you say he's an arms dealer as well. Can he be arrested or somehow be made accountable?"

"Sorry, Doctor. For now, Langley just wants us to watch him and report back on his activities."

"He needs to be stopped," Morales murmured. "He may give a lot of money to worthy causes, but the misery of his kind of business that spreads to the region is unconscionable."

As she spoke, a camera shutter clicked and captured Ross and Morales in a frame.

THREE

The home of Dr. Lisa Morales was an average size apartment in a nondescript complex near the small town of Barranca. Very middle class. It was far from the luxury of Costa Rican resorts that catered to foreign tourists, primarily American tourists, on the Atlantic and Pacific coasts. The structure was concrete and glass set in sterile architecture—a building that attracted no attention. Perfect for someone who wanted to avoid notice and therefore perfect from the CIA's standpoint for one of their informants.

Lisa Morales had been the resident physician for Doctors Without Borders in Barranca for almost a year. She had made her small, one-bedroom apartment as homey as she could. She was reasonably well paid for her work, including a stipend from the CIA, but her life was designed to look like that of a young, idealistic physician on a modest salary. A rattan sofa and loveseat set, along with a bamboo-and-glass coffee table, took up most of the space in the small living room. The secondhand furniture was underlaid by a worn light-brown carpet. Cheap curtains adorned the two street-facing windows in the room. The adjacent kitchen sported only basic cookware and an ancient refrigerator. There was nothing high-end in the apartment. A small card table with four folding chairs served as the kitchen table. The only thing special about her furnishings was the secret compartment in the back of a battered end table. She seldom kept anything of a confidential intelligence nature, but it was there if she needed it. To even a critical eye, all was average and uninteresting.

"Okay, Lisa, you've got eighteen points with a double-word score. But watch this," Ross said.

"Go for it, Mr. Wordsmith," she replied as Ross laid down his tiles.

"There it is, 'seizure,' that's twenty-nine points, triple-word score."

"You don't like to lose, do you, Walter?"

"After twenty-five years with the Company, if I could stand losing I'd probably be dead by now," Ross replied.

It was always this way with them whenever Ross visited. They took a simple game of Scrabble and made it a highly competitive exercise. It fed both of their type-A personalities and took their minds off the deadly serious business they worked at—gathering intelligence on drug traffickers so that others in the CIA bureaucracy could take action.

"You getting hungry yet?"

"Yeah, as a matter of fact, I am," he replied. "What did you have in mind?"

"How about Chinese?"

"Here? You've got to be kidding."

"No, Chinese is universal, you know that. You can get Chinese anywhere. Where have you ever been that you *can't* get Chinese? And besides, I order from them all the time. How about chow mein?"

"Works for me," Ross replied as he continued to fiddle with his Scrabble tiles, rearranging them on his tile holder and plotting his next move.

Morales got up and walked to the phone hanging from the kitchen wall to put in their order. *"Si . . . si . . . A que tiempo? . . . si . . . Gracias."* As she returned to join Ross, she passed in front of one of the windows. From across the street and unseen, a camera clicked. As she passed in front of the second window, a camera clicked again.

"So how long?" Ross asked as Morales sat down again on the loveseat in front of the Scrabble board.

"A half hour. I know, I know, you get it much faster in the States."

Ross grinned. "What would I know about ordering Chinese in the States? Listen," he continued, lowering his voice, "we got a response from our last cable to the embassy." He was referring obliquely to his reporting senior in Mexico City. "We're still waiting for the Chief of Mission to finalize an updated list of requirements for you. Apparently one of the operations types had some additional questions. We should have it for you in a couple of days."

Morales merely shrugged on hearing this and laid down her tiles. " 'Broken' . . . that's twenty-one points."

"Y'know," Ross said almost to himself, "I'll never

understand why good old boys from Princeton, who haven't been in the field since Nixon was in the White House, are the ones who control our playbook." He stared at the board and put down three of his tiles. "Double-word score. Eighteen points."

"'Dumb,'" Morales replied, shaking her head. "Easy word, good score."

"Read it and weep."

"I'm trying not to," Morales replied.

The game and their banter continued, mixing Scrabble challenges with quiet shoptalk. It was familiar and comfortable. They were intelligence operatives, even though Morales was more informant than agent. They were both, as Robert Heinlein would say, strangers in a strange land. The game progressed, and as the board became a tiled mosaic, they continued to discuss ways their seniors could act more quickly on the information they were providing. Ross, the senior spook, easily shared his experience and his ideas with Morales. And while there was no sexual tension between them, he couldn't help but embellish on his espionage exploits. For her, it was a cause; for him, it was a way of life.

Morales looked up at Ross and smiled as she put all her tiles on the board. "Thirty-four points!"

"'Adumbrating'? That's not a word!" Ross exclaimed.

They both paused a moment as the doorbell rang.

"Finally!" Ross said. "I'll get it."

"Here," Morales replied as she threw a dictionary at him. "It's pronounced *ADAM-brating*. It means 'portending' or 'foreshadowing.' You're buying dinner."

Ross fumbled with the dictionary, looking for Morales's word as he ambled toward the front door.

"Nice," he said. "Most case officers get tactical partners. Langley sets me up with some kind of Scrabble hustler."

"Scrabble Yoda," Morales replied, leaning back on the loveseat and kicking off her shoes.

Ross looked through the peephole and saw the delivery boy holding their Chinese takeout. He undid the security chain, opened the double bolt, and turned the doorknob to the right. As he swung the door open, he reached into his back pocket for his wallet.

"How much do I owe . . ."

PSSST! PSST! There was only the metallic clatter that followed the muted explosions as the suppressed automatic chambered new rounds. The silencer and the downloaded rounds did their work as two 9mm hollow points slammed into Ross's forehead.

Morales looked up just in time to see the back of Ross's head expel a curtain of red mist that dusted the entryway walls.

Tommy and two of his men charged through the door, stepping over Ross's lifeless body. Morales froze for just an instant, then rolled off the loveseat and dived for her weapon. Tommy and the two men charged directly at her.

The Agency firearms training Morales received at the Farm served her well. She moved instinctively and managed to double-tap the man closest to her. The explosion inside the small apartment was deafening. He went down hard, but she stayed with her first target a fraction of a second too long. As she pivoted to take aim, Tommy elbowed her square in the face, knocking her gun away.

Momentarily stunned, Morales was helpless as Tommy picked her up and slammed her through the coffee table, shattering the glass. Snarling, the enforcer picked her up and again threw her to the floor, knocking the wind out of her. Gasping, she came to her knees when the third man kicked her in the ribs. Fighting back and on an adrenaline high, she somehow struggled off the floor and was almost standing when Tommy took a sap from his back pocket and neatly clipped her on the back of the head. This time, she melted to the floor like a wet towel and did not move.

Tommy and his man quickly duct-taped her arms and legs, and shoved a cloth into her mouth. Then, as Tommy knelt over Morales's hog-tied body, his man used a razor-sharp carpet knife to cut a section of the dung-colored carpet from around Morales's bound body. The two men rolled Morales up like a tortilla in the section of carpet. The two hoisted her onto their shoulders and, half stumbling over the inert form of Ross, quickly left the apartment. They dashed down the single flight of stairs to the back alley and threw the carpet holding Morales into the back of a battered pickup truck.

The entire operation had taken less than two minutes. Only the two shots from Morales's pistol and the roar of the speeding pickup disturbed the still evening. When the police finally arrived, they asked few questions. And if any of the neighboring residents saw anything, they were not talking, nor did the Barranca police expect them to.

They began to arrive at Gator Beach just after 5:00 P.M., and by 5:30 there were kids racing between the picnic shelters and the water, often with mothers chasing close behind. Two of the younger platoon SEALs had arrived earlier and had three of the beach fire pits burning gently with a nice bed of coals. A platoon family outing was a logistically intensive affair, and there were coolers, beach bags, food containers, diaper bags, and paper dinnerware stacked on the picnic tables. The beach toys, including boogie boards, soccer balls, paddle balls, and a Nerf football, were soon fully deployed. The platoon was at full strength with sixteen SEAL operators—two platoon officers and fourteen enlisted SEALs. A few single men had their girlfriends in tow, but most of the men were married with kids. The average age of the Bandito Platoon SEALs was just under thirty. When Roark and Jackie Engel arrived, the gathering had swelled close to fifty. The surf was low and the water chilly, about 62 degrees, but that did not deter the kids or the dads—the former too excited at the prospect of playing in the water and the latter professionally immune to cold water. So the women organized and talked, while the kids and SEALs splashed about. The kids outlasted the SEALs in the water.

Jackie Engel moved easily among the other SEAL wives. She came from a prominent family in Indianapolis, and her father was a senior executive at Eli Lilly. She had met Roark during his junior year at Notre Dame while she was a freshman. They dated for two years and became engaged when he graduated. It was a long-distance engagement while she finished college and he completed SEAL training. She would have left school to be with him, but he insisted she stay and graduate. "We'll have a lifetime together," he told her, "so stay and get your degree." They'd talked about her finishing at

San Diego State or USD, but neither offered a degree in her field—microbiology. When she offered to switch majors to be near him, he again rejected it. "I plan to be in a dangerous line of work for quite some time," the ever-practical Roark had told her. "You have to be prepared to step up and be the breadwinner." He also knew that a SEAL officer in training was seldom home. So they were together for part of the summers and during Christmas and Easter breaks, and they were on Skype nearly every night. It was good training for marriage to a deploying Navy SEAL.

Jackie was tall, blond, and thin. As a young girl she had been awkward and angular, and since she was clumsy, she hated sports. Her ears back then had been too big, and she had always felt disproportionate. But as a teenager she caught up with herself and began to move with a newfound ease and grace. She grew into her features, and although not quite beautiful, she was attractive—striking even. Her parents had sent Jacquelyn, their only child, to the private Park Tudor School, where she excelled academically and dated very little. As she matured, she acquired a soft, ethereal presence that made her appear aloof and often made boys reluctant to approach her. Her grades and College Board scores were such that if her family had not had the means, she would have attended college on an academic scholarship. When she came home for Thanksgiving her freshman year at Notre Dame, she told her parents she had met the man she would marry. They brushed it off as infatuation and inexperience. Still, they were concerned that this attachment would distract her from her studies—or, worse, cause her to drop out of school. Yet her first-semester grades reflected no such problem. Still, they were wary of this first boy in her life. Jackie's parents did not meet him until later that spring.

They met Roark during a parent's weekend at South Bend and quickly realized that this boy was a man, that he was courteous and polite to a fault, and that he was as much in love with their daughter as she was with him. While Jackie completed school and he completed SEAL training, her parents found themselves worrying that the separation might cause the relationship to end. The wedding took place a week after her graduation, followed by a reception at the Meridian Hills Country Club. Jackie was radiant, and the Navy groomsmen were just as handsome and polite as their new son-in-law. And they all wore the same shiny gold pin on their starched, white uniforms—the one they called the Trident.

When Engel returned to their small Coronado efficiency after his lunch with Nolan, he was worried about having broken the news of Jackie's pregnancy to his chief. He was still trying to figure out how to tell her when she saw him and smiled.

"You told Dave, didn't you?"

"Well, you see, he just sort of found out. I didn't actually tell him."

"And he's the only one who knows, right?" she asked, knowing the answer full well.

He shifted from one foot to the other. "Well, it sort of went a little further than that."

She came to him and they hugged. "Yeah, I know. Brothers by different mothers and all that." They had stood in the kitchen-dining-living area for some time and just held each other. That afternoon they went for a long, easy bike ride together, their last for a while. Then they loaded the cooler in the car and headed for the platoon beach party.

The sun dropped behind the clouds before it dropped behind the ocean. No green flash tonight. The SEALs and the kids gradually played themselves out and began to straggle back to the food tables. It was a standard beach spread with chips, burgers, hotdogs, potato salad, and coleslaw. The other wives fussed over Jackie, and Roark moved from one table to another, taking a few moments with each extended family group. Dave Nolan was on the move as well. Their circuits converged when they reached a couple comfortably ensconced in two beach chairs on the edge of the group. Their kids were older and off doing what teenagers do on a Sunday night.

"Evening, Senior Chief. Hello, Mary. Good to see you again."

"Evening, sir," he replied. Then to Nolan, "How goes it with the Bandito, Jefe?"

"It goes well, Senior—even better knowing that you'll be with our detachment."

Mary, sensing they needed to talk, pushed herself to her feet. "Think I'll go and see what the girls are doing." She paused, then gave Engel a hug. "I just heard the news, Roark. I couldn't be more tickled. Blessings to you and Jackie."

"Thanks, Mary. We won't be long."

They watched as she made her way over to a group of wives. Engel sensed that the collective mood of their ladies was much lighter than it had been during previous pre-deployment parties. Those rotations had been to Afghanistan or Iraq, with the prospect of certain and continuous combat. This deployment, with the task unit away from the active theaters in a contingency posture, held the prospect of probable engagement, but not the daily combat operations nearly all of them had known since 9/11. On this rotation, they would be looking for opportunities to get their guns in the fight. Currently in Afghanistan, as it had been in Iraq a few years before, the environment was target rich, and quite often, the fight found you.

The SEAL wives were for the most part bright, attractive, outgoing women and, in many cases, much more than the home half of a marriage. SEALs tended to marry women like themselves—capable, self-reliant, and independent. Many, including Jackie, were professionals whose income exceeded that of their husbands. Most worked until the children arrived. Some then became stay-at-home moms while others retained nannies and continued their careers. Yet because many SEALs and their wives shared the type-A gene, divorce rates were high—not noticeably higher now than before 9/11 but still high.

"Senior, I didn't speak with you before I asked the skipper if you could detach in support of us. I hope you don't mind."

"No worries, sir. I've been to Southeast Asia many times, and before this deployment's over, we'll all probably be back out in WESTPAC with the rest of the task unit." He grinned with some satisfaction. "It's a chance to work a new area of operations. Other than that, I go where they tell me, just like you do. That much hasn't changed."

At thirty-nine, Senior Chief Otto Miller was older

than any of the platoon SEALs and one of the older hands at Team Seven. He was also a legend in the SEAL Teams. As a platoon leading petty officer at SEAL Team Five, he had been badly wounded in an urban firefight during the Battle of Ramadi in 2006. His squad had gone out to rescue an Army patrol that was pinned down by insurgents. Early in the fight, his face had been raked by shrapnel, and a bullet found its way under his body armor and lodged itself in his spine. Yet he kept his gun in the fight, and his actions saved many lives in the beleaguered patrol. The bullet left him with permanent nerve damage and only the partial use of his left leg. He could have taken his Navy Cross and a substantial disability pension and retired, but Otto Miller was not finished serving his country. While he was still in physical therapy, he asked to have his Navy rating changed from Special Operator First Class to Intelligence Specialist First Class. Intelligence Specialists are among the Navy's smartest sailors, and their rating is known to be one that demands a great deal of ability. Miller got his rating change, but he also had to pass the IS1 exam to keep it—no easy task for someone new to the specialty. He passed the exam and then some, exceeding the scores of other more-seasoned sailors, specialists who had been working in military intelligence for years.

The ten years of continuous combat since 9/11 produced a good many wounded SEALs, men physically unable to return to duty. Not all of them handled it well. They had not joined the Navy and the SEAL Teams because they couldn't find work or because college proved too difficult or to receive job training. They joined to become professional warriors. Once in the Teams, they

entered this elite brotherhood and came to know the
sometimes-narcotic thrill of special-operations combat.
When their battle wounds forced them out of combat
rotation, either they adjusted or they did not. Most got
to where they were because they were goal oriented and
success driven. The disabilities imposed by combat simply brought on a new set of challenges. A great many left
the Navy and began a new life, usually with great success. Others, like Otto Miller, found a different way to
serve in uniform. For a few, what they had come to know
and what had been taken from them proved to be too
much. They became the emotional casualties that every
war produces.

Miller was heavily scarred about his mouth and neck,
and no amount of plastic surgery would ever make him
what he was. He wore a beard and mustache that hid
most of the damage, but that was not why he let his facial
hair grow. Among his many talents was his knack for
languages and his skill as an interrogator. In Iraq, a man
wore a mustache; and in Afghanistan, men wore beards
and mustaches. So did most of those detained as terrorist
suspects. He was merely conforming to the culture of
those from whom he wished to extract information.
Miller's record of successful interrogations now exceeded
his considerable operational success. It was said that he
could get a hardened criminal to dime out his own
mother and to feel good about having given her up.
When he was an operational SEAL, he was in high
demand in the platoons. Now every task unit wanted
Miller in their intel shop. Both Engel and Nolan considered it something of a coup to have him in support of
their detached squad. That they were given Miller was a

further indication that there could be some activity in or around Central America that might require an on-call, special-operations response element.

"Any idea what's going on down there?" Engel asked the senior chief.

Miller considered this, thoughtfully pulling his hand down his beard in a professorial gesture. He wore his hair longish and combed it straight back over his head. His deep green eyes seemed to be backlit. During interrogations, they became incandescent and piercing, and he used them on his opponent like he had once used the targeting laser on his automatic weapon.

"It could be just about anything," he finally replied. "Drugs, extortion, a kidnapping. I'll know a little more tomorrow morning once I've had a chance to run the agency alphabet trapline. But something's got someone's attention, that's for sure."

After more than ten years of war, the military special operators and the diverse appendages of the national intelligence apparatus had finally become synched. They now talked to one another, and the talk led to cooperation—the kind of cooperation that had resulted in the killing of Osama Bin Laden. Miller had good contacts at the CIA, FBI, DEA, NSA, and DIA, and with their human and technical collection organizations. The intelligence community and the military were also now linked by sophisticated and secure communications networks. Early Monday morning, Miller would be pushing his agency and military contacts in Central and South America for any breaking leads. Usually, but not always, bits of information came from the opposition's use of unencrypted cell phones or some other technical collector. There was also the occasional agent on the payroll of some hardworking CIA case officer who came up with some obscure but related fact. And that fact could be linked to another fact and to still another until the mosaic produced operable intelligence in the form of a target folder. This was called operations-intelligence, or ops-intel, fusion, and it was making life dangerous for terrorists worldwide.

"It's like this, fellows," the senior chief continued, "over in the sandbox, in the jihad-land, it's all about religion and tribalism. Down south, it's all about money. The money comes from drugs. There are the drug-support industries like gunrunning, the bribing of officials, assassination, and so on, but the big bucks come from producing drugs and moving drugs to the U.S. and European markets. It's a sixty-billion-dollar-a-year industry. The U.S. military mission down south has to do with training—training the Colombians and the Salvadorians to fight drugs. But we don't fight drugs down there, they do, or at least that's the idea. We've had the Green Berets and some of our special boat teams helping with this training, but not a SEAL direct-action element in this mix, which, gentlemen, is what you are."

"What *we* are," Engel interrupted. "You're a part of this team."

"Thanks, sir. The money from drugs only comes when the product gets moved north. So the druggies have some very efficient and sophisticated ways to get the stuff across our southern border. And God knows there are plenty of illegals moving south to north. The big concern has always been that the jihadists and the druggies might climb into bed with each other. It's got the boys and girls at Langley scared shitless. See, the jihadists have money and motivation, and the druggies have the mules to move contraband into this country. So the fear is that some deal gets cut to bring chemicals or radiological materials across the border. I know the Agency and Homeland Security have people working on this. So our going south may have something to do with this. My guess is they wouldn't pull a SEAL detachment down there unless there was something afoot. Someone's concerned about something. There are probably indicators, but nothing solid yet. But, hey, you fellows have been around long enough to know it could be something or it could be nothing."

Engel nodded. It made sense. "Chief, what else?" he asked, looking at Nolan.

Nolan simply shrugged. "It is what it is. We're ready to fight—as a platoon or now as a detached squad. All we need is a target folder and a mission-support package, and we're good to go." He paused and glanced over to where the platoon SEALs were gathering expectantly, in two separate groups: one, the squad that would be deploying with the task unit to the Philippines, and the other, the detached squad that would go south. "Boss, the guys all know about the change, but a little fatherly platoon officer advice might be in order right now."

"Understood. Senior, you want to excuse us for a moment."

"No problem, fellows. I'll let you know if and when I learn anything."

It was the custom on the eve of a deployment for the senior platoon officer and the platoon chief to each give a short, private out-the-door speech to the SEALs before they broke off to finish the evening with their families.

Since the Bandito Platoon would be splitting into two squads for at least the initial part of this deployment, Engel had elected to make the break now. His assistant platoon officer and the next senior enlisted leader, the platoon leading petty officer, would caucus with the task unit squad, while he and Nolan would quickly meet with their detached squad. The platoon SEALs sensed this, and the two groups of SEALs separated and moved apart—from the families and from each other. Engel and Nolan led their group to one of the outlying picnic tables. There were five others besides the two of them, making it a light squad. The task unit squad would have a total of nine SEALs, which Engel knew would make his task unit commander more comfortable. He had his own responsibilities. Engel and Nolan had selected the five for their individual skills but had not cherry-picked them; they would fight alongside any of the Bandito Platoon SEALs.

There was Diego Weimy, or just plain Weimy. He was one of the platoon snipers and now the lead sniper for their squad. Like many SEAL snipers, he did not grow up hunting or shooting with his father or uncles. In fact, he grew up on the south side of Chicago, where the closest he came to a rural experience was the trash-strewn vacant lot where the kids played baseball and hid from local merchants after they'd boosted a candy bar or a radio from their store. The SEAL sniper instructors liked men who had limited shooting instruction, as it meant there were fewer bad habits to break in teaching them long-range shooting. Weimy had been stocking shelves in Albertsons when he decided to go into the military. He chose the Navy because he wanted to get away, and there was no saltwater near Chicago. He volunteered for SEAL training on a whim, having no idea what he was getting into. In training, Weimy had been what they called a gray man—someone you never noticed. But after Hell Week had caused most in his class to quit, he was still there. He was good at all SEAL skills, but by SEAL standards, not great at any except for shooting. Still, he had the right temperament, the shooting mechanics, and the cold efficiency of a natural-born sniper. Weimy, like the rest of them, was now anxious to learn more about the squad's detached duty. He was also anxious to get back to his wife and infant son.

Ramon Diamond was the one SEAL they selected because he was the best. He was the most experienced of the two platoon radio operators, and since they would not have the support of the task unit's communications team to draw on, they drafted him for the squad. Ray was an electronics geek first and a SEAL second. Everyone came to Ray—with a new cell phone that they needed to learn how to operate or with a laptop that had fallen prey to a particularly nasty virus. Engel suspected that Ray quietly hacked into national-security databases for satellite imagery. On their last deployment to Afghanistan, he always seemed to come up with great aerial imagery of their targets. When Engel had asked where he got them, Ray had been evasive, saying that you just had to know where to look. They had worked well together on that last deployment. Ray normally stayed close to Engel, as communications were critical in the modern fight—comms with the engaged SEAL fire teams as well as comms with the support elements and higher headquarters. During one particularly vicious firefight, Engel had looked around and couldn't find Ray. A team-mate had gone down, and Ray had raced through a hail of fire to drag the injured man to safety. That action led to Ray's second Silver Star. One of the big dichoto-mies with their platoon geek was that his arms were cov-ered with gang tats, which he refused to discuss. "Some guys are reborn in Christ," Ray would say when asked. "I was reborn in the Navy. That's all you need to know." In addition to his IT skills, he had a dry sense of humor and a knack for pushing other people's buttons.

Sonny Guibert was perhaps the only one of the group who looked like a SEAL, or what those outside this tight-knit community thought a SEAL should look like. In a word, he was a wall. At six feet two and 225 pounds, he was the largest SEAL in the squad or the platoon, and movie-star handsome. He had thick blond hair and per-fect teeth. When the Bandito SEALs parachuted with-out equipment, they often said they were jumping Guibert rather than jumping Hollywood. He towered over SEALs like Weimy and Ray, who were under six feet and fifty-plus pounds lighter. Dave Nolan accused him of having weight-lifter genes, as he was naturally cut and buffed. For that reason, he did only nominal upper-body work, but he was a highly competitive triathlete. He was the squad's automatic-weapons man, which meant he carried the M48 machine gun—a compact SEAL weapon that digested the heavy 7.62 NATO rounds—and in a squad action, his weapon was the biggest dog in the fight. He also served as the squad's armorer, which meant he had sub-custody of all the squad weapons and night-vision equipment. He made sure the detached squad had extra weapons and spare parts, so they could operate independently from the task unit. In one word, Sonny was reliable. It was Chief Nolan's job to check all those with platoon and squad responsibilities, but he did so very carefully with the big SEAL. Sonny took an immense amount of pride in knowing that he kept the squad's weapons package up to standards and that everyone's work gun was up and running. Sonny's personal responsibilities also extended to a wife who could pass for Miss California and two blond, towheaded daughters. The family was Hallmark material.

Alfonso Joseph Markum had joined the Navy in his late twenties and needed a special waiver to enter basic SEAL training at twenty-nine. A.J. was born in Trinidad and came to Miami with his mother when he was six. She married a Cuban exile and they all settled in little Havana. Neither spoke English; they were poor but proud. A.J.'s stepfather worked as a security guard and his mother cleaned homes. A.J. was left alone after school and had flirted with gangs, black and Cuban, but two things kept him from serious trouble: One was the example and sacrifice of his mother and stepfather. The other was a youth-club mentor who introduced him to Muay Thai fighting, or Thai kickboxing. A.J. was small, compact, and quick. His heroes were ranked fighters like Tony Jaa and Buakaw Por. Pramuk. Had he been introduced to the sport earlier, he might have become a professional, but it was a discipline that took decades to master at that level and he had started too late. His inclinations led him into security work and to several years with the Dade County Sheriff's Department. But he found police work frustrating, and he ran afoul of department politics. His troubles usually began with a fight between his large Anglo partner and a local gangbanger. When things began to go badly for his partner, A.J. would step in and settle things. Three Miami hoodlums, albeit ones with criminal records and aggressive personal-injury lawyers, were left with permanent physical disabilities. While A.J. Markum was protecting and serving the citizens of Dade County, the lawsuits against the county began to mount, and he was let go. So A.J. went looking for work where a man was supposed to have his buddy's back, and this took him to the Navy SEALs. Most who survive the rigorous SEAL training have to dig deep within themselves to make it through. A.J. was not one of those. He was the squad's point man, and he was one of the best with Team Seven. Contrary to popular myth, SEALs seldom killed silently with their hands; they had suppressed weapons that did that at long range and up close. But if it came to a quiet kill, hand-to-hand, then the go-to SEAL would be A.J. Markum.

Finally, there was Mike Bennett, or Mikey. The youngest and least experienced SEAL in the squad, this would be his second deployment. Mikey was one of the platoon's two medics. In dividing up the platoon talent, Chief Nolan had chosen Mikey first. When Engel had lifted an eyebrow in question, Nolan simply shrugged. "He's good to go, but I'd like him where I can keep an eye on him." Nolan had no need to explain himself. Engel felt the same way. Mikey would win the nicest-guy-in-the-world award. He'd been an Eagle Scout and a National Science Fair finalist. He had a degree in sociology from the University of San Diego, he'd married his high school sweetheart, and he came from family money. He struggled in basic SEAL training, failing once and finally making it on his second try. On his first deployment, he had done well, both with the dirty jobs assigned new SEALs on their first rotation and with the running and gunning that were an every-night occurrence in Afghanistan. He'd taken life quickly and professionally, so his SEAL skill set was good—even better than good. If Engel or Nolan could put their reservations into words, it would be about the dial. All SEALs have to dial it up in the fight and dial it down in garrison or at home. This allowed them to be tenacious and lethal during the adrenaline high of a firefight and still be able to lose graciously at cards in the barracks or read bedtime stories to their kids at home. Mikey's dial didn't seem to be calibrated like the others. On the everyday/normal side, it extended to a range well past the others; he was simply an easygoing, nice person. On the combat side, he did his job, but with seemingly no aggression or emotion. On his first patrol, an insurgent stepped from a doorway and brought them under fire. Everyone reacted, but Mikey was the fastest, ringing the insurgent up with a perfect double tap to the head. He looked back at Chief Nolan with that gee-whiz, how'd-I-do-it grin and simply continued on the patrol. He might well become the best among them, but he *was* different.

Engel surveyed the men around him. "Guys, I only have so many stay-tight, stay-focused, stay-professional speeches in me. You've all been there; you all know the deal. I know nothing more about what may be waiting for us downrange than you do. I do know that while we're detached from the task unit and the squadron, the communications back home may not be what we've enjoyed in the past. Let your families know that there may be times when we'll be in the wind, and they'll not hear from you." He paused to carefully frame his words. "Regarding families, I'll say again what goes without saying. If there are any issues—personal, emotional, financial, whatever—get them fixed. If you need help, there's the chief and myself. Our wives are there to help as well. We're all here for you. But get it right and get it locked down. When we leave, I want a total front-sight focus on the mission. Everyone's got everyone else's back. That's how we go to war; that's how we all come back from war. We good with that?" He met each man's eyes in turn, and each nodded in agreement. "Chief?"

"You've said it all, Boss. So let's drink to our brotherhood." Nolan raised his beer and was quickly followed by others, including a few who were raising water bottles. "For all of those who go downrange—to us and those like us—damn few."

"Here, here."

"Friggin' right."

The two squads broke from their separate gatherings, much like they had peeled from their free-fall V-formations, and rejoined their families. It was full-on dark, and most people had pulled in close to the fires. The wives handed off sleeping kids to their fathers. The older kids drifted back to sit between their parents. Mikey and his wife joined the Nolan tribe and took one of the little boys between them. Ray and A.J. sat near Engel and Jackie and observed a comfortable silence. Some talked quietly, others just listened. An occasional joke or war story kept the melancholy at bay, but it was a holding action. Finally, the Banditos and their families began to drift away. Jackie walked Julia Nolan back to their car, leaving only Nolan and Engel. Always the good Scout, Mikey had doused and inspected all the fire pits. No glowing embers or rekindles while he was on duty.

"That's it, Boss. I think we're ready."

"I think you're right."

"And don't worry about the other squad—they have good veterans and good leadership."

Engel smiled. His chief knew him well; he was thinking just that. "I'll do my best. Can't worry about what you can't control, right? Just like back here on the home front."

Nolan nodded. "Two days and a wake up, then the long good-bye."

Engel again smiled, but it was a sad one. "Yeah, the long good-bye."

The following day, despite Senior Chief Miller's best efforts, there was no further clarity on what might await them. Something seemed to be brewing, but no one seemed to be able to communicate what it might be. The day after that, the task unit and their single Bandito Platoon squad mustered at the North Island Naval Air Station for the flight that would take them west, halfway around the world. Actually, they would fly north on a great circle route, pausing at Kadena Air Force Base on Okinawa for fuel before continuing on to Manila. Lieutenant Engel and Chief Nolan were there to see them off. Following the good wishes and the good-byes, the big C-17 swallowed up the SEALs, the task unit combat support team, and their gear. For Engel, Nolan, and the remaining Bandito squad, they and their support team would be staging gear at this same location for most of the day. Their departure was scheduled for early the following morning.

Every SEAL leaves on deployment in his own way. For some it's highly ritualized and formatted. Others go to great lengths to make it just another day. A few try to make the last minutes pass slowly; others want it over and done so they can begin the countdown to the homecoming. Above all, it's individual—each SEAL and SEAL family handle it in their own way.

The night before, just as he had for previous deployments, Roark Engel arranged for the Coronado Livery, the oldest cab company on Coronado, to call for him at the street entrance to their condo building. For him, the leaving was in the details, and he busied himself with them. Roark Engel faced a common special-operator's dilemma. His professional calling was that of a combat team leader in combat rotation. He loved his wife dearly, yet his calling demanded that he leave her for long periods of time. So he immersed himself in the details.

For Jackie Engel, the last days were measured in the degrees of seriousness that began to overtake her husband as the time for deployment drew closer. She knew he held it off as best as he could, but as the time to leave approached, he took on responsibility like the layers of clothing one puts on to go out into a cold night. She could almost see him bend under the weight of it. She knew it was a double burden. He was bending under the weight of the responsibility of taking care of his men *and* of leaving her and their unborn child. She also knew that once he was gone and could focus only on the men and the mission, he would do fine. Jackie Engel didn't resent this; she understood and accepted it. More than that, a part of her welcomed it. She knew that his total attention to his duties was the best insurance she had that he would come home to her intact.

The day before, he and Jackie had gone over everything that needed to be in place before he left. This morning he wanted to think about nothing; he wanted to make their parting as gentle and painless as it could be. Mechanically, he showered, shaved, dressed, and got ready for the day just like any other. They shared a simple breakfast and tried to be cheerful. These little practiced routines helped him fight through the emotional strain of leaving his wife. So they went through the routines together. They talked about their next breakfast together, and future breakfasts with a high chair between them.

His operational gear, uniforms, files, computer, and the few civilian clothes he would take were long since packed and staged for the deployment. The only thing he put in his bag the night before leaving was always the flag. His flag had adorned the coffin of his grandfather, who was killed in action in World War II. His grandfather on his father's side had piloted a B-24 during the Ploesti raids. On his final mission, he kept the dying Liberator in the air until the rest of the crew had bailed out. Then he rode the stricken aircraft to a fiery grave. There was no question: Warrior blood coursed through Roark Engel's veins. Roark always took the flag with him on deployment; he said it kept him safe—that the spirits of the warriors in his family would protect him while he was in harm's way. The day before, the flag had been over the mantel in a small rectangular shadow box. The next morning, it was gone, spirited quietly into the canvas document case that contained his orders and deployment authorizations.

Then it was time. He was dressed the same as he was every morning—camouflage uniform, rough-out desert boots, and utility cap. For Roark and Jackie, their established point of departure was the front door of their little condo. He would go out the door, and she would remain behind.

"Got the flag?" she asked, just as she had on previous deployments.

"Got the flag," he responded. Then came the litany of advice and cautions that she knew was coming and for which she loved him.

"Now, promise me you'll stay away from your sister Carol. I know it's only secondary smoke and she sits by the fireplace, but its still bad news."

"And stay away from processed food," she said, mimicking him, "and deli meats and diet anything."

He smiled affectionately and added, "And sushi and ice cream and alcohol," even though neither had touched a drop, save for his Bushmills at Danny's, since they learned she was pregnant. She pulled him close and rubbed his closely cropped head. "It'll be okay, Lieutenant. Just come back to me with a decent head of hair."

"You know, Jackie, I not only love you, I'm very proud of you."

"Ditto, Boss,"

"Any other orders?"

"Yes. I want to look into your eyes when our first child is born."

"Honey, you know I'll do my best."

Both were misty eyed and holding each other closely.

He bent over and kissed her gently on the mouth. "I love you."

"And I love you."

They continued to hold each other for another long moment, then he took up his document case, turned, and walked away. Only after she had gently closed the door did tears flow, and once they started, there seemed to be no end to them.

At the North Island terminal, there were the squad SEALs and the hastily configured support package that would accompany the squad. The aircraft, a newer C-130J, had arrived at noon the day before, so all of the gear was aboard and strapped down. Those like Engel who had said their good-byes at home were essentially already on deployment. For those whose families came to see them off, they were still multitasking—juggling their family and team responsibilities. Julia Nolan was there with all five kids and seemed surprisingly cheerful, but then she'd had far more practice at this than Jackie. Engel greeted each of the kids, then turned to Julia.

"Ready to go, Roark?" she said as he hugged her.

"As ready as I can be," he replied.

"Got a deal for you. You take care of Dave and I'll look in on Jackie, okay?"

He gave her a feigned look of surprise and a smile. "But isn't it Dave's job to look after me?" Then more seriously, "You got a deal, Julia, and thanks—I really appreciate it."

Engel said hello to Mikey's wife, who was dressed as if she were going to a garden party and crying as if she were at a funeral. Like himself, Sonny had also said his good-byes at home and was ready to launch. At this point, there was little else for Engel to do. The loading and the manifesting were Nolan's responsibility, and he knew that all was well in hand. Senior Chief Miller had taken charge of their support package, and that, too, was done. He found the pilots standing off to one side and joined them. They looked on while the others completed their farewells.

"Ready when you are, Lieutenant," the pilot said.

"Then let's do it," Engel announced. Nolan had kept an eye on Engel for the high sign, even as his family pressed closely about him. Engel had only to nod his head; his platoon chief would do the rest. Engel boarded the plane, stowed his case under his seat, and strapped himself in. Then he closed his eyes and thought of Jackie, totally detached from the commotion of the others clamoring aboard the aircraft. Twenty minutes later they were climbing out over the Pacific and turning south.

The compound was designed to blend into the dense foliage and surrounding mangrove, and it did just that. The few dilapidated buildings that were scattered over the five-acre compound were completely hidden by the vegetation. It would have looked like any other poor Costa Rican jungle enclave were it not for the eight-foot-high chain-link fence topped with barbed wire surrounding it, the two forty-five-foot wooden guard towers, and the armed men patrolling the area. The property was ten miles from the coast but at least an hour's travel over the unimproved roads. There was standing water on one side of the compound and a brown, slow moving river that crawled past a quarter mile north. Any aircraft flying over would not know it was there, save for the two rut-filled dirt roads barely wide enough for one car to navigate, and they were but shadowy creases in the canopy. The small compound was protected by its remoteness as well as its security force.

Several miles away, a small village provided a link to civilization and housed an additional security force. Like numerous small inland villages, there was a main road; a cluster of huts; and a central building that was a cantina, a general store, and a Pemex station. There were two armed forces in the area: the Costa Rican national army and the local drug cartel. The cartel considered the village and this isolated compound a part of its turf and under its protection. These two forces seldom confronted each other. This was not because of the normal practice of bribing officials, at least not out here at the foot-soldier level. Theirs was a practical accommodation. Both were well armed, and neither the cartel security men nor the *federales* wanted to end up facedown in the mud and the mangrove. So they gave each other a wide berth.

Inside the compound's largest building, a long, low structure, Lisa Morales hung from a rafter in a 20x20 foot end room—the tips of her bare toes just able to gain a purchase on the plank flooring. Old Spanish newspapers and mildew covered the room's peeling clapboard walls, and a single yellow bulb dangled overhead. It was just enough light to cast her slim shadow on the wall and floor. The door pushed open from the exterior and filtered daylight spilled into the room, illuminating Morales's bloody face and filthy clothes. Tommy filled the door for a moment, then walked up to the battered physician. She raised her head and peered at him through slitted, swollen eyes.

"I am a doctor, and my organization will pay a generous reward."

Tommy stood a foot from Morales and smiled. He was a brutish figure with a pocked face, narrow eyes, and a thatch of unruly, unkempt hair. He wore a rumpled polo shirt and pleated slacks—both with streaks of blood on them. Just under six feet, he weighed close to 250 and was running to fat. Yet he exuded a raw animal power that was both compelling and cruel. He held a cell phone on speakerphone in front of her swollen and bruised lips.

"I am a doctor, and my organization will pay you a reward," Morales said again, her voice pleading and weary.

Half a world way, sitting in a Lincoln Town Car on a deserted street in Brovary, Ukraine, Christo sifted through a collection of photos of Morales and Ross. They showed the two of them in her apartment window, sitting at a café, and walking through the streets of Barranca. Christo himself was dressed in a hand-tailored Bond Street suit, with a crisp white shirt and floral tie. He frowned, shifted in the soft leather seats, and gave his attention to the image of Morales on his iPhone.

"Tell me, what is it about you Americans that makes you feel entitled to interfere in my affairs—affairs which are of no concern to you whatsoever." He was smiling, but there was a hard edge to his voice.

"What . . . what are you talking about? My name is Lisa Morales. I am a physician, nothing more." She struggled to continue as Tommy held the phone closer in his enormous hands, but she could only squint at the cell-phone screen through blood-laced eyes.

"I know who you are, Miss Morales, and I know who you work for. I know who Mr. Ross works for, or worked for. What I don't know is how much you know. So why don't you make this easy on both of us and tell me just exactly what you think you know."

"I'm a doctor. I try to prevent mothers from dying at childbirth," she replied, rallying somewhat. "I treat children with malnutrition who are half starved because of you and your dirty business. I work with—" but her sentence ended when Tommy slammed his open palm into the side of her head.

"How did that feel, Miss Morales? Not good, I think. So I want you to think about what I have just said," Christo replied with the same forced smile, "and what I want from you. Now, you have a nice day at the spa." Then to Tommy, "Take me off speakerphone."

Tommy disengaged the speakerphone, put the cell phone up to his ear, and stepped away from her.

"Keep her alive, and don't call me back until she talks." Then, thinking of Tommy and the headache that this meddlesome woman and her CIA handler had caused him, he added, "And after she talks, you may do what you want with her."

"As you say, *Patron*," Tommy replied with a twisted grin.

Christo rung off and exhaled deeply, suspecting it would take a while to get what was needed from Morales. He sensed that she might be a tough one. The women, he mused. They were always the tough ones. He paused a moment to reflect on the passion and stubbornness of the ideologically committed. Fools, he concluded—an irritant but nothing more. He sighed and stared passively out the window of the Town Car into the bland Brovary landscape.

At the compound, Tommy cupped his hand and slammed it against Morales's left ear.

"Diga me," Tommy shouted. He was close enough to spray spittle across her cheek.

"Diga me," he shouted even louder and aimed another blow at the near-lifeless Morales.

High above the dense, emerald-colored jungle canopy, a King Air 350 twin-engine turboprop flew at fifteen thousand feet. It was stacked with the finest high-end monitoring equipment U.S. taxpayers could buy, all focused on the compound directly below.

The American Surveillance Technical Officer—or STO—monitoring the plane's equipment had his headphones on as he huddled against a rack of electronic listening gear. He put his hands over the headphone ear cups to seal out the whine of the aircraft's twin PT6A-60A engines. The STO nodded his head slowly as he listened.

Finally satisfied that he had heard all he needed to hear, his hands flashed to his laptop and raced over the keys. After no more than a few minutes of typing, he hit the SEND key. His message, and a copy of the intercept, was encrypted and uploaded to an orbiting communications satellite.

FOUR

Prior to 9/11 and the ramped-up tempo of operations that evolved in Iraq and Afghanistan, the work of U.S. Special Operations Command and their ground-combat components revolved around proficiency training here at home and joint training exercises with allies overseas. Periodically, they were called into action for short engagements like the incursions into Panama, Grenada, and Somalia. Even the Gulf War was short-lived. The pre-9/11 life of a special operator was one of continuous training and perhaps, if he were lucky, an isolated mission tasking. Things began to get interesting during the 1990s as terrorists were tracked and chased, but SEALs, Green Berets, and Rangers, like most of the conventional forces, remained a garrison force and a force in waiting.

To keep forces poised in a forward-deployed position, the United States had gone to great lengths and expense to maintain bases around the world. Yet the United States had few such bases in Central and South America. One reason for this was that, aside from the issue of drugs, there was no threat from this region. The other was that the Central and South Americans did not particularly want *Norte Americano* bases on their soil. So U.S. force projection into this area was done offshore from units of the fleet or from hastily constructed, temporary land bases, usually at some leased complex near some little-used outlying airstrip. This was where the Bandito squad found themselves shortly after their departure from Coronado.

They occupied a portion of a disused industrial park next to an abandoned airstrip, surrounded by dense tropical vegetation. Occasionally, some unidentified aircraft set down and quickly took off at the nearby strip, usually at night, but there were no aviation services. Their own C-130J delivered them at night and quickly departed. A single dirt road serviced the airstrip. They occupied two warehouses that had cracked concrete floors and leaky roofs but were nestled inside a surprisingly secure chain-link enclosure. Periodically, they were visited by two dated tanker trucks that alternately delivered water and diesel fuel. All business was done in cash, American greenbacks. The buildings where the SEALs and their support team slept on folding cots were kept at a habitable human threshold by generators. Everyone wore civilian clothes—mostly cotton slacks, T-shirts, and shower shoes. There were portable restrooms and a single makeshift shower. They ate MREs and drank bottled water. Two very hardworking Navy Seabees kept the mini-base functioning, and a security detachment of Marines dressed like locals provided unobtrusive security. Lieutenant Engel, Chief Nolan, and the other SEALs went out of their way to thank those who worked around the clock to provide for them and watch over them.

The seemingly hasty operating base was, in fact, a very well-rehearsed and orchestrated mobile presence. It could be set up and taken down in a matter of hours, and moved as conditions dictated. Even though a temporary, transitory facility, it was still an armed presence in a foreign country. Yet it was no rogue operation. This forward operating base was established after careful negotiations with the host nation and the U.S. State Department. While it could have been anywhere in the world, this particular base was in a remote area of Costa Rica, an allied nation. And it was of no small concern to that nation's American ambassador and his country team. Engel and Nolan had flown to the capital to meet with the embassy chief of staff and the CIA station chief. The two were supportive but cautious; they engaged in diplomacy and espionage, not shooting and killing. Yet they had read the message traffic, and they saw much of the raw intelligence. They knew that there indeed might be a need for a special-operations direct-action team. So the presence of this special-operations strike element was official and sanctioned but could be denied by all concerned should that become necessary—clandestine but not necessarily covert.

The only part of the complex that was habitable by accepted standards of comfort or military-like in its construct was their little tactical operations center, or TOC. In deference to the computers, the communications equipment, and the large flat-screen monitors, the temperature in this small enclosed area tucked into a corner of one of the warehouses bordered on chilly. There, Senior Chief Otto Miller set up shop, directed his two intelligence specialists, and coursed through the volumes of electronic message traffic that came across his comm nets. Everything about where they now found themselves was an inconvenience or an accommodation, but their computer and communications suites were state of the art. The operational SEALs could live anywhere and under any conditions—not so their hardware. In his little TOC, the senior chief could video-teleconference with anyone, anywhere, and transmit and receive text and imagery to and from anyone, anywhere. The senior chief even had an espresso coffee machine set up and was seldom without his favorite coffee mug, a chipped ceramic relic that had been around since Moby Dick was a minnow. Engel and Nolan began to find reasons to visit the TOC—for the coffee, for the company of the senior chief, and for the chance to learn if there might be a target folder taking shape. The latter came about on their fourth day there, but not during one of their nightly visits.

Roark Engel was back on the beach on Coronado with Jackie. The tide was way out, and they were running on a flat, firm expanse of wet sand. He was pushing one of those jogger's strollers in front of him, and he could just see the sunbonnet of their child over the stroller canopy. For some reason, his dream's eye could not tell, nor could he remember, if they had a little boy or a little girl. Jackie was radiant, running beside him and smiling. She knew, but somehow he didn't. He kept trying to peer around the bonnet for some clue—boy or girl. Jackie laughed gently, as she often did when she understood something and he didn't. Then she put a hand to his shoulder. Only it wasn't *her* hand.

"Hey, sir, wake up." Suddenly, Engel clamped the offending wrist in a viselike grip. "Easy there, sir. It's just me, Lance Corporal Jennings from security. The senior chief wants you in the TOC right away."

Engel shook himself awake. "Sorry, Corporal. I'll be right there. Wake Chief Nolan as well."

"That's already been done, sir. He'll meet you there."

Engel glanced at his watch; it was 2:00 P.M. local time—1400. If they were assigned a mission, they would undoubtedly go in at night, so the SEALs were already into their daytime sleep cycle. They called them vampire hours. Engel and Nolan arrived dressed alike: olive drab T-shirts, running shorts, and shower shoes. Both had the beginnings of an on-deployment beard. Nolan's hair was matted and askew, while Engel was still resplendent in his pre-deployment buzz cut. Nolan headed for the coffeepot, Engel for Miller.

"What's up, Senior?"

Miller didn't answer immediately. He was focused on his secure laptop, electronically flipping through secret message traffic. Engel waited patiently while Nolan joined them. The senior chief then turned from his computer, all business.

"Lieutenant, Chief," he began. "The listening posts down here have been following a series of intercepts that are a little out of character for the normal flow of druggie chatter. We have computer programs in place that listen, sift, track, and correlate information—words, speech patterns, voice inflections, and a whole array of programmable anomalies. They're at work twenty-four/ seven. Over the past several weeks, there seemed to be some new players in the game. At first the analysts weren't sure if it was a rival cartel or someone else. We're not here to get involved in turf wars or domestic disputes. We were sent down here to stand ready if it was, in fact, something else. That now appears to be the case.

"Three days ago, two CIA types were attacked in a residential apartment complex outside of San José. One was a case officer and the other an agent. The case officer was killed and the agent abducted. There was gunfire and a lot of blood, and in the commotion, one of the opposition was killed and left behind. The dead guy didn't fit the mold of your run-of-the-mill druggie. And as you know, druggies here in Central America don't grow or refine the product; they're just in the distribution chain. From what we can gather from the local *gendarmes*, he may be Eastern European. On top of that, there's something of an unwritten rule that the cartels leave Agency personnel alone, and we don't bother them. The CIA's priority is terrorism, and as long as the spooks are looking for terrorists, they're given a free pass. Also, the agent in question was someone special and something of an embarrassment. She was a medical doctor associated with Doctors Without Borders."

"Aw, for Christ's sake," Engel blurted. "What the hell's the Agency doing putting someone like that at risk?"

"You gotta be shitting me," Nolan added.

"Yeah, I know, but it is what it is, and it looks like we might have to deal with it."

The CIA recruits their agents from any number of sources, always looking for a way inside the group they wish to penetrate. They often provide intelligence to other agencies on the illegal drug traffic, but they seldom work penetration agents on the cartels. The Agency also made a point of staying away from NGOs, especially the big ones like Oxfam, World Vision, and Doctors Without Borders. Everyone recognized and applauded their work, and to use someone under the cover of an NGO or even a nonprofit was a big no-no.

"Susan, maybe you can help us out with this."

Lieutenant Susan Lyons was a trim woman in her mid-thirties with wavy, auburn hair pulled back in a short, no-nonsense ponytail. She was dressed in the khaki uniform of a Navy lieutenant, complete with a Surface Warfare pin and a modest row of campaign ribbons. Ostensibly, she was a Navy intelligence officer. She'd arrived in a light plane early this morning and immediately met behind closed doors with the senior chief. She seemed to wear the uniform well, Engel noted, thinking that she might even be a reservist. But he doubted that she was active-duty Navy. The senior had called her by her first name, and he was religious about military courtesies. Whoever she was, she was something more than a Navy lieutenant.

"My name is Lieutenant Susan Lyons, and I'm attached to the embassy," she began, casting a thanks-a-lot look at Senior Chief Miller. "I'm going to give this to you as straight up as I can, and I hope it'll be enough. The two people involved are Walter Ross and a Dr. Lisa Morales, both U.S. citizens. Your concerns about Dr. Morales working for American intelligence and an NGO are noted. But why she was doing this is not relevant; that's well above all our pay grades. I can, however, tell you that issues of national security and homeland defense are very much in play here. She was not there just to spy on drug lords, okay?"

It was not okay, but Engel held his tongue. Nolan started to say something, but Engel put a hand on his knee. "Okay for now, Susan. Please, we're all ears."

She gave him a measured look and then continued. "Ross and Morales were tracking some undesirables that were known associates of one Mikhail Troikawicz, better known in the international arms trade as Christo. Morales had even had contact with Christo in her DWB work. Now, we care a great deal about Christo. He supplies a lot of people with a lot of weapons." She pulled a notebook from her briefcase, flipped to a page, gave it a quick glance, but never looked at it again. "Christo was born in Grozny on 15 April 1964. His uncles were all Chechen separatists; they fought the Russians and profited from the fighting. Christo was not a fighter, but he gravitated to the profit side of the war. After most of his relations were killed, he relocated to Central America, retaining his Chechen clients and taking on the Sandinistas and cartels. He's a smart guy, with a degree in business from the University of Virginia and an MBA from Wharton. He works all sides of the street, to include legal government purchases for many Central and South American nations." She hesitated a moment, then continued. "Our side has even used his organization to get weapons to national liberation movements we support. He also supplies weapons to the Russian mafia, the FARC, the Muslim Brotherhood, and just about every al-Qaeda splinter group you can name. When he can, he stays away from the business of drugs, sort of a self-imposed, non-compete agreement. When he can't, it's usually as an accommodation for one of his cartel clients. He's important, and he's a bad guy. We've wanted him for a long time. But he's a slick one. He's very wealthy, and he spreads a lot of money about—in the pockets of politicians and for worthy regional and local charities. He makes a sizeable annual contribution to Doctors Without Borders.

"While he's tried to upgrade his image, Christo's Chechen roots have recently dragged him back into the sewer. He's had a long-standing, on-again/off-again relationship with a character named Abu Shabal. Shabal *is* a terrorist—a terrorist bent on mass murder. He was involved in the Beslan School Massacre in 2004, and the Russians have a price on his head. He's reportedly been jumping in and out of training camps in the southern Philippines and in Indonesia. We think he may have even been personally involved in the killing of Ambassador Marguilles in Jakarta, along with thirty-seven school-children. If Christo is bad, then Shabal is evil—evil in the worst kind of way. This is what may have gotten Ross killed and Morales taken alive, and God only knows what they're doing to her."

"All this is interesting, ma'am," Nolan said, "but what's the executive version of all this; what's our bottom line here?"

Senior Chief Miller smoothly intervened. "Just before sunrise today, we got an ISR platform aloft and on station near where we think they might be holding her. Here's an overhead shot of the place about a week ago."

He brought up a blurred, thermal image of a scattering of huts that appeared to be a small base camp most likely used for transshipment or repackaging of narcotics on their way north. There was modest activity. "Now this is the way it looked earlier this morning."

Miller brought up another thermal/low-light-level video composite of the same camp. It rotated slowly in a clockwise direction, which meant the ISR bird was circling high above in a counterclockwise orbit. The intelligence, surveillance, and reconnaissance aircraft were marvels of technology in integrated imagery overlay. They could lock onto a piece of earth like this base camp and, using a combination of visual, thermal, infrared, and radar sensors, deliver an enhanced picture that was both encrypted and real time. They were now looking at imagery that was eight hours old. The best imagery was obtained at night when the ISR platforms could fly lower and see better than in the daytime. Neither Engel nor Nolan asked if this was a drone or a specially outfitted light aircraft flown by a military contractor. It didn't matter. They could see that the number of people in the camp had risen dramatically, as had what appeared to be an increase in security activity in and around the camp.

"As you guys can see, something's going on down there, and it doesn't fit the normal pattern of drug activity. This building here," Miller said, pointing to a single structure at the edge of the main encampment grouping, "is probably where they have her—if she's there. We've been able to establish that this hut gets traffic at all hours, suggesting this may be where she's being held and where they're probably interrogating her. Earlier today, we got a cell-phone intercept that all but confirmed she's in the camp. So it's a straightforward personnel recovery mission. It won't be easy, but it's doable." The senior chief smiled wolfishly, "But, hey, easy for me to say. I'm not going in." He tabbed a key and the image went to a smaller scale showing a river snaking past about a quarter mile from the camp. "We can insert you here by parachute, probably a free-fall drop since the drug-traffic trapline is alert for low-flying aircraft. As for coming out, we have a special boat team with the amphibious ready group cruising offshore. They can be inserted well downstream and be standing by for an extraction. And, who knows, you might need some on-call firepower."

"Any intel on the opposition?" Nolan asked.

"Not much. It's my guess—our guess," Miller replied, glancing at Lyons, "that security will be in tiers and on loan, or on lease, from the cartels. From the imagery, there'll be a dozen or more at the site, but there are sure to be plenty more in the area. So you'll have to limit your time on target. As for Morales, they know what they have and who they have. They'll interrogate her and either put her up for sale, what's left of her, or just kill her. Given the connection to Christo and Shabal, they'll probably just kill her. So a high-value target but not necessarily high-value security. Standard druggie armed thugs but good ones, and they'll probably be reasonably alert. They will be well armed with minimal training, but not afraid to fight and die. Lots of collective bravado, tactically primitive, and unpredictable. Most certainly, dangerous." He gave them a palms-up gesture. "Wish I could be more specific, but that's about it."

"It's like this, gentlemen," Susan Lyons said in a quiet

voice. "She put herself and her organization at risk to help us. Now she needs our help. A very brave lady is going to die a horrible death unless you can do something about it. And she does have information we'd like the opposition not to have. Yet I know how it is—that on a mission like this, it's your call. All I can ask is that you please try and help her."

With that, she rose and exited the TOC, leaving Miller, Engel, and Nolan sitting in a tight little circle around the flat screen. They were quiet for a long moment before Engel broke the silence. "She certainly does know how it is," he said, "and she put the turd in our pocket."

They all, in fact, knew. Personnel recoveries were dangerous and chancy business. Balanced against the chance of success was a significant risk of failure. Failure came in at least two forms: getting the subject of the recovery killed or getting some of your own guys killed, or both. Ultimately, unless it was a rare issue of immediate national security, the go/no-go decision to commit a team to a personnel recovery operation rested at the task force or local level. Since they were operating as an independent detachment, it was their call—they could be ordered not to go, but it was their call to go. It was Nolan who finally spoke.

"If it was just some do-gooder who had gotten lost or pissed off the locals, I'd say she made her bed and let her sleep in it. But since she was working for us, well, that makes it different. Kind of binds the cheese, so to speak."

Engel nodded. "Yeah. Technically, this makes her one of our own, and we don't leave one of our own behind.

Senior, you're more read into this than either one of us. You think the good lieutenant is leveling with us?"

Miller leaned forward, elbows on his knees over steepled fingers. "I think she is. She didn't say as much, but I think she knows and admires this Morales lady. But I give her credit; she seems to be giving us the straight stuff. Either we go get Morales or she dies badly. Sir, it's your call. That's why they pay you the big bucks, and chiefs like Nolan and I have to make do on starvation wages."

"Well, shit," Engel said. He pushed himself to his feet and began to pace about the TOC. The call would be his—his and Nolan's. But ultimately, the responsibility was his alone. As with all small-unit commanders, there were three things he must weigh and weigh quickly, as the mission was time sensitive. He had to balance the mission, the lives of his men, and any risk to noncombatants. Noncombatants would be a side issue on a mission like this, but even in a druggie camp there could be women and children.

"When can we go, Senior?" Engel knew Miller would already be staging assets and arranging clearances to support the mission, should he elect to go.

"I can have your support package in place by midnight. It would seem a predawn hit would be in order, with an after-dawn extraction."

Engel again nodded, this time with some finality. He had only to glance at Nolan for his input—he nodded imperceptibly. "Okay, then, it's a go. Senior, you know what to do. Chief, roust the boys, and let's get at it."

"You got it, Boss."

Nolan left the TOC to get the other SEALs up and moving. Miller returned to one of his communications terminals and set in motion the mechanics of a special-operations personnel-recovery operation. Engel stepped out to find Susan Lyons. He wanted to see if he could get a little more straight talk from her.

Once alerted for a mission and briefed on the mission basics by Chief Nolan, the SEAL Bandito squad set about their business. They'd done this many times before and needed little direction. Each had his own area of responsibility. From now until they launched for the mission, the squad would collectively prepare equipment, plan the mission, brief the mission, and rehearse their actions on target. This is what they would do if they had two days, two weeks, two hours, or, in this case, about eight hours.

Sonny checked with each SEAL to confirm what weapon he would be carrying and began to set out ammunition, grenades, and special weapons systems accordingly. Since on this mission he would be engaged in room clearing rather than fire support, he would carry the lighter M46, a belt-fed .556 submachine gun. As the squad member tasked with air-operations responsibility, he would also see that the parachutes were laid out and inspected along with the gear bags they would use in the jump. Ray, as the primary communicator, began work on the comm plan with primary and alternative frequencies. He would work closely with Lieutenant Engel to manage the on-call support assets and to monitor the command-and-control net. He also set up the tactical

SEAL net, which would drive the flow of the operation on the ground. Part of Ray's job would be to ensure that each multiband inter-squad team radio was inspected, encrypted, mated to a fresh battery pack, and fully tested. They would not have a dedicated sniper overwatch team for this mission, but Weimy would carry a suppressed Mk12, a sniperized version of the M4 assault rifle that was sniper-accurate for the ranges they'd be working. He, too, could be tasked with room-clearing duties, and the Mk12, if a little long, would still serve in that role. But his primary job would be to kill quietly at a distance. There was little for Mikey to do, as each SEAL medical kit was up to date, as was his own squad medical bag, but he knew he would be responsible for tending to Morales and getting her ready for travel. He haunted the senior chief and Lieutenant Lyons for any updates on her condition. A.J. was the squad point man. His job would be to take the team from the insertion point to the target and from the target to the extraction point. Although the waypoints to the target and the extraction lanes would be GPS-driven coordinates and azimuths, he also needed to be able to find his way by compass and pace count should their GPS fail. For most of the afternoon, A.J. pored over maps and imagery to establish insertion points, extraction sites, and alternative extraction sites.

Nolan and Engel spent the balance of the afternoon reading intelligence reports and looking at imagery of the target. They focused on developing the plan of attack and the all-important actions on target. They'd done this many times before in Iraq and Afghanistan, but in the sandbox they had two very distinct advantages. First, they were blessed with good intelligence on the opposition and precise, state-of-the-art targeting imagery. Second, there was always an overwhelming quick-reaction force on standby if they got into trouble. On this mission, they had sketchy intelligence on the bad guys and the target area, and if they ran into problems, their contingencies were limited. They grabbed a quick MRE and worked into the evening. By 2200, they had constructed a reasonably accurate sand-table terrain model of the target encampment and what they hoped was the building where Morales was being held. Nolan stood back to inspect their work.

"It's not great, Boss, but it's probably as close as we're going to get."

"I agree," Engel replied. "You never know enough, but in this case I'd sure like to know a helluva lot more."

Nolan shrugged. "In the end, it all comes down to the basics—the element of surprise and violence of action. If we get that, then we'll get this done."

"And God help us if for some reason they know we're coming."

"Amen to that. You ready for operational briefing?"

"As ready as I can be. Let's do it."

Fifteen minutes later, the squad was assembled in the TOC. The senior chief and Lieutenant Lyons updated them on the intel picture. Then each member of the squad gave a short briefing on his area of responsibility. Engel then gathered them around the terrain model and walked them through their actions on target—what they *planned* for actions on target. After a short rehearsal behind the warehouse using an old shed as a target building, they began to gear up for the mission. At midnight, an MC-130H landed at the remote airstrip and paused to receive the squad of heavily armed SEALs. As they moved out onto the tarmac, Lieutenant Lyons stepped from the shadows.

"Guys, I'll not be here when you get back, but I wanted to thank you for what you're about to do. Good hunting and Godspeed."

The SEALs clambered aboard yet another C-130 airframe, but this one was different. It was an MC-130H Combat Talon II—a special-operations, deep-penetration bird. At more than three times the cost of a C-130H or one of the later variants, the Combat Talon had an electronic suite that allowed it to "feel" its way through commercial and military radar coverage to stealthily deliver its cargo. But for the guys in the back, the cargo, there was little discernable difference; it was still a 130. For this clandestine pickup, there was the noise of the aircraft coming and going, but no lights. It was a black operation—literally. As they gained altitude, Mikey, who was seated next to Engel, leaned close and shouted in his ear.

"Hey, Boss, me and the other guys have been talking. When we get back to Coronado, we're gonna get that guy."

"What guy?"

"The guy that gave you that fucked-up haircut."

Across the bay of the 130 and to either side, broad white smiles cut the blackened faces of the squad SEALs. A short time later, the drop aircraft approached the target at twenty-two thousand feet, well above an altitude where some notice might be taken on the ground. The ramp/door combination ground open and the heavily laden SEALs shuffled to the rear, bunching up on the ramp. The smiles were gone; now was the time for business. The red lights on either side of the ramp winked out and were replaced by green lights. The SEAL squad tumbled from the rear of the 130 as a single mass.

As the SEALs tumbled into space over Costa Rica, two Sikorsky CH-53E "Super Stallion" Marine Corps helicopters sat turning on the massive flight deck of the USS *Bonhomme Richard* (LHA-6). The "*Bonnie Dick*," as she was known in the fleet and by those who served on her, was a U.S. Navy big-deck amphibious ship steaming fifty miles off the coast of Costa Rica—forty-one thousand tons of versatile U.S. Navy expeditionary muscle. The *Bonnie Dick* had an impressive array of defensive armaments, as well as a wing of AV-8B Harrier II attack jets, a fleet of assault helicopters, and close to two thousand marines. The downdraft from the Super Stallion's seven-bladed rotors washed the ship's flight deck with gale-force winds as the bird's pilots performed their final prelaunch checks.

"Tower, Bulldog Six-One and flight, ready to lift."

"Bulldog Six-One and wing, cleared to lift, winds eighteen knots on the nose and stay with me on this net."

"Roger, Tower."

With that, both birds lifted gently from the deck. The intensity of their downwash increased to hurricane force as they pulled into a hover.

The Bulldog wingman, Bulldog Six-Three, dipped his nose and thundered straight ahead into the blackness, the helo's rotating red anticollision beacons and tiny red, green, and white position lights providing the only light, save that of a full complement of stars overhead. Bulldog Six-One, the lead helo, slid smartly to the *Bonhomme Richard*'s port side and remained in a hover, sixty feet above the black ocean below. Once in a stable hover, the big helo began to drift back to the port stern quarter of the *Bonnie Dick*.

As Bulldog Six-Three turned lazy circles directly above the ship and Six-One hovered, one of the two Special Operations Craft-Riverine, or SOC-R for short, was positioned on the aft portion of the *Bonhomme Richard*'s flight deck. The flight-deck drill this night was to hang a thirty-six-foot, fourteen-thousand-pound combat craft from each helo. Inside each bird, a five-man boat crew from Special Boat Team 22 looked on anxiously. For these highly trained Special Warfare Combatant-craft Crewmen, or SWCCs, this was high drama—and more than a little nerve-racking. All they could do was watch as the twenty-ton helicopter hovered over the beloved boat.

Bulldog Six-One's pilot carefully lowered his hover to just ten feet over the first SOC-R combat craft. A flight-deck crewman in his yellow flotation vest and flight-deck helmet reached up with a long pole and attached the steel cable from the SOC-R's boat harness to the large cargo hook on the underside of the Super Stallion. Once complete, the landing signals officer standing directly in front of Bulldog Six-One raised his spread arms up and up again, signaling the pilot to lift his hover and accept his burden. Gradually, the Super Stallion took tension on the four-point sling, and the SOC-R was airborne.

The Bulldog lead pilot, moving more carefully now that he had his cargo slung underneath and making small cockpit corrections, dipped the nose of the Super Stallion as he began to creep forward. Once through translational lift, he increased speed to ninety knots and took up position on the *Bonhomme Richard*'s starboard side, orbiting in circles five hundred feet above the black ocean. The Super Stallion and the SOC-R now moved as one.

With Bulldog Six-One's pickup complete, Bulldog Six-Three's pilot spiraled down from five hundred feet and followed the ship's wake until he was at *Bonnie Dick*'s fantail. He then eased over and above the second SOC-R boat. The pilots and crewman on the deck completed the same maneuver as with the lead bird. Bulldog Six-Three, mission ready and transitioning to forward flight, eased away from the *Bonhomme Richard*'s port side. Thanks to the skill of the Marine pilots, the delicate maneuver had taken less than fifteen minutes.

"Bulldog Six-One and flight, you are cleared to switch control frequency; come up 262.5 megahertz and have a safe flight."

"Bulldog Six-One, roger," the lead pilot replied as he flew straight ahead, still at five hundred feet. Within a minute Bulldog Six-Three was formed up in loose cruise formation on Six-One's starboard side as the two Super Stallions turned gently east toward the west coast of Costa Rica.

Forty-five minutes later, the two CH-53Es thundered over the treetops of the lush Costa Rican jungle, their slung matte gray SOC-R boats conforming to their every move. They remained just above the treetops to avoid any commercial radar detection, and they showed no lights. The Marine pilots, relying on their Helicopter

Night Vision Systems, their GPS navigation systems, and hours upon hours of night-flight training, made their way precisely toward their insertion point with no ground reference points or electronic emissions.

The two Super Stallions slowed as they found the river, Bulldog Six-Three pulling into loose trail behind his leader. Established in a hover over the wide river, the Super Stallion's pilots gently lowered the SOC-R boats into the water. As they did, each boat's five SWCCs, with a great deal of relief, clambered down rope ladders into their boats. Once waterborne, they were back in their element.

The "boat guys," as their SEAL brethren called them, traced their roots back to the U.S. Navy torpedo boats of World War II. The SWCCs, called "swicks," could take the SEALs where deep draft Navy ships couldn't—into shallow water and far up rivers like this one. The SOC-Rs drew just twenty-four inches. Their mission this night wasn't to deliver the SEALs to the fight; it would be to extract them.

The coxswains gave their respective Super Stallions a thumbs-up, and the bird's pilots cut the umbilical holding the boats underneath them. Their mission complete, the CH-53Es turned west toward the blue water and their home plate, the *Bonnie Dick*. The boat crews immediately began to prepare their craft for high-speed travel into harm's way. The well-tested engines roared to life at the touch of the ignition. The coxswains then pointed their bows upriver, the engines at an impatient idle and the two Hamilton waterjets holding each craft steady against the gentle current. Each boat leader, a Navy chief petty officer, took charge of his boat and directed his small crew to "armor up." The SOC-R carried a formidable arsenal of .50-caliber machine guns, 40mm grenade launchers, and 7.62mm mini-guns.

Chief Ricardo Bautista—the officer in charge, or OIC, of the lead, or One Boat—quietly barked orders to his crew. The noise of the departing helicopters marked their presence, but no use letting those who might be listening know there were *North* Americans on the river.

"You know the drill, Wilson. I want the .50-cals fore and aft, and the mini-guns port and starboard."

"Got it, Chief."

"Bachmann, have the grenade launchers at the ready in case we need them."

"Roger that, Chief."

There was a flurry of activity as both crews removed the weapons systems from their tied-down, stored positions and mounted them on their craft's gunwales and fixed stanchions. Heavy cans of ammunition were broken out and made ready. Neither boat showed a light as the crews went about their business in total darkness. There was the occasional flicker of a well-hooded red penlight. The swicks knew their boats, and they knew their systems. On the lead SOC-R, each crewman reported when he was up and ready. It was much the same on the Two Boat.

Bautista watched from his coxswain's flat, missing nothing. When all was ready, he pulled himself up to his full five feet eight and turned to the others. "Okay, guys, bring it in." His four swicks collapsed in around the helm. "Now, listen up. We got SEALs on the ground in bad-guy territory. Our job is to extract them safely, and the recent intel says there's a good chance it'll be a hot extraction. Everyone, stay focused and stay professional. Call out your targets; do it just like you trained. There'll be bad guys out there as well as our SEAL brothers. Make damn sure of your targets, then bring the pain. Got it?"

Bautista's crew nodded in unison. They got it.

"Two Boat, One Boat, over," Bautista said into his encrypted lip mic.

"Two Boat here, manned and ready, over."

"Roger, Two. Standby to get underway, One out."

With that, Bautista slammed the SOC-R's throttles forward, and the twin 440 Yanmar Diesels went from their idle grumble to a full-on roar. First one craft, then the other, leapt up on step and roared up the river at forty knots. The Two Boat followed a hundred meters behind the One, its crew undoubtedly motivated by a talk just like Bautista's.

As the two boats sped upriver, their crews, all wearing the latest generation night-vision devices, scanned the shorelines, where the jungle ran right into the water. The river was flat-black under the stars and narrowed imperceptibly as they made their way upstream. Bautista wore a singular night-vision optic. This allowed him to see the dark ribbon of river ahead and to monitor the nav-aids on his console. His primary aid was an enhanced Garmin GPSMAP 720 Marine Navigator, not unlike those found on mega-yachts. The river, the riverbanks, the Two Boat, and any above-water features were easily seen on the color monitor. Even without the night-vision ocular, he could find his way. Getting there was one thing; getting there at the right time was yet another. A hot extraction could be chancy, high-risk business.

They needed to be on time to recover their SEALs but not too early, as the SOC-R's roaring engines could be heard for miles. Timing was everything, and in this case, "everything" meant life and death. His split concentration, half river and half electronics, was broken by Wilson on their tactical net.

"Shit, Chief, this jungle looks really thick, probably just like the jungle your pappy saw when he was driving Swift Boats in Vietnam."

Wilson, Bautista said to himself. It was always Wilson. He was the crew clown—the two-boat section clown, actually. But Petty Officer Josh Wilson was a superb gunner and considered one of the best in Special Boat Team 22. So Bautista put up with him—even indulged him. The boy was a surgeon with a mini-gun.

"That was my *grand*pappy, Wilson. Now keep your eyes on your sector and your mind on your job."

"No worries, Chief," Wilson replied, stroking the barrel of his 7.62mm mini-gun.

"Bachmann, you awake?"

"Roger, Chief, right here." The reliable Petty Officer Ted Bachmann was both awake and ready. He was the team's electronics and communications specialist.

"Let's get the Raven ready to launch."

"Roger that, Chief."

Bachmann had carefully assembled and tested the RQ-11 Raven drone. He had only to reach down into the bottom of the boat and carefully lift the little aircraft from its cradle. Less than three feet long and weighing only four pounds, the Raven was one of the better and more useful unmanned aerial systems. The SEALs and the Special Boat Teams depended on it for tactical surveillance and reconnaissance. The Raven's digital data-link was capable of pushing streaming video of everything its sensors could see from just overhead to the bird's ten-thousand-foot operational ceiling. This Raven variant has an extended-range capability that allowed it to stay aloft for close to three hours. It was a lot of capability in a small, portable, combat-ready package. And it was operator friendly. Both SEALs and swicks used it extensively.

"Ready, Chief."

"Make it happen, Ted." Bautista slowed the One Boat to twenty knots; the boat was faster than the bird.

Bachmann activated the Raven's sensor package and checked to see that he had a presentation on his laptop computer. Then he switched on the battery-driven electronic motor and held the little drone over his head. Usually it was "thrown" into the air for a launching. This night, with the movement of the boat, the Raven just floated up and away.

"Raven's airborne, Chief," Bachmann reported. "I have good copy on all sensors."

"Good job. Keep it headed upriver and just ahead of us." Bautista touched a key on the front of his body armor to shift frequency. "Two Boat, One here. Be advised our Raven is away. We'll continue upriver at this speed. Estimate we'll be at our initial layup position in fifteen mikes, over."

"Ah, roger, One. Initial layup in fifteen minutes, Two out."

Ten minutes later the two SOC-Rs cut their power and came off step. From there to their initial layup or standby position on the river, they would move at idle speed. At a predetermined 45-degree bend in the river, first one craft, then the other, folded itself into the foliage on the left outside bend of the riverbank. They tied off on mangrove trees with quick-release mooring lines. Both boats shut down and waited in a deafening silence. Each had an unobstructed view up and down the river, and they were virtually invisible along the bank. Ten minutes later, the UHF SATCOM radio crackled to life in Bautista's headset.

FIVE

All seven SEALs hit the same partially cultivated field within seconds of each other and in a tight group. That was the beauty of a free-fall insertion with steerable parachutes. The seven had formed up on Sonny after they left the MC-130H, fell three thousand feet, and opened their chutes at the same time. Then, under canopy, they followed him to the precise drop zone location he'd selected in planning the jump. Without a word, the squad rallied and moved into the shelter of an abandoned banana grove, stashed their parachutes, and began to quietly strap on their body armor, operational gear, and weapons. It was doubtful that they had been seen, but they were taking no chances. Once geared up, they went into a security perimeter and listened for five minutes in complete silence. Engel called Ray over to him. Ray passed him a handset that was on a coiled tether to his satellite radio.

"Mother Goose, this is Blackbeard, over," he said in a low voice.

"This is Mother Goose, over." Through the encryption and the space-borne relays, he could make out the controlled voice of the senior chief. And, Engel thought, perhaps a note of relief as well.

"This is Blackbeard. We are at Point Alpha, how copy, over?"

"Mother Goose. Copy you at Point Alpha, over."

"Blackbeard, roger, out."

While Engel called in their safe insertion, Chief Nolan began to work his way from man to man around the circle, making sure there were no issues from the jump.

"Nicely done, Sonny," Nolan said in a low voice when he came to the big SEAL. "Couldn't have picked a better DZ."

When he got to A.J., "Ready?"

"Ready, Chief. Target is two eight zero, about four clicks."

Finally, he made his way to Engel. "We're up, Boss. A.J. has us about two and a half miles east of the target. Y'know what I really like about an operational jump?"

Engel paused, rolled his eyes, knowing he would have to hear this.

"You don't have to hump your shit a mile or so off some big Army drop zone, and there's no rigger standing by to give you crap about how you coiled up your chute."

Engel couldn't help but grin. "Okay, Chief. Now that we've got that settled—let's go to war."

Nolan turned and signaled to A.J., pumping his fist in the air. The Bandito point man turned, rose, and began to move. Without another word, seven dark forms filed out of the banana grove traveling east—A.J. on point followed by Engel, Ray, Sonny, Mikey, and Weimy, with Chief Nolan bringing up the rear. Periodically, A.J. would halt the patrol, and they would all listen and then move out again. Their drop zone was at one thousand feet elevation, just above the coastal mangrove that bordered the edge of a deciduous forest. As they descended to lower elevation, the ground became incrementally wetter. A.J. picked their way through small groves of ceiba and bamboo with an occasional fig or mango tree. The undergrowth was a mosaic of saw grass, low palms, ferns, and flowering shrubs. Had it been daylight, they would have been amazed at the variety, density, and coloring of the orchids. Since they had left the banana grove, they had encountered no sign of cultivation or any structures, but that was expected. They were making their way toward the marshy coastal lowlands. Apart from a dog barking in the distance and the occasional scurrying of an animal or a reptile, they moved in complete silence and solitude. They also moved quickly with the help of their night observation devices, or NODs, and a sliver of a moon that would not set until just before dawn. A.J. had planned their route well, keeping them on solid ground. Only as they approached the target did they begin to walk through marshy areas. At a security halt some four hundred meters from the target, Engel again turned to Ray, who was just behind him in the patrol. This time Ray took a pigtail from his satellite radio and plugged it into one on Engel's combat harness.

"Mother Goose, Blackbeard. You still with me, over?" he now spoke into his encrypted helmet mic.

"Mother Goose, here, over."

"Roger, Mother Goose. Approaching target from the east per our planned route. Anything from Whiplash, over?"

Miller paused a moment and then, "Whiplash is on the move and expects to be operational at his insertion point in ten minutes, over."

"Roger, ten mikes to his insertion. We are moving to the pre-assault position. Estimate forty mikes to beginning the assault, over."

"Copy forty mikes to the assault. Mother Goose, roger, out."

At a hundred meters from the camp, they smelled the damp smoke of a wood-burning stove. At sixty meters, they began to hear voices, but there was no alarm in them—mostly coughing, bursts of guttural Spanish, and an occasional laugh. Otherwise, there were only the normal jungle-swamp noises. A.J. halted the patrol forty meters from the encampment, and no one moved for ten minutes. Then he called Engel forward, and the two lay side by side. They could clearly see the long, low building that was the compound's central structure, plus two outlying structures that were more distant and partially shrouded in the mist rising from the swampy ground. The area immediately in front of them was dark but for dim interior lighting in the main building. This was where they were holding Morales—if their intelligence was accurate. They could see what appeared to be security lights on poles on the other side of the camp, the side served by the main access road, but from their vantage they appeared only as distant and luminescent balls of cotton to the naked eye. In their night optics,

they were fireballs. They knew there were other structures near the main access road, but they were lost in
mist and mangrove. That there were lights but no gen-
erator sound meant there was electricity and perhaps
even phone service. What was not shrouded in the rising
mist they could see well with their night-vision devices.
These were the latest generation of NODs, with low-
ambient light and thermal capability. The huts were
cheap wooden-framed constructions—cottage-like affairs
with corrugated roofing. All were built a few feet off the
ground on stilts. There were planks leading from the
front and rear of the main building in deference to
the muddy ground. Almost all the camp, except what lay
directly before them, was protected by a crude eight-foot
chain-link fence topped with barbed wire. Between the
SEALs and the huts, there was twenty meters of a shallow estuary that joined the main river several hundred
meters north of the compound. The SEALs had pur-
posefully selected a route that would bring them in this
way; it was the most difficult and therefore the least
likely avenue of approach.

The encampment was served by a dirt road that led
from the far side of the camp due west toward the coast.
A secondary road led north from the main building to
the river some four hundred meters beyond. A.J. brought
them to the eastern edge of the encampment exactly as
planned. Engel squeezed him on the shoulder—good
job. A.J. had secured his GPS receiver and continued to
study the camp with his NOD.

"Security?" Engel whispered.

"I've seen two. One is on roving patrol, and the other
is seated on a bench just outside the front door to the

main building. And off to the right, about forty-five feet in the air, see it?"

Engel did, easily. "Got him." Both knew that the glow of a cigarette tip that high, which looked like a flare with the NODs, could only mean a sentry in a guard tower. Everything else, including a second guard tower on the far side of the camp, was obscured by a stand of mangrove and the night mist.

The plan called for a predawn assault with an after-dawn extraction. Dawn was still an hour away, which meant they had ample time to scout the encampment and carefully ease into position before moving on the target building. Engel moved back close to Ray.

"Tell the senior chief we're at the camp and have the target structure in sight. Proceeding according to plan."

Ray nodded and quietly called Mother Goose on his radio with their position and information. Then Engel keyed his tactical radio, speaking quietly into the boom mic from his helmet. Due to the marvels of technology, SEALs and other special operators all wore headphones that allowed them to hear radio traffic clearly, and they had only to whisper into their boom microphones to transmit. The headphones were also equipped with sound-canceling and enhancement features that blocked loud noises, like gunfire and explosions, but amplified all other sound. They could hear footfalls, quiet conversation, leaves rustling, and the buzz of the swamp sounds quite clearly. Engel carried two radios, one tuned to the frequency of his support net and the other to the frequency of his squad tactical net. He keyed his tactical net freq.

"Okay, Banditos, radio check." They answered in turn.

"A.J. here."

"Ray here."

"Sonny here."

"Mikey with you."

"Weimy here."

"All present," Nolan added.

"Okay, guys," Engel whispered into his mic, "we're at the camp and at the jump-off point. Stand by to move to your pre-assault positions. Boss out." Then he keyed his other radio, the one that connected him to his support net.

"Whiplash, this is Blackbeard. You with us, over?"

"Whiplash is standing by and in position. Laying up thirty mikes at a fast run from your primary extraction site, over."

A wave of relief swept over Engel. His boat support team was in place, according to plan and just as he had expected. Had it been otherwise, the senior chief would have told him. Still, it was comforting to know there were friends nearby.

"Good to have you with us, Whiplash. We are on target and moving to our pre-assault positions. Our Raven airborne, over?"

"The Raven is airborne and headed your way, and Whiplash is standing by. Good hunting, out."

Engel paused to take a deep breath, then keyed his tactical radio.

"Chief, come up here."

"Roger, moving."

Nolan moved up the file, dropping to a knee between A.J. and his lieutenant. The three of them again studied what they could see across the short expanse of dirty water. For a security force, the water represented a barrier and security; for SEALs, it meant concealment and sanctuary. A few minutes earlier, A.J. had spotted another two sentries on roving patrol on the far side of the camp. That made a total of five. But to get across the water, the sentry in the guard tower would have to be dealt with. Engel bent close to his chief.

"We're a bit ahead of schedule. Believe we should bring the squad up online and hold here for another ten minutes or so, then begin working our way across the water toward the target hooch. There's a shallow rise just a few meters to our right and just above the water. I can control from there, and it's a good perch for Weimy."

Nolan studied the ground. "From the looks of the security on this side of the camp, there may be a few more Tangos than we bargained for." Tangos, in the SEAL lexicon, were terrorists, but the term could be applied to any member of the opposition. "Might be we could use your gun in this fight."

Engel considered this. In a small-unit engagement, the platoon or squad leader needed to keep himself in a position where he had oversight of the ground action and could coordinate the supporting elements. His weapons were his radios. If he were in the fight, he could not do that as well. So, as was often the case, the leader positioned himself to control the fight, and his number two led the fight. Given what he was seeing across the canal in the way of security, another gun in the assault element would certainly help, maybe even be a game changer. But this assault might well turn into a melee, and he needed to stay above it.

"That's tempting, but I better be where I can control the action." He glanced at his watch. Then, "Let's get 'em online and do this thing. Let me know when you're ready to cross."

Nolan nodded and keyed his tac radio. "Okay, guys, let's go get this lady. Weimy, you're with the Boss. The rest of you, on me."

The five SEALs moved as one across the short piece of open ground to the edge of the estuary, making good use of the palmetto growth at the water's edge. Engel and Weimy moved off to their right to a gentle rise that afforded them a good view of the encampment and the main camp building. Weimy began to scan the camp through his Mk12 optic sight, noting targets for future attention and looking for others not yet found. Engel laid his M4 to one side and pulled a small case from his rucksack. Using the lid as a light shield, he flipped on the Toughbook laptop. It took a few moments for the device to find the satellite and bring up the preset program. Then the screen filled with an infrared presentation of a jungle canopy moving slowly from the top of the screen to the bottom. He keyed his radio on the support net.

"Whiplash, this is Blackbeard. I'll take control of the Raven now, over."

"Blackbeard, Whiplash. You have the Raven, over."

"Blackbeard, roger, out."

Engel typed in a set of GPS coordinates, and the presentation began to rotate as the little drone responded to new guidance. Within minutes, the camp came into view. Engel put the aircraft into an orbit over the target, brought it down to a thousand feet over the camp, and adjusted the camera zoom. He began to pick up details of the camp, the long central building, and finally the two guards on the ground, plus the third in the guard tower.

Nolan came up on the tactical net. "Okay, Boss, we're in position."

"Roger, stand by to move when I give you the word."

"Roger."

The delay before an assault, when everyone was in place, was important. It allowed the SEALs in the assault element to become oriented to the camp, the swamp sounds around them, and the target building. It allowed Engel and Weimy time to study the layout in front of them and become familiar with the movement of sentries. After close to ten minutes, Engel came up on the tac net.

"Ready, Chief?"

"Ready, Boss."

Engel leaned close to his sniper. "Okay, Weimy, he's yours."

From his perch, Weimy could clearly see the guard in the tower a hundred meters away. Through his AN/PVS-4 low-light scope, it was as if the man was just twenty-five meters away in broad daylight. It was by no means a difficult shot, but he didn't want the guard to fall from the tower and create a disturbance. The guard was no longer smoking, but he was leaning against the rail of the tower's small elevated platform, an AK-47 held loosely in the crook of his arm. His head periodically bobbed as he fought going to sleep. Weimy centered the crosshairs as he went into his breathing cycle, then pressed the trigger.

The guard dropped silently to the tower platform like a wet rag, but his canteen tumbled over the edge. Weimy and Engel winced, but there was no sound as it fell into the soft mud at the base of the tower. The only sound was the cough of the suppressed rifle and the audible *snap* of the bullet cracking the sound barrier on its way to the target. Following the shot, they all waited in silence for any reaction from the crack of the round. There was none.

"Okay, Chief. You're good to cross."

"Roger, we're moving."

Each SEAL entered the water in turn, slowly moving from the bank until only their helmets and NODs were visible. They fanned out as they approached the other side, no noise and no ripples. This was something the SEALs had rehearsed dozens of times; this was their element. The estuary was not deep, yet only their heads crested the water. A.J., Mikey, and Ray slowly emerged on the far bank, crouching low as they moved to the cover of the mangrove and low palm growth. They then carefully dewatered their weapons and took up security positions, slightly flanking the building. Nolan, Sonny, and Mikey remained immersed.

"We're set, ready to move on the target, over," Nolan reported.

Engel keyed his tactical radio. "Okay, Chief, give me a paint."

"Roger that. Coming on now . . . and off."

First Nolan, and then the other four SEALs in turn,

activated their IR beacons so that Engel could identify them on the Raven presentation and Weimy could see them with his NOD. "Okay, guys, we can see all of you. Be advised, guard one is still seated at the front entrance, and guard two is on the far side of the building. Two other guards that we can see are on the far side of the compound. Chief, you and Sonny are clear to move from where you are to the side of the main building. Everyone else hold fast."

Nolan rogered up and started to move from the water, then froze. Between Sonny and him was a small wooden platform stilted a few inches above the waterline. It was too small to be a dock but would serve as a small-boat tie-off and loading pier. The big SEAL and his chief were still shoulder deep in the dark water on either side of the structure. As they waited motionless, a sentry stepped from behind a tree and out onto the platform. It was always the one you didn't see. As Engel, Nolan, and Sonny held their breath, Weimy sighted in.

"I have him," Weimy whispered over the tac net, and he did.

The shot took him just over the heart on his left side, spinning him to his left and over backward toward Nolan. Nolan reached up and caught him before his body splashed the water, and eased him below the surface. Not yet dead, the guard jerked involuntarily as he inhaled water, but it did not last long. When he stopped moving, the chief released him and pushed him under the wooden pier.

"Nicely done, you guys," came Engel on the tac net.

"Yeah, just like we rehearsed it," Nolan replied. "You ready, Sonny?"

"Ready, Chief," and the two SEALs emerged from the water, carefully draining their primary weapons as they advanced on the target hooch.

The plan called for them to move slowly and deliberately on the target, locate Morales, and, if possible, bring her out without alerting anyone. This meant inching forward and avoiding contact with the camp security force, or at least delaying any contact until they could find Morales and gain control of her. It's said that most battle plans go out the window when the first shot is fired. On this night, it was the first scream.

The back room of the long, squalid hut had become a torture chamber. Heeding Christo's instructions to keep her alive and not call back until she talked, Tommy did what he did best. He tortured the young doctor. Yet in doing so, he was careful to prolong Morales's life. He had never let Christo down, and he didn't intend to do so now. He knew the stakes and knew that if he failed, his life was worthless. Christo would have *him* tortured and find someone else to extract what he wanted from Morales.

The look on Tommy's face was one of determination laced with frustration. He had slowly increased the pressure on Morales, from slapping her face bloody to burning her flesh with a lit cigar to cutting her and rubbing salt into the wounds. Earlier that day, he had had her gang-raped by the camp sentries; he had applied electric shock to her breasts and genitals. Nothing had worked. Now, Tommy reached into his bag of sick tricks for what he was sure would finally bring her around. He'd only had to go this far with a hostage once before, a tough Costa Rican paramilitary officer, and the man had broken in less than five minutes. This . . . *Yankee bitch* wouldn't hold out half that long. He permitted himself a smile; he was going to enjoy this.

Lisa Morales was chained to a sturdy wood table. The rusty metal dug into her wrists, which were made dark red from both dried and oozing blood. Her hands were splayed out on the table, the tops of them swollen and bruised. She hung from them, with her head just below the tabletop. Her feet, stretched out behind her and tied to ring bolts in the floor, were black and swollen from the stick beatings on her soles. Dozens of large flies buzzed around her, licking at the open wounds. She was naked save for her bloodstained bra and panties, and her face was so swollen from Tommy's beatings that her mother would be hard-pressed to recognize her. Blood seeped from multiple cuts on her torso and legs. The table and floor about her were slick with blood, urine, and feces. It looked like a scene from the Spanish Inquisition.

"*No mas . . .*" Morales moaned, the words almost unrecognizable as she struggled to form them through swollen lips. Her moans were drowned out by a high-pitched electrical whine.

"*Por favor . . . no . . . por favor,*" she moaned, barely audible.

Tommy stepped in front of Morales holding a power drill with a 1/16th-inch bit and leaned into the drill as it bit down and through Morales's left hand.

"*Arrrrrrrrrgh . . .*"

The shriek was not loud, but primal and guttural—a

sound more animal than human. Her cries were so shrill and wrenching that Tommy raised up, extracting the drill bit from her hand. Enraged that he had let her cries interrupt the flow of his work, Tommy aimed the drill bit at the top of her right hand and shoved it through. Morales's legs jerked uncontrollably and her head slammed into the top of the table, her body now in an uncontrollable seizure. The look on Tommy's face had changed from determination and frustration to pure rage.

"Speak to me, you bitch! *Diga me!*"

From deep inside Morales, some small reservoir of adrenaline gave added strength to her voice, and she emitted a howl that pierced the thin walls of the building, spilling into the still night outside. The terrifying screams that echoed through the camp and the surrounding mangrove transfixed the SEALs, freezing them in place. Even the roving guards paused in their lazy patrol routes and turned to listen. After a long moment of the unbearable, heart-wrenching cries, Chief Nolan came up on the tac net.

"Sir, we got to go."

"Roger that. Everyone get ready to move, but hold where you are and wait for my command." Then on his support net, "Whiplash, Blackbeard, over."

"Whiplash here, over." The two SOC-R craft were still nestled against the bank at the bend of the river, tied off on mangrove trees and virtually invisible in the low vegetation.

"This is Blackbeard. We are about to go hot. How soon can you get to my primary extraction site, priority one, over?"

"This is Whiplash. We can be at your primary

extraction in thirty mikes, maybe a little sooner on priority one, over."

Engel did some mental calculations. It did them no good to have Morales, and in all likelihood a small army of pursuers, if they had no extraction platform. Neither did it do them any good for the boats to arrive too soon. This was going to be close, one way or another.

"Roger, Whiplash. Start making your way here quietly, and stand by to respond at your best speed, over."

"Understood, Blackbeard. We are moving toward primary extraction at slow speed, over."

"Blackbeard, roger, out." Then on the tac net, "Okay, guys, smooth is fast. Go get her, and call out the security as you see them."

Some fourteen miles downriver, Chief Bautista had the order he'd been waiting for and switched to his tactical net.

"Two Boat, One Boat, we're moving upriver at idle. Follow me at loose trail. Man-up on all weapons systems, and be ready to put the pedal to the metal. This extraction will most likely be a hot one."

"Two Boat, roger."

No more words needed to be exchanged between Bautista and Chief Tom Dial, the Two Boat's captain and coxswain. The two SOC-R craft fired up their engines and eased out from the bank in unison. With the Yanmars purring at a soft growl, they began to work their way upstream toward the extraction site at a reasonably quiet five knots. They all felt it; they were headed for a fight. As Bautista and Dial held their craft in the current, each swick crewman at his individual station checked and rechecked his weapon and ammo supply.

* * *

As the two SOC-R craft worked their way upriver, Engel was now completely focused on visual presentation on his screen, shifting back and forth from low-light level color to infrared. The SEALs had all switched on their IR markers so he could track them easily as they advanced on the target building. The sounds now coming from the long low hut were moans punctuated by howls of pain and pure terror.

The assault element was now on the move in a modified skirmish line, with Chief Nolan walking point and two SEALs to either side, trailing and slightly behind— five silent forms rhythmically sweeping the area in front of them with the barrels of their weapons as they closed on the low silhouette of the main structure. On reaching the side of the building, they flattened against the plank siding with the now plaintive screams urging them forward. Nolan then moved to the van and led the file to the entrance end of the building. The others bunched closely behind him.

Lieutenant Engel brought the Raven even lower, optically sweeping the area around the SEAL squad. He then saw the roving sentry moving from behind the rear of the building toward the side where the SEALs were queued up by the front entrance. In another few steps, he would be sure to see them.

"Chief, hold up!" Nolan and the other SEALs froze.

"Got him?" Engel whispered.

"Got him," Weimy echoed.

As the guard stepped from behind the building, he was caught mid-chest by a .556 round from Weimy's

Mk12. Again, there was only the spit of the rifle and the brief *snap* from the round's sonic path. The Tango's heart exploded from the impact of the round. He dropped to his knees and fell face forward into the mud.

"Okay, Chief, you're clear."

"Roger that. We're moving."

Nolan moved carefully around the corner of the building, looking over his rifle across the front porch and entryway. The guard, having been alerted by the sonic crack of the last shot, was now on his feet near the door, with his back to Nolan. If he turned, Nolan knew he'd have to shoot him, and that would alert the camp. "Uh, Weimy?" he whispered into his mic.

"No worries, Chief." This time it was a head shot and the guard collapsed. Again, another sonic crack parted the silence, this time accompanied by the clatter of an AK-47 falling onto the hut's wooden porch decking. This may or may not have alerted those in the building or other sentries. Nonetheless, Nolan and his teammates knew they had to act swiftly now. They quickly moved to a stack at the door. A.J. carefully tried the knob and, finding that it turned, pushed it carefully open. He led the file inside, unchallenged. They crept silently down a short, dimly lit hallway. As they entered, they flipped up their NODs; there was enough light to work without them. Ray remained at the door as rear security, leaving the others to press on.

On the rise outside the camp, Engel and Weimy could only watch as the SEALs disappeared into the building. Engel continued his eagle's-eye survey of the surrounding buildings and Weimy looked for targets. He watched the two roving sentries on the far side of the compound but elected not to kill them. Double kills are sometimes difficult, and until something alerted the camp, he would do nothing to disturb things. For now, they weren't a threat. The real concern was that for every sentry they could see, there could be a dozen or more off duty nearby.

The four SEALs in the hut's short hallway paused to listen. All they could hear were low moans coming from deeper inside the building. The interior walls were a combination of plywood and wallboard. The doors were cheap hollow-core wood. Nolan knew they had to get to Morales quickly, but they couldn't advance without neutralizing any threat behind them. There were three doors at the end of the hallway. They smoothly set up at the left-hand door—standard room clearance. A.J., Sonny, and Mikey popped through the door and pried it out. Nothing but trash and two soiled mattresses. It was the same for the door on the right. The center door led to a larger room with dirty dishes on card tables and a half dozen rusted metal folding chairs. They cleared it quickly. Another door led to an adjacent room; Morales had to be behind that door. They moved quickly to the door and were about to make an entry when the door and wall in front of them exploded.

Nolan and the other SEALs dove for the floor as the automatic-weapons fire scythed back and forth, chewing up the wallboard, belt high. All made it safely except Mikey. A round caught him just under the lip of his helmet, snapping his head back. Blood immediately washed his face as he lay inert on his back in front of the door. Chief Nolan, seeing him go down, grabbed him by the collar and dragged him to the relative safety of the exterior side wall.

The gunner in the next room was relentless. After a quick magazine change, he again opened up, but this time he was clearly shooting high. Sonny low-crawled to the door, kicked it open, and rolled in a flash-bang grenade. Following the explosion, A.J. dashed through the door in an instant and double-tapped a Tango trying to work the bolt on an AK-47 that had jammed. But it was a small room, more of an anteroom, with yet another door behind it. A.J. and Sonny were now on their own, and both knew they had to keep moving. Stepping over the body, they paused for a fraction of a second. Then A.J. gave the door a strong kick.

Just before the shooting started, Tommy—having abandoned the drill and donned leather gloves—was about to give Morales yet another vicious backhand. She was now semiconscious and probably wouldn't feel it, but he really did enjoy hitting women. Yet he knew he had to be careful. Fun was fun, but Christo wanted information, and he couldn't take the chance of killing her—yet. But just one more backhand would probably be all right. Then the guard in the next room went full automatic with his AK-47. The sound through the thin walls was deafening. There was a brief silence and then more firing. There were two others there in the room to help Tommy with the interrogation. They were both cartel security retainers and stood by passively while he worked on Morales. When the firing started, they reacted much more quickly than Tommy did. Both turned in unison and bolted through the rear entrance. Tommy, not wanting to leave Morales, took up his Glock .45 and turned back to the sound of the shooting. A loud explosion followed by more shots caused him to hesitate, but then he put his eye to a crack in the door to try to see what was happening—at the precise moment A.J. kicked the door in from the other side.

Stunned, Tommy staggered back and tried to raise his pistol just as Sonny barreled through the door. The two crashed against the opposite wall chest to chest, too close for Sonny to get the barrel of his SAW level, but he managed to block Tommy's gun hand, forcing it up and away. Tommy was bigger than Sonny but not nearly as strong. Locked together, Sonny forced Tommy back against a wall and drew his Sig Sauer 9mm. He rammed the barrel of the automatic under Tommy's chin, and while he was eyeball to eyeball with the big Chechen, he blew off the top of his head. A.J., having no angle to get off a shot, could only clear the rest of the room and watch.

"Clear," A.J. shouted. Then turning to Morales, he keyed his radio. "Hey, Chief, I think we got her."

Nolan quickly came back on the net. "Roger that. Ray, get in here. Mikey's down and I need you with him."

Ray raced through the building to where Nolan was tending to Mikey. He was unconscious and making incoherent sounds. But his airway was clear and he had a strong pulse. Mikey was the squad medic by training, but every SEAL is a medic through cross-training. Now those men Mikey had trained would have to try and save him.

"He's bleeding but he's breathing," Nolan told Ray. "Do what you can to stabilize him and get him ready to travel." Then he went to find Morales. Ray knew the drill—keep him breathing and keep the blood inside, and there was plenty of blood. He removed Mikey's helmet and began to apply a pressure bandage.

An instant later, Nolan was at Morales's side. She was

semiconscious and could only mumble over and over, *"Bastante—no mas."*

Nolan took her face in his hands, none too gently. "Miss Morales. We are Americans, and we are going to get you out of here." He wasn't sure, but he thought he saw a glimmer of recognition.

On the rise across the estuary, Engel and Weimy heard the shooting and saw the flash-bang, but there was little they could do. At the first burst of gunfire, Engel radioed Whiplash and requested they come at top speed. Both he and Weimy were on the tactical net, so they both knew that the team had Morales and that Mikey had been shot—neither knew how bad. Engel had been here before: There's a fight, he has men down, and he's tethered to his radios. But he knows Nolan and the others can do the job, and though he's anxious to know what's going on, he also knows Nolan will tell him when he's able. All he could do now was to focus on the Raven presentation and look for threats. Then the two men bolted from the back door of the long hut.

"I got two squirters," Weimy said on the net.

"Take 'em," Nolan confirmed immediately.

Weimy sent a round between the shoulder blades of the first man, just missing his heart but collapsing a lung. He staggered on a few steps before a second round, two inches left of the first, severed his spinal cord, pitching him face forward to the ground. The second Tango made it to a beefy, extended-cab pickup truck and slipped behind the wheel. Before he could close the door or start the engine, Weimy took him through the rear window of the cab with a head shot, painting the inside of the windshield with bone fragments and brain tissue.

Inside, Nolan snatched a curtain from the wall and covered Morales's bruised and battered body. She was bleeding from cuts and burns all over her torso and limbs, as well as from her nose and mouth. He took a scarf from his neck, wet it, and dabbed Morales's dry, cracked lips. She was now weeping softly. "Okay, listen closely—this is important. What is your mother's maiden name?"

"R-Rosales," she whispered.

"What street did you grow up on?" She gave him a puzzled look. "Please, what street did you live on when you were a little girl?"

"Hot Springs."

"Good girl." He keyed his mic. "Boss, we have her and a positive ID, stand by." Then he went over to where Ray was tending to Mikey. "How's he doing?"

"Hard to tell, but I've slowed the bleeding. No way to tell how bad it is, but it's not good. We need to get him help." Ray had his head swathed in bandages. Mikey looked like a mummy.

Nolan again keyed his mic. "Okay, Boss, Mikey is down with a head wound—looks serious. We're getting him and the package ready to move."

"Roger, copy. Put a rush on it—we got company."

"Say again."

"I said we have company. There are two trucks inbound from the west on the main road. They appear to be loaded with Tangos. Get out of there, Chief. You've got five minutes at best."

"Christ, the fun never stops."

On the rise outside the camp, Engel could do nothing but watch on his computer screen as the quick-reaction force, a crew-cab pickup with eight or ten men in back and a Ford Explorer loaded with men, made their way down the access road toward the compound.

"Whiplash, this is Blackbeard, over."

"This is Whiplash, over."

"Whiplash, we have a QRF inbound, and I have wounded. How far out are you, over?"

"Blackbeard, I'm fifteen mikes from the primary. How many pax, over?"

"Six effectives, two wounded. Plan for a hot extraction, over."

"Blackbeard, I copy six effectives and two wounded for a total of eight pax, and a hot extract, over."

"Good copy, Whiplash. Blackbeard, out."

"Two Boat," Bautista said on their tac net, "you copy that?"

"Roger that, One," Dial replied. "I'm right behind you."

Ricardo Bautista had been a Special Warfare Combatant-craft Crewman since their small, tight-knit community was officially formed in 2000—back when he was a second-class petty officer and still new to the Special Boat Teams. He knew that as leader of a two-boat SOC-R element, it would all be on him. A hot extraction meant that his SEAL brothers would be running for their lives and that he and his boats' gunners could mean the difference between getting them out safely and watching them perish. He had to stay cool, yet his excitement was palpable. Ten years of ground wars in the Middle East and Southwest Asia in landlocked places like

Afghanistan generated few combat opportunities for his fellow swicks and their highly capable watercraft. Now, for better or for worse, they were in the mix.

The two SOC-Rs came up on step and leapt forward as Bautista and Dial slammed their respective throttles forward and the crafts' twin 440 Yanmar Diesels responded at full power, thrusting each boat forward at their redline speed of forty-plus knots. It was showtime, and Bautista was both in charge and on the spot. The mission would succeed or fail, and men would be saved or would die, based on his decisions over the next few minutes. He had a good crew; he knew that—he'd trained them. But they were green. For most of them, this would be their first combat engagement.

"Okay, listen up. This is gonna be a hot extraction—damn hot," Bautista said into his boom mic. "I want all weps-trained to starboard. We're still," he paused, glancing down at his Garmin 720 Marine Navigator, "about eight miles away from the primary extraction site. I want the Two Boat in loose trail until we get to where we're going. Then, at the extraction point, I want us no more than ten yards offshore and ten yards bow to stern. Remember, get a clear field of fire for every weapon. Got it?"

"Yep, Chief . . . Got it, Skipper . . . No worries . . ." and other short replies told Bautista his crews were up on step, just like their boats. "Remember our creed, boys," he said, referring to the six-paragraph SWCC Creed each of them knew by heart: "'I will close and engage the enemy with the full combat power of my craft. I will never quit and I will leave no one behind.'"

The answering mic clicks told Bautista all he needed

to know. The boat guys, *his* guys, were ready. What they had trained for, for most of their professional careers, was about to go down.

At Engel's position on the shallow rise, the first hint of dawn was creeping into the eastern sky. All he could do for the moment was stare at the scope and watch the quick-reaction force close on the compound. Daylight would make their movement out of the camp easier, but they would also lose their night-vision advantage.

"Get out of there, Chief."

"Working on it, Boss."

Occasionally, there was the soft bark of the Mk12 as Weimy found a target. The Tango sentries on the far side of the camp who responded to the initial bursts of gunfire were quickly taken out. Several others appeared but soon went into hiding when they realized there was an accomplished sniper out there. They were content to remain hidden and alive, at least for now.

Sonny searched the room while A.J. did what he could to get Morales ready to travel. Suddenly Nolan was at his side. "How's she doing?"

"She's passed out, and there's no way she can walk. How's Mikey?"

"Not good. Sonny, we done here?"

"Yeah. I got a laptop, a cell phone, and two flash drives. That's about it."

"Bag it and go help Ray with Mikey. We got a QRF breathing down on us. I'll take her, and we'll go out the back door. A.J., take us out of here and make for the first rally point."

"Hurry, Chief." There was an urgency in Engel's voice. "They're closing fast."

"Copy, Boss. We're out the door now."

Engel and Weimy watched as A.J. led them from the building toward the first rally point, a predetermined meeting place on the road that led north out of the camp toward the river. They left the building at a slow run, with Sonny carrying Mikey like a sleeping child and Nolan with Morales draped over his shoulder. A guard along their route saw an opportunity and moved from behind a tree. Before Engel could shout a warning, Weimy's rifle spat a round and took him in the chest. He went down to all fours, and a second round knocked him flat.

"Good shooting. Now, we gotta get out of here." Engel no longer needed the Raven display to track the QRF; he could hear them coming. He snapped the Toughbook computer shut and stowed it. Seconds later he and Weimy sprinted down the hill toward the rally point. Just outside the camp, this initial rally point was also only about a quarter mile from the river. If they could meet there and get into the bush before the QRF trucks were on them, they had a chance. If not, the trucks would run them down and that would be that.

Nolan and his team were moving at a jog trot at best, and he knew they were moving way too slow. But once clear of the building, he saw the truck with the dead guard slumped at the wheel.

"A.J.!" he shouted. "The truck!" but A.J. was already heading for it. He grabbed the dead Tango by the collar and jerked him from behind the wheel, dumping him unceremoniously into the mud. The keys were in the ignition. The engine turned over once, then twice, and finally caught. Nolan laid Morales into the truck bed as gently as he could and jumped in after her, followed by Ray. Sonny put Mikey in the rear seat of the extended cab and jumped in with him.

"Any time now!" Nolan yelled to A.J., who had just wiped away the last of the blood and brains from the windshield. He jammed the truck into gear and mashed the gas. In a flurry of mud flying from all four tires, the truck slewed around and headed for the back road that would take them from the camp. As they cleared the compound, Nolan saw the two trucks from the QRF enter the compound on the main road and charge after them.

"Damn," he said, to no one in particular, "we were almost home free." He keyed his mic. "Hey, Boss, we're clear of the camp en route to the rally point, but we got two Tango vehicles on our tail, and they look pissed. The good news is that we have wheels and should be at the rally point in less than a minute."

Engel and Weimy got to the road and the rally point just ahead of the SEALs in the truck. Engel carried the squad's one and only LAAW—a light anti-tank/assault weapon that was more than capable of dealing with a truck. He pulled the launcher over his head and discarded the carrying strap, slinging his M4 rifle in the LAAW's place. He quickly extended the launching tube, removed the safety pin, and kneeled down with the rocket on his shoulder, just as A.J. and the SEAL truck rounded a bend in the road. They flashed past him and slowed to a halt.

Weimy was at Engel's side with a hand on his other shoulder. They were both breathing hard from the dash to the rally point. "Steady, Boss. Sight picture and trigger squeeze."

"Sight picture and trigger squeeze," Engel repeated.

The pickup truck rounded the bend well ahead of the Explorer. It was a big Ford extended-cab 250, and its bed was crowded with armed men. Engel pressed the trigger detent and the rocket leapt from the tube. It took but a nanosecond for the missile to cover the thirty meters between the LAAW launcher and the grill of the Ford. The force of the blast pushed the engine back through the firewall and essentially buckled the frame from the dashboard forward, causing the truck to hinge, nose down. With the nose of the truck burrowing into the mud, the inertia of the vehicle generated a forward flip, with the truck bed careening over its front bumper, tossing close to a dozen stunned Tangos into the dirt in front of the two SEALs. Engel, momentarily frozen from the blast of the rocket, recovered in time to dodge a bouncing tire that almost took him out. Weimy calmly shot two of the shaken Tangos who tried to get to their feet. What was left of the pickup slid into the far ditch on its top.

"Today, gentlemen, if you don't mind!" Nolan yelled at them. "There's another fuckin' truck coming!"

Weimy and Engel turned as if poked by a hot iron and ran for the truck. They dove into the bed, careful to avoid hitting Morales, who was curled into a fetal position. A.J. stomped the accelerator. With the other vehicle in pursuit, there was no time to unload everyone and carry their wounded through the bush to the primary extraction site; they had to keep moving. Engel keyed his support-net radio.

"Whiplash, Blackbeard, over."

"This is Whiplash, go ahead, over."

"Make for the secondary extraction site—I say again, secondary extraction site, how copy, over?"

"Blackbeard, Whiplash. Understand secondary extraction, over."

"Roger that, Whiplash. Blackbeard, out."

Nolan put a hand on Engel's shoulder. "Good show, Boss. Now what are you going to do with that?"

Engel glanced at the empty, now-worthless rocket-launcher tube. "Oh, yeah," and tossed it from the truck. He then took his M4 from his shoulder and checked the action. "How's Mikey?"

"He's holding his own, but we got to get him some attention."

On a straight stretch of road, the Explorer came into view. It was gaining on them. Several rounds pinged on the tailgate as Tangos leaned out the window to shoot at them. Nolan dropped onto the curled form of Morales to shield her from fire. Ray and Weimy began to return fire, with steady well-aimed rounds. A puff of smoke was emitted from the Explorer, and there were several spiderwebs in the windshield, but still they continued to come.

"A.J.," Engel called over the tac net, "how far to the secondary?"

"Maybe five minutes, maybe less."

A lifetime, Engel thought, wondering how A.J. could drive so well and still key his radio. "Drive on, brother.

Smooth is fast." Then switching radios, "Whiplash, Black-beard, over."

"Whiplash here, over."

"We'll be at secondary in four mikes, over."

"Copy four minutes. See you there. Whiplash, out."

The secondary extraction site was four miles down-stream from the primary. While this meant four miles in the truck getting shot at, it also meant four fewer miles for the SOC-Rs to travel. At the secondary site, the road passed close to the bank of the river before veering away. Again, Engel reckoned it was going to be close.

The Explorer was still coming after them, but no one was leaning out the window shooting at them anymore. Ray and Weimy continued to fire—steady and measured, with each round finding the windshield or the grill of the vehicle. Then the Explorer slowed and began to drift back. Either the truck or the men inside, or both, had lost the will to continue. Nolan looked up from where he was shielding Morales and grinned.

"Guess we showed those assholes what they get for tailgating a bunch of SEALs."

Weimy and Ray matched Nolan's smile, each slump-ing into a corner of the truck bed at the tailgate. For Engel, it was a wave of relief, now that they had a clear shot to the secondary extraction site. Then, suddenly, a Dodge Ram crew cab swung in behind them from a side road, and they were again under small-arms fire. If pos-sible, there were even more Tangos in the Ram than in the first pickup.

"E-fuckin'-nuff already," Weimy shouted as he and Ray began to return fire. There was no burst of fully automatic fire or even rapid fire. They both went back to steady, rhythmic shooting, making every round count. The truck dropped back momentarily in the face of this precise fire, but it was still coming. Behind the Ram, a stake truck appeared with a dozen or more Tangos. Suddenly, the back window of the SEAL pickup exploded, which for some unknown reason revived Mikey, who popped upright.

"Will someone get some goddamn suppressing fire on those fuckers, for Christ's sake?"

As Sonny grabbed him and pulled him down in the seat, several more rounds came through the nonexistent rear window and stitched the windshield. A.J., in the act of a contortionist, kept his left foot on the gas and kicked out the spiderwebbed and brain-streaked windshield with his right. Nolan continued to shield Morales while Engel joined Ray and Weimy returning fire. They came to another straight stretch in the road, and someone in the bed of the Ram fired an RPG that whizzed just over their heads and exploded in a stand of trees well in front of them. First one rear tire, then the other, began to come apart from multiple bullet strikes. They slowed, and the pursuing trucks drew nearer. Engel dumped the rest of his magazine on full auto and keyed his mic.

"Whiplash, you with us, over?"

"Whiplash here. We're thirty seconds from the secondary extraction, over."

"So are we," Engel replied, having no idea how close they were and not even sure they could last another thirty seconds in this wild chase, "and we are *extremely* hot, over." He did a quick mag change and rejoined the fight.

A.J. felt the truck dying underneath him. At every bend in the road he expected to see the river, but each time he was disappointed. Then, suddenly, he saw it at the end of a long straight stretch. He stomped on the gas pedal even though it was already on the floor. He rammed the shift lever into low trying to gain more purchase on the muddy road. The engine screamed as the truck slewed side to side. The rear wheels were still shedding rubber and spitting mud—the front wheels were dragging the truck along. Suddenly he lost the right front and it was all he could do to keep the truck on the road.

"Come on, bitch!" he screamed. "Just a little farther."

They were losing speed rapidly, but they were almost at the bank. He could see the shallow berm ahead on the right that separated the road from the river. "Hang on!" he yelled over his shoulder, both hands on the wheel, "we're going in!" The road veered sharply to the left and there was a barrier straight ahead. Just before they got to the barrier, A.J. swerved to the right, never taking his foot off the gas. The truck climbed the berm, just missing the barrier, and nosed over into the slow-moving river.

In the rear seat, Sonny grabbed Mikey and held his head to his chest for the impact. In the back, Chief Nolan wrapped his arms around Morales from behind, clamping her hips between his thighs. Engel, Ray, and Weimy knew what was coming, but they kept shooting until they were airborne. Just before Engel hit the water, he caught a glimpse of two shapes on the water about twenty meters from the shore and thirty meters downstream, gliding toward the extraction point. When his head broke the water after the dunking, he was wearing a grim smile. They'd been outmanned, outgunned, and running for their lives. Now all that was about to change.

Chief Bautista saw the SEAL pickup charging toward the river and the two Tango trucks in hot pursuit. He quickly grasped the situation. He turned the One Boat to port so that the Two Boat following closely in his wake would also have a good field of fire. Moments earlier they had cut their engines, come off step, and were now coasting toward the extraction site, pushing a large bow wave into the gentle current.

The men in the two pursuing trucks held on as their vehicles skidded to a stop right where the SEAL pickup had jumped the berm. They were suddenly and acutely aware of the two strange craft closing on their position. Some of the Tangos were training their guns on the heads that were popping up to the surface as the pickup began to drift and sink lower in the water. Others were turning their attention and their guns toward the two strange craft. For most of them, it would be their last conscious thought. As the two trucks slammed to a halt, Chief Bautista came up on his tactical net.

"Okay, boys, bring the pain."

Simultaneously, four Dillon M134D electrically driven Gatling guns, often called mini-guns, opened up on the two trucks at a range of thirty yards. In the first five seconds of this one-sided encounter, the two trucks absorbed close to two thousand rounds of 7.65mm NATO standard coming at them at 2,800 feet per second. In those five terrible seconds, the two trucks received more than forty pounds of brass-encased steel in 150-grain increments. That was in the first five seconds, then there was another five seconds, and another five seconds after that. Incidental to the mini-guns were the four .50-calibers that contributed another two hundred rounds in focused bursts of fire during each of those five seconds. The .50s deal out far fewer rounds, but the armor-piercing, incendiary, and tracer slugs go through *everything*, save for the few rounds that found the engine blocks. The sound was deafening, and the carnage unimaginable. Trucks and Tangos shredded into an amalgam of blood, bone, mud, and metal.

In less than twenty seconds, it was over. The silence was deafening as the echoes from the gunfire reverberated from the foothills. While several gunners panned over the two steaming hulks, the boats and crews began to maneuver to pick up those in the water. The One Boat recovered Engel, Nolan, Morales, and Weimy. The Two Boat got the others. The corpsman/gunners on each boat quickly checked them all and then began to treat Morales and Mikey. The gunfire was quickly replaced by the roar of diesels and the boats sprung up on step, now running west with the current. Before Engel could ask, Chief Bautista was up on the support net to give him an update.

"Sir, we have all eight of you and are heading for an extraction site about nine miles downriver. I've alerted a MEDEVAC chopper and they're already inbound. We'll have you airborne in about fifteen minutes. They'll take you all back out to the *Bonnie Dick*. And my corpsman in the Two Boat says your wounded SEAL is now conscious. Good chance he'll pull through."

Engel paused to say something, but then realized normal speech was impossible with the roar of the engines. He keyed his support net. "Chief, what kind of premium whiskey do you drink?"

"Uh, I don't drink, sir, but maybe a couple of bottles of Wild Turkey for the boys might be in order."

"Done, and Bravo Zulu all around. You guys saved our asses."

"Just another day in the Special Boat Teams, sir, but thanks."

As he slumped back, Engel caught Nolan's eye. Both men felt the overwhelming exhaustion that came after a sudden ultra-adrenaline high. Nolan would have given him a mock salute, but his arm was too heavy to raise. Anyway, he didn't need to. The look that passed between them said it all. *We went to the very edge, and we came through it alive—again.* After this brief moment of silent communication, they both summoned the energy to move aft to where the corpsman was tending to Morales. With some effort, she focused on the two strained and grizzled faces, and a look of pure gratitude washed over her face. She mouthed, *Thank you.* Then Engel made his way back to where Weimy, the consummate professional, had his Mk12 trained over the gunwale, still looking for targets along the wooded riverbank. Engel put his hand on Weimy's shoulder and leaned close to make himself heard.

"Thanks, brother. You were there every time, all the time. We wouldn't have made it without you."

"Hey, Boss, the only easy day was yesterday."

Moments later, the two boats came off step and

gently nosed into a bank that abutted a flat grassy area. The grass was close to two feet tall but was now blown flat by the prop wash of two MH-60S Navy Knighthawk helicopters. One was a slick—a MEDEVAC bird with several corpsmen and two litters. The other was the chase bird, amply armed with two M240 machine guns mounted in the doors behind each pilot and four Hellfire rockets on the Knighthawk's batwings.

The deafening noise of the Knighthawk's howling GE T-700 turbo-shaft engines and the slapping four-bladed rotors drowned out any attempt to talk. The swick crewmen carefully handed Morales and Mikey over the blunt bows of the SOC-Rs to the waiting arms of a team of corpsmen. They were quickly tied into litters and rushed to the MEDEVAC chopper, which lifted off immediately, heading west back toward the *Bonhomme Richard*.

Engel and Nolan, after shaking hands with every SWCC sailor, made their way to the waiting chase helo. The lieutenant and the chief quickly embraced A.J., Sonny, Ray, and Weimy as they climbed aboard, then scrambled in after them. They were soon airborne and out over blue water. The six SEALs sat around the small compartment grinning at one another. They were the sheepish, holy-shit-I-still-don't-believe-it grins of men who had just cheated death. Sonny, seated next to Engel, leaned close to be heard over the rotors.

"Here you go, Boss. A souvenir of your visit to Costa Rica."

Engel opened the waterproof bag, which proved not to be entirely waterproof. It contained the laptop computer, two flash drives, and a cell phone from the Tango compound. He regarded Sonny, who even sweat stained and mud splattered looked a lot like Brad Pitt on a good day.

"This could be valuable intelligence, Sonny," he said in mock solemnity. "I hope you didn't let it get banged up."

Sonny's grin, with those perfect, even teeth, got even bigger. "No more so than me, Boss."

SIX

In Kherson, Ukraine, the administrative center of the oblast, or province of the same name, near the southern reaches of the Dnieper River, Shabal walked past rows of abandoned warehouses ten kilometers east of one of Kherson's major shipyards. Once a busy industrial center making machinery for Kherson's thriving shipbuilding industry, the district, like the shipyard to the west, fell into disuse when Europe's tanking economy decimated Ukraine's shipbuilding industry.

A pack of rats feasting on the carcass of a dead cat scattered as Shabal kicked a board at them. Fucking parasites. The dead cat called to mind his younger sister, who now worked as a waitress in Odessa. There she flirted for tips with the vacationing capitalist swine who visited her restaurant. With those tips, she supported herself and her four cats, all adopted from the street— something this poor creature would never know. Shabal hated rats almost as much as he hated capitalist swine. If he wasn't expected by Kerimov, he'd stop and put a bullet in every rat. A bullet was too good for the capitalists. So he had other ideas.

But he was expected and he had come a long way to complete his mission. He knew Kerimov had what he wanted, and although he would bargain with him—it was always about bargaining—what he was about to obtain was priceless. He knew Christo would have to pay dearly for them, but he did not care. This was jihad, and no price could be placed on that which served the Will of Allah.

Shabal feared nothing but was wary of Kherson's drug dealers. This area was theirs; the Kherson police had stopped patrolling this district long ago. If one of those drug dealers even half suspected Shabal was a rival dealer trying to muscle in on their territory they'd put a bullet in his brain. He didn't slow down as he approached the warehouse entrance in the dark alley.

He rapped twice on the heavy metal door, all the while keeping his head on a swivel. Christo would never come here. That's why he had to do this.

The peephole clicked open and the voice merely said, "Who?"

"Shabal."

The door creaked open and the bulky man with the AK-47 in his right hand waved Shabal inside the dimly lit vestibule. Once Shabal was inside, the man slammed the metal door shut with a resounding *thud* and waved the AK-47 at him in an upward motion. Shabal knew the drill. He raised his arms high above his head as the man unceremoniously jerked Shabal's heavy overcoat to the side and removed the Russian Kobalt 9mm revolver from Shabal's belt.

That done, the man grunted and waved the weapon at a flight of stairs. Shabal descended as the guard followed him down, the Kalashnikov pointed at his back.

As he negotiated the last dozen steps, Shabal heard the music of a violin. When he reached the bottom steps, he surveyed the room. It was a cavernous bunker at least forty meters by eighty meters, easily five meters high, with raw concrete walls. There were numerous metal tables and working lights suspended from the ceiling. Clearly, this was a serious work area, one that no one was supposed to stumble onto.

Shabal looked at the thick Russian playing the violin. He was an unpleasant-looking man with a flat, Slavic brow, and the instrument looked tiny in his enormous, calloused hands. Yet he was accomplished and played with feeling and passion. Shabal ignored everyone and everything in the room and addressed the man.

"Is that Mendelssohn?"

"Brahms," replied Kerimov, the correction delivered without emotion but with an air of a man who was self-assured regarding his music.

"I came to speak to Kerimov."

"I see. And you must be Shabal," the Russian replied, extending his hand to shake Shabal's.

Shabal looked at Kerimov's hand disdainfully, did not take it, and then looked him directly in the eye. His cold stare conveyed that he was here for business, nothing more.

Kerimov recovered quickly. It was all business for him, too, and he knew Shabal needed what he had. He wouldn't be bullied—or taken lightly.

"As I explained to you on the telephone, I have exactly the thing for your needs," Kerimov continued. He lifted two heavy duffel bags sitting in front of him and placed them at Shabal's feet.

Shabal leaned down and unzipped one of the bags, lifted out a thin vest, and held it up with one hand. He looked at it quizzically, as if he were expecting something different.

"They are light, yes?" offered Kerimov, smiling. "You could wear one under a tuxedo or simply a light shirt," he continued.

Shabal continued to inspect the vest, holding it up close to one of the suspended working lights, examining it from all angles.

Kerimov turned on a handheld metal detector and passed it slowly over the vest, covering every inch of it. The metal detector didn't make a sound.

Shabal put the vest down on the table.

Kerimov opened the vest and ran his hands over it, continuing his explanation.

"Inside, tiny ceramic ball bearings—five hundred of them—are woven into the vest. The inner lining of the vest is filled with a new generation of explosive gel." Kerimov spoke with pride; he was a craftsman, and he wanted his work appreciated—as well as paid for. "The new explosive will propel the ceramic balls at a velocity close to that of a chambered rifle round.

"It is truly devastating. It does not look like much, but believe me when I say it would take dozens of your martyrs and your vests to do what one of these can do. They can kill everyone on a city bus or a subway car. Others in the vicinity would die as well. There are few weapons in the world a single man can operate that are more deadly. And not one that is more discreet. You could take a tour of the White House with one of these or board an airliner."

Shabal trembled imperceptibly as he considered the possibilities. "Can I see a demonstration?" he asked.

"You would have to drive to Siberia," Kerimov replied, chuckling. "When this explodes, no one is safe. No one inside a kilometer radius is safe."

Shabal knew there was no possibility of a demonstration, but to ask was part of the negotiation. Kerimov could see that Shabal needed little convincing; now they were talking about the price.

"Walk with me," he said to Shabal, picking up the vest and walking past tables where women were constructing other vests.

Shabal followed as they moved toward a corner of the bunker where a number of workers were sitting on metal folding chairs, hunched around a small TV. They were eating lunch and watching a soccer match.

Kerimov nodded toward the TV. "You take one of these into a place like that and you will kill hundreds—perhaps thousands—as panic sets in and they begin trampling each other heading for the exits."

Just then, several of the workers let out a cheer as the home team scored. The roar of the crowd on the TV broadcast became a continuous roar as the TV camera panned the stadium, a vast sea of people leaping and cheering ecstatically.

Shabal stared at the TV, consumed by what he envisioned the vests could do—the casualties they could cause.

Christo stood before the floor-to-ceiling windows of his office on the thirty-fifth floor of Kiev's Esplanada Continental office building looking down at the landscape of Ukraine's capital city. From his vantage point in the center of the city, more than five hundred feet above the sprawling cityscape, it seemed as if he could see all of Kiev—from Independence Square to Saint Andrews Church to Mariyinsky Palace to the Verkhovna Rada building, seat of the Ukrainian Parliament, to every monument and building in the city.

But unlike the slow-moving, winding, Dnieper River far below him, Christo's brain was moving at warp speed. He knew what he had to tell Shabal, and he thought he knew what Shabal's reaction would be. He wrestled with what to say and just how to say it. He knew he had to keep Shabal and his terrorist plot moving forward at any cost. This was the key to his own plan and, for that matter, the life he envisioned with his wife, Dominga, and daughter, Solana.

"Your guest is here," a voice called from over his shoulder. His secretary, per his instructions, ushered Shabal in.

Christo spun and looked directly at Shabal. "Look at you, my friend! You look the same—older, harder, but the same."

Shabal lowered his head in a neutral gesture but said nothing.

"May I take your coat?" the secretary asked politely. "Or get you something to drink?"

"That will not be necessary," Shabal replied.

Christo sat down heavily in his chair and exhaled deeply, partly a natural reaction and partly to convey his apprehension—his uneasiness. He wanted Shabal to know he was troubled—to understand the difficulty of his position. Christo also knew this would be hard for Shabal to believe given Christo's privileged upbringing, his wealth, and the well-appointed office suite in Kiev's most prestigious building. Shabal now sat across the desk from Christo, shucking his coat onto the arm of the chair.

"From time to time I see former friends—people from my old life—and it's almost always a disappointment," Christo began wearily, speaking in their native Chechen dialect. "They've become distant or they've become boring or, more often than not, they have crawled into a vodka bottle."

Christo's remark accomplished its purpose and brought a small smile to Shabal's face. He swirled the ice in his water glass and raised it to Shabal.

"It's nice not to be disappointed for a change, Hubie." It was a name they used as childhood friends.

Shabal's smile vanished as rapidly as it had appeared. "That's not my name," he replied, all but spitting out the words as he turned his face away from Christo to look out at Kiev in the distance.

Christo recovered quickly, measuring Shabal and his mood. As difficult as this man could be, he still needed him.

"I know, I know. Mohammad Abu Shabal. The son of

Shabal. Come, my old friend, your father's name is Afghan."

Shabal bristled and continued to stare outside, ignoring the man behind the desk. Christo thought he knew him, but he did not. Yes, they had been schoolmates as boys. And yes, they were once close. Christo was sent to the upscale boarding school by his indulgent parents; Shabal had attended the same school on scholarship. But he had had to work two jobs after school just to dress like Christo. No, the man behind the desk did not *know* him. And now, what the hell was he up to?

"Things change," Shabal replied, "as have the times we live in."

"Yes, things have changed," Christo began, leaning across his desk to get as close to Shabal as he could. "That's why this might be the last time we meet like this. For I must find myself a hole to hide in—for me and for my family."

That got Shabal's attention, and he finally turned to look directly at Christo.

"I don't understand."

"It's like this," Christo continued. "I'm being watched by the CIA, and I can afford to take no chances. As soon as arrangements can be made, I am taking my family away. I have neither the energy nor the will to fight the Americans, and I will not endanger my family."

"But what about our plan, Mikhail?" Shabal protested, shock registering on his face at this unanticipated announcement. "My men have been training for close to a year. I have devoted almost all my resources to this project. Much of what we have worked for is in place."

"And our plan," Christo interrupted, "this arrangement between us, will be honored. Just because I have chosen early retirement doesn't mean my promises will go unfulfilled," he continued, holding Shabal in his gaze.

"But there is still much to be done."

"And it will be. However, I must insist the completion of our plan be done through associates of mine—trusted associates. I am being watched. It is for the safety of all concerned. I simply must distance myself from you and the execution of what you are planning."

"This is not good, not good at all!" Shabal exclaimed, leaping up from his chair. "I trusted you, not your associates. Now you wish to run and hide. You are a coward!"

Christo paused to frame his words. They were now on unequal footing. Shabal cared nothing for his own life. If it was forfeited in serving this plan or the cause, so be it. Christo did not share this commitment, nor would he put his family at risk to serve "the cause."

"Yet I must insist," Christo replied, also rising, trying to be firm but calm. He would not have Shabal towering over him. And, he reminded himself, not for the first time, that he was dealing with a zealot. "You have your plan, and I respect that. You have had my help and the help of my organization. And you will continue to have it. But I have my family to think of. I ask that you respect that as well."

"You are a coward!" Shabal repeated. "This is bullshit and you know it. This work and this plan are too important for you to turn it over to your . . . your 'trusted associates,'" he spat out, his anger boiling over. "It's too late. You can't change this and run away."

"Nothing changes," Christo said evenly, his voice

conveying resignation and the fact that he was trying to be reasonable.

Shabal could no longer stand still. He began to pace, throwing his hands into the air as his anger turned to rage—rage now directed at Christo.

"You just told me that now you want out—that others will act for you, in your place. Do you know what I had to do to get here? Do you know the men I had to sacrifice to get here? No, you have *no* idea. No, you are shit and a coward! You live up here in your ivory tower. You don't know and you don't care!"

Shabal turned his back on Christo and walked to the other end of the massive office suite, muttering to himself, too agitated to continue or to stand still.

Christo lowered himself to his chair and watched Shabal closely, unsure of how to proceed. And, he asked himself, could this have gone down any worse? Or any better? He had counted on Shabal wanting to go forward, with or without him. Now he was not sure. Dealing with men who refused to compromise was difficult at best. In business, Christo reflected, one compromises often.

He had tried to put himself in Shabal's shoes. He knew Shabal was a Muslim zealot with a single mission. He had no family, no money, and no other life. He had nothing Christo had, nor at this point, did he want to. He, Christo, was a businessman. Yet they had a common interest, did they not? There was no reason they shouldn't be able to come to an understanding.

Shabal wanted to kill as many Americans as he could, and he had recruited and trained a small army of martyrs committed to this same goal. And now he had just the right weapon—these vests Shabal had told him about—but he would need Christo and his resources to purchase them and to get them onto American soil.

While Shabal paced, Christo considered his position. The CIA was on to him. They had been on to him for some time, but then he was just *another* drug smuggler. It had been his ties to Shabal and the issue of terrorism that had elevated his profile at Langley. Otherwise, he would have been content to keep plying his trade and adding to his billion-dollar-plus net worth. Thanks to his links to Shabal, that was past. And now this new plan promised to double—or triple—his net worth overnight.

And he marveled at the simplicity of the plan. Just before Shabal unleashed his legion of martyrs armed with their explosive vests in the United States, Christo would short-sell a broad bundle of U.S. stocks. Others, such as American defense stocks, he would buy long on margin. When the markets crashed and corrected following the attack, he would sell. Then and only then would he have all the money he, Dominga, and Solana would need for the rest of their lives. They would relocate far from Costa Rica, in some Muslim country where the CIA was unwelcome.

It was a brilliant plan, and the only thing that could wreck it was for Shabal to balk. And now he had—or seemed to have. He had to fix that. This was business, he reminded himself, and there was always room for compromise. He would simply have to reason with the man.

"Abu Shabal, please, sit down. I know we can work this out . . ."

* * *

Later that morning, as the *Bonhomme Richard* steamed north off the west coast of Guatemala, Lieutenant Roark Engel made his way to the ship's sick bay. He had changed from his blood-and-mud-encrusted battle dress into a clean set of camouflage utilities, but his face was marked by dried sweat and residual black face paint that still rimmed his eyes and mouth. He looked like a Shakespearean actor who had only partially removed his makeup. The medical facility was amidships near the waterline, so the movement of the big ship was barely discernable. He stepped through a bulkhead coming just outside the door to sick bay and into a large triage area. In doing so, he moved from Navy haze gray into a world of white linen and stainless steel. The sick bay suite was quite spacious, as it was designed to handle the combat casualties of a Marine Expeditionary Unit. There was no reception area, just a large treatment room that ran athwartships with a long line of critical-care treatment tables. Engel paused to allow his eyes to adjust to the bright lights, and then moved cautiously past the line of tables. A corpsman, recognizing him as one of the embarked SEALs, pointed him to a series of patient bays off an adjoining corridor. He nodded his thanks as he moved along the line, glancing into two empty bays before finding the one that was occupied.

Mikey was awake and lying on his back. He had tubes in each arm and one running up his nose. His head was wrapped in white gauze, with one bandage drifting down to secure a cotton pad that covered his left eye. A monitor just above his head beeped regularly as it issued a series of green squiggles that marched left to right across the screen. Mikey sensed someone at the foot of his bed and lifted his head. He regarded Engel with his one good eye and smiled.

"Hey, Boss, what's happening?"

"The usual after-action debriefings." Engel stepped to the side of the bed. "I hope you feel better than you look, Mikey, 'cause you look like someone in an *ER* episode."

"I think I'm good, but there may be an issue with my left eye. The doc says there's a lot of nerve damage and that I might lose the eye. The bad news is that I can't see out of it; the good news is that it's my non-shooting eye. How's the rest of the squad? Am I the only malingerer?"

"We're all good. As you may or may not remember, it was touch and go for a while, but the boat guys pulled our chestnuts out of the fire—once again."

Mikey looked off into space for a second. "Yeah, I kind of remember that. Sort of like Mr. Toad's Wild Ride. And the Morales lady. We get her out all right?"

"We got her, but she's pretty beaten up. They really worked her over. Anything I can do for you?"

"Has anyone told Debbie yet? She's gonna freak out when she hears about this."

"I talked with Jackie before I came down here. She and Julia Nolan are on their way over to your place now." Engel took an Iridium satellite phone from a cargo pocket in his trousers and put it on the nightstand. "This is tied into the ship's comm system and will ring down here. Jackie will give you a call when she gets there. She'll break the news to Debbie, and then you can talk to her yourself. And talk as long as you like; it's the Navy's nickel. Just no operational details, okay?"

"Got it, Boss."

Normally, Engel would not have to caution him about security, but he had no idea just what kind of pain medicine he was on. Given what had happened, he seemed remarkably coherent, with only a slight slur to his speech. He was also just a little drifty, but then he was Mikey.

"You going to be okay there, brother?"

"I'm okay, Boss, really. My head throbs and I get nauseous now an' then, but it's not bad. I'd like to get some sleep, but I think Doc wants me to try and stay awake. I will until I talk to Debbie, then I'm going to get some shut-eye—shut-eye, get it?"

"Yeah, I get it." Engel had spoken earlier with the doctor, who was guardedly optimistic about Mikey's overall condition but was worried about the eye. Still, he had no clue why Mikey had no sight in his left eye—or why he was otherwise fine. The bullet entered his left temple, skirted his cranial cavity, and exited through the back of his head. That the apparent damage was no worse was something of a miracle; just how bad it *really* was or how much permanent damage there might be was still unknown. The *Bonnie Dick* was now steaming north at twenty knots, and they'd soon be within CH-53E Super Stallion range of San Diego and Balboa Naval Hospital. If he remained stable, they would fly him off as soon as they were in range.

"I'll check back with you later. Take it easy and do what the docs tell you."

"Roger that, Boss. Oh, what about my gun, radio, and NOD? Sonny will have my ass if I've lost my gun and any of the other gear." Engel grinned. By nature, SEALs were hard on their equipment, but they were paranoid about losing sensitive equipment—equipment they were signed out for. The paperwork was onerous.

"We left a lot of shit back in that river, including your gun. Your night-vision goggles and MBITR are trashed, but Sonny has them, and the serial numbers are readable. We'll get you a new gun when we get back to Coronado."

"Thanks, Boss. Thanks for everything."

Thank you, Mikey, Engel thought as he stepped from the bay. Just as he did, he heard the electronic ring-tone of the Iridium.

"Hello? . . . Hi, honey . . . Yeah, but it's not all that bad . . . Well, sort of in the head, but it's not all that bad . . . Aw, don't cry, baby. The round went in just above my hairline, so I'm still a handsome devil . . . That's right, the hair will grow right over it."

Engel smiled, shaking his head, and headed for the SEAL berthing area and his communications laptop. He had more combat duty ahead—his after-action reporting.

In another portion of the sick bay, there was yet another visitor to yet another patient, only this visit was not going well at all. The visitor was confronted just outside the patient bay by an attending hospital corpsman who was standing his ground.

"I'm sorry, but it's like I said before. She's a very sick lady, and that means no visitors and no exceptions."

"Look, I'm only going to need about five minutes tops. It's really important, or I wouldn't be asking."

"Hey, I hear you, but this is from the senior medical

officer—no visitors, period. And besides that, the lady's had a pretty rough go of it. She was semi-coherent when she arrived here, and they've got her pretty well sedated. Not sure if she could be of any use to you even if I could let you talk to her. Besides, we'll be flying her off some-time this afternoon, along with the wounded SEAL."

"Yeah, I know that, and that's why I need a few min-utes with her now, before she gets flown off."

"Hey, I'd like to help, but I have my instructions. There's nothing I can . . ."

"Are you one of the SEALs?" Both men turned to see Morales standing at the door of the bay, dressed in a hospital gown. Her face was swollen and starting to bloat from the beatings, and both her hands were bandaged like those of a prizefighter before the gloves are laced on. There were dark rings under both eyes, and one of them was swollen shut. Several of her front teeth were chipped.

"Close enough," Senior Chief Otto Miller said as he tried to step past the corpsman, but the young medic intervened.

"Hey, look, I said no visitors—doctor's orders. And, ma'am, you need to get back to bed."

"I am a doctor," Morales replied with some effort through puffy lips, "and I'm giving new orders. Let this man through."

Miller followed her into the small bay, catching her by the arm and helping her back into the hospital bed. She was very unsteady.

"And you are?" Morales asked as she gathered the sheet up around her chin. The bile rose in Miller's mouth as he saw the still-weeping cuts and cigarette burns on her arms. Engel and Nolan had said that she was a gutsy lady, but here was the proof.

"Ma'am, I'm Senior Chief Otto Miller. I run the intelligence section for this SEAL detachment. I'm no longer operational, but I am a SEAL. Listen, I know you're hurting, but I've got just a few questions if you can manage it. I'll be as quick as I can."

"Sure, fire away," she replied, avoiding Miller's gaze, seeming to look past him.

"Thank you. I know you've had a rough time of it, but we're trying to track down those responsible." Miller fished a small notebook from his pocket and flipped a few pages back. "We picked up a cell phone, a laptop computer, and some flash drives at the compound where they were holding you, and there are some things on those devices that are both troubling and confusing. I was hoping that you might be able to help us with this." He looked at her closely, but she remained passive, still looking past him. A single tear rolled down a bruised cheek from the one open eye. "There were cryptic references to 'transportation support' and 'critical funding requirements' and finally to 'the pilgrims.' And the cell phone we recovered had several calls to numbers we've traced to the Philippines and to Indonesia. Does any of this mean anything to you, or did you hear anything while you were being held that might help us—anything at all?"

Miller waited for close to a minute and was about to repeat himself when she held up a hand, a white mitt actually, to forestall him. She then wetted her lips.

"Th-the man who beat me was on the phone a great

deal. He spoke a language I did not understand, but I think it was Russian. But I understood a few words, or at least I thought I did. One was 'Christ' or 'Christo,' but it did not seem to be in reference to God. Perhaps someone's name. And I distinctly heard the word 'Somalia,' but I had no way of knowing if they were referring to the country or something else. I don't know if it was in the context of funding, but they did talk about euros. On occasion they lapsed into English, and on one of those occasions I heard him mention 'the big event.'" She paused and then slowly shook her head. "I'm sorry, that's all I can remember. I wish it were more, I really do."

Miller was about to respond when she raised her hand. "One more thing. I was aware when it was daylight and when it was dark. Most of the calls were late at night or early in the morning, like he was calling someone somewhere around the globe. And when the locals there spoke to him, they addressed him as 'Señor Thomas.'" She paused, and what might have been a frown crossed her swollen features. "I-I guess that's about it. Sorry."

"That's just fine. Every little bit helps." Miller quickly scribbled a number on a page of his notebook. Then he tore it from the pad, folded it, and tucked it in the wrapping on top of her wrist. "If you think of anything else, call me from any secure military or government phone. That number will reach me anytime, anywhere in the world. Thank you for this, and thank you for what you've had to endure. You're a very brave lady."

Just then, the curtain to the bay was jerked back, and a Navy commander in a white smock stepped in. He had a stethoscope draped around his neck, as if to announce that he was indeed a medical officer. "I thought I left instructions that this patient was not to be disturbed." He was about to continue, but then he glanced from the determined look on Morales's face into the cold green eyes of Senior Chief Otto Miller.

"By your leave, sir, but this is important. Please, I'll not be but another minute. And I'll have to ask you to wait outside . . . sir."

Again, the serious look on Miller's face brooked no argument, the difference in rank notwithstanding. The commander hesitated, but only for a moment. "Keep it short, Chief. She needs her rest."

"Aye, aye, sir," he replied as he pulled the curtain to reestablish their privacy. Miller and Morales regarded each other for a moment. Morales, even in her battered and medicated condition, knew this man was a serious professional. And Miller, knowing people as he did, knew that this gallant woman would carry scars from her ordeal, scars that were both physical and emotional, forever. But with a little time, she would get through this; she was a survivor. She'd not forget, but she could and would move on. He leaned in close to her.

"How much do you remember from the time the assault team burst into the room where they were holding you until you were airlifted out of there?" he asked in a quiet voice.

She closed her one good eye a moment, and then opened it, meeting his gaze for the first time. "Not much. There were shots, then an explosion, then more shooting and yelling. It was all kind of a blur. The whole time, though, I was aware that I was with the good guys. And that helped a lot. Before that . . . well, I'd rather not talk about it."

Miller nodded. "I understand, but since I debriefed the assault team, let me fill you in on what happened after the good guys arrived. The big guy who questioned you and hurt you—you know the one I mean?" She blinked rapidly and nodded. "Well, one of the good guys painted the ceiling of that room with his brains. I'm sorry to report that he died quickly, but the son of a bitch is now burning in a special hell reserved for that kind of scum." Miller again paused, watching her very closely, and just as carefully framed his words. "And the rest of those cockroaches—the ones who had their way with you?" Another nod and another tear. "Most of them are dead. Some of them died quickly, but a great many probably bled out from mortal wounds. A few may have escaped with their bullet wounds, but you know better than anyone what a high-velocity, jacketed round does to surrounding tissue. Those who may have managed to crawl away will probably lose a limb to gangrene or die of it—if they're lucky. The *federales* will be on the lookout for men with gunshot wounds; I made sure of that. They'll not get anything close to decent medical treatment. You, ma'am, were their worst nightmare." He stepped back to regard her, nodding his head. "And you're a lot like those good guys on the SEAL Teams. You'll get through this; you'll move on." He stood erect and saluted her, even though he was without a cap, and Navy men never salute uncovered. "Good luck, Doctor. Thank you for your service to our country."

After the senior chief left, Morales, for the first time

since that Scrabble game so very long ago, smiled—even though it hurt to do so.

That night in the *Bonhomme Richard*'s SCIF, or secure classified information facility—the most secure environment on the ship—Lieutenant Engel, Chief Nolan, and Senior Chief Miller sat around a small conference table with three onboard senior intelligence types. One was the *Bonnie Dick*'s senior intel officer, a full commander, and another, the senior enlisted intelligence specialist, a master chief. The third was a civilian analyst from NSA, the National Security Agency. The contents from the cell phone, the laptop, and the two flash drives had been sucked dry by the *Bonnie Dick*'s cryptologist and the information sent by dedicated satellite link to their intel counterparts at NSA, NCIS, CIA, and DIA. Plus, analysts on the *Bonnie Dick* were not without resources and had been poring over the data since Engel had handed the devices to Miller the minute they touched down on the ship. The laptop, phone, and flash drives had been whisked off to the intel spaces, where the technicians had been working on them nonstop. Engel and Nolan were now fresh from a nap, a shower, and a late afternoon shipboard breakfast, and into what, for them, was their morning routine. Engel was drinking tea; Nolan black coffee from his battered mug.

"So she said Somalia," the NSA man said. "You're sure about that?" He was dressed in an open-collar shirt and, in deference to the cool air pumped into the spaces to satisfy the requirements of the computers, a corduroy jacket with patches on the elbows. A mustache drooped around the corners of his mouth like a set of parentheses. It was as if he were cultivating the clandestine-service look.

"Absolutely," Miller replied, "Somalia. And she said she thought they were speaking in Russian."

"Close," the NSA man said. "Based on some of the text we took from the devices, it was Chechen. But what are the Chechens doing right in the middle of the drug trapline in Central America? That encampment in Costa Rica neither refines nor processes cocaine. It was strictly a transshipment operation—Colombia to the U.S. border. We know Chechens deal in cocaine, but Costa Rica? They take their drug deliveries from the South Atlantic cross-ocean connections, up through and across North Africa. Something's all out of whack here."

Just then a ship's messenger buzzed at the SCIF access door to gain entry. The intel master chief went to the door, took the proffered message, and signed for it. It was on a clipboard with red stripping on the border, marking it as a top secret communication. The master chief handed it to the NSA man. He lifted the cover sheet and studied the message for a long moment.

"Well," he said at last, "this fits, but I'm not sure what it means. The tech people back at headquarters managed to get into the cell-phone memory deletes and retrieve some coded text messages." He smiled. "We have some exceptionally talented geeks back there, and there's very little they can't get from a cell-phone record. What we have from one message is a set of coordinates ten miles inland along the northeast coast of Somalia. From another message, we have a date. The two seem to be related, as they and they alone have the same encryption protocols. So something seems to be happening in Somaliland three days from now. Given what we know about those involved, namely *Messieurs* Christo and Shabal, this can't be good."

"Any exact time that goes with that date?" Nolan asked.

"No, just a date, but there's more," he replied. "On one of the flash drives and on the laptop, there are references to retribution and vengeance on the Great Satan, and of revenge for the death of Osama Bin Laden. One reference said," he donned a pair of half-moon reading glasses and consulted the message, "'We will continue jihad against those responsible for the martyrdom of the holy one and exact a revenge as is befitting our great departed leader.' Sounds like they're planning something big, and it seems to be related to whatever it is that's to take place in Somalia three days from now. And it may or may not have anything to do with what happened in Costa Rica. Or it may have been that this Chechen guy was just there to interrogate Dr. Morales."

"Have we learned anything about him," Engel asked, "other than that he's dead?" Whenever possible, enemy combatants killed are photographed, as are those subjects of field interrogations. The NSA and agencies maintain huge data banks of persons of interest that could be accessed and IDed by facial recognition software.

It was the naval intelligence commander who spoke. "The guy who interrogated Morales was one Toma Zaurbek, a Chechen national who goes by various aliases, including Teddy, Tallin, and Tommy. He's a known member of the Chechen mafia and for the last several years has been in the employ of our friend Christo. From what little the Agency has released to us, Morales and her case officer were there to gather information on Christo, and somehow that came to Christo's attention. So that might be why Christo had them hit. From the debriefings of you and your team, it would seem that Tommy was the only semi-gringo at the compound. The rest of the goons were hired help."

"So it would seem reasonable," Engel offered, "that what is going down in Somalia has nothing to do with Costa Rica and everything to do with Christo."

"That's right," said the man with the mustache, "and with the other mystery man, Shabal. We know he's a sometimes associate of Christo, and he was referenced on yet another text message on the encrypted cell phone. Besides the texting, we've seen a spike in suspicious cell-phone traffic that relates to this quote, 'big event.' A lot of this traffic is localized along the known drug trans-shipment points as well as Cedros Island off Baja. Cedros is well down the coast from the border, but it's a known transshipment point for maritime smuggling."

"And it gets even better," the intel commander continued. "With all this information in place and collated, the red lights are flashing all over the alphabet agencies. The General has just made this a code-word operation. From now on, you, your detachment, and all of us are effectively in isolation until this gets resolved. So, Lieutenant, let your people know that their movements and communications are now restricted. And be ready to go operational as required. I know you're a man down in your assault team. If you need additional personnel, let me know, and I'll see that the request gets priority going up the line. You might also want to start thinking about an SR mission to Somalia. Since we're code-worded, they may want you to conduct the mission rather than assign it to another unit." He looked at his senior enlisted advisor. "I miss anything, Master Chief?"

"No, sir. I think that about covers it, at least for now."

"Lieutenant Engel?"

Engel looked from Nolan to Miller and back. Both their looks said they had nothing now but that there was a great deal they needed to talk about as soon as they could get off by themselves.

"Sir?" the commander said to the NSA man, who was now camped behind a laptop that was configured to handle classified message traffic.

"I have nothing else, but my boss at NSA just sent me a back-channel text. He says this has the look, feel, and smell of the real thing. I agree with him. And by the way," he glanced at his screen. "This is now Operation Desert Flower. Makes you wonder what idiot comes up with these supposedly random code words and phrases."

Nolan headed back to the SEAL compartment to get the other SEALs up to speed on the recent developments and to let them know they were now code-worded and in isolation. Code-word protocols were both precise and strict. When a situation or series of events reached a certain threat level, it was assigned a code word. This segregated all message traffic that referred to the code-worded operation; it was classified top secret, special handling. Those associated with or read into the operation were restricted in their movements, and their contact with those not associated with the operation or situation was also restricted. A Marine sentry would be stationed at the door to the SEAL compartment, and all comings and goings would be logged, along with the destination and purpose of any time away from their compartment. The decision to make this a code-word operation could only come from a very senior level. In this case it came from the man whom they now referred to as The General—General David Petraeus, the director of the Central Intelligence Agency.

A code-worded operation was indeed rare, and many SEALs and special operators went their entire careers without being assigned to one. They were reserved for issues of immediate national security. But a code-worded op was a dual-edged sword. On the positive side, it was a chance to be part of a meaningful operation—something important. On the negative side, their movements would be severely restricted, and they would have little contact with the outside world. They could receive e-mails from their families, but there would be no outgoing replies. As far as those back home were concerned, they would have dropped off the face of the earth.

Engel followed Senior Chief Miller back to the *Bonnie Dick*'s tactical operations center and began to log into the special, stand-alone communications nets that had been set up for this operation. It was a lengthy log-in process, one that isolated any code-worded message traffic from the normal military and government-agency communications channels. This procedure would not only provide hypersecure comm links but also, in the unlikely compromise of security, would track the security breach to its source. There were few security services capable of tracking the telltale nuances of military-activity and communication-traffic spikes. Only the Chinese, Russians, British, Israelis, and possibly the Iranians could do this, but they were taking no chances, or at least The General wasn't. Engel had just finished his log-in procedures when Nolan stepped into the TOC.

"Hey, Chief," Engel said as he turned from the computer console, one specially shielded to allow for top secret traffic. "How are the boys taking to their first code-word operation?"

Nolan shrugged as he handed a small canvas bag of cell phones to Engel. "They're pretty stoic about it. Excited but stoic. That little adventure in Costa Rica has left them a little spent. Give them a little time and they'll start to whine about the restrictions. And they all want to know what our next move might be. I told them we'd get back to them when we know."

Engle nodded. He took out his personal cell phone and dropped it into the bag and handed it to the senior chief. They would be locked up for the duration of the operation. It wasn't that Engel or Nolan didn't trust their SEALs not to sneak a call home, but if there was a security breach, it would probably come from the unauthorized use of a cell phone. If their phones were all locked up, they would not be hassled by the cell-phone traces and embarrassing questions.

"Well, what *are* we going to do?" Engel said, looking from Nolan to Miller. "I'd rather send a course of action up the line than have someone else calling our shot. Senior?"

Engel and Nolan were SEAL operators and more than capable of operational planning as it related to the tactical execution of a special operation. But when it came to the evaluation and distillation of intelligence from a variety of sources, assessing various courses of action, and plotting the next move or a succession of moves, Senior Chief Otto Miller ruled. So both Engel and Nolan now sat in silence, waiting for the oracle to speak. They were seated in a quiet corner of the TOC, away from the bustle and activity that buzzed about the rest of the secure facility. Miller carefully stroked his beard, ordering his thoughts.

"There are a lot of unknowns in this, but I do agree that there seems to be an unnerving aggregate of information that suggests some very bad people are up to no good—perhaps some major no good. This Christo is a bad one, but he's just a businessman. It's Shabal that has me concerned. He's ideologically committed, and his kind scares me." Miller was again silent, then leaned forward with his elbows on his knees.

"It would seem that the business in Costa Rica had only to do with Morales and Ross getting too close to Christo, and they paid the price for that. But it stands to reason that Christo's up to something or they would have just killed them—made it look like a drug hit or a botched kidnapping. They took the time and the associated risk of capturing her and conducting an interrogation, which means there's more to this. But unless I miss my guess, it has nothing to do with Costa Rica—it was about Christo.

"Then there's this business of what may take place in Somalia. We need to know more about that and how it relates to Christo and any Christo/Shabal tie-in. Is it about drugs? Arms? Money? What's going on and why? I think we need to put some eyes on whatever is about to take place there, and since we know where and roughly when, it shouldn't be too difficult. Logistically complex, but not too difficult. The good news is that since we're under code-word protocol, we can ask for just about any support we might need for a special reconnaissance mission, and we'll get it. The bad news is that since it is a code-word operation, we may not have the luxury of assigning that SR mission to another team in the time available to us."

Miller lapsed into a moment of silence before continuing. "And finally, there's this business of phone intercepts and traces that lead from Christo's Costa Rican operation to the Ukraine, Russia, Indonesia, and the Philippines. We have no idea where Shabal is, but we do have indications that Christo is no longer in Central America or Eastern Europe. He does have an oceangoing yacht that was just sighted in the Strait of Malacca. So there's a good chance he may be coordinating things from there. Or if he's not there, he soon will be. He's a careful one, and there's a good chance that he'd like to be aboard his yacht and halfway around the world if there's some kind of attack on the homeland. I don't think that yacht is over there for crew training; he wants it there for a reason. And that brings us to what these two might be planning, and we have to assume it's an attack on U.S. soil.

"If that's the case, it seems reasonable that Christo's connections with the cartels in South and Central American might well figure into this, which means some kind of breach across our southern border. Until we get better information, or information to the contrary, I think we have to play it that way. You currently have only six in your team, and that may be enough for a small direct-action assault or a raid, but not enough for backup or a blocking force. SEAL Team One is midway through their deployment preparation. I recommend that you ask that a full platoon be put on an eight-hour flyaway standby in case you get a mission tasking. No need to read them into code-word protocols, but have them on standby in case you need them, okay?" Both of them nodded, and Engel made a note on his scratch pad. "Then, even though it's going to be a pain in the ass, send two of your guys on a special reconnaissance mission to Somalia. You can plan it from here while they're in transit. I know it cuts your team by two more, but it leaves both of you here to work the traffic and intel picture, and plot the next move as more information comes in."

"Roger that, Senior," Nolan said, "but couldn't they pull a small SR team from a deployed East Coast squadron, even maybe one that's deployed to Iraq or Afghanistan? I hate to be down two more guys."

Miller lifted an eyebrow as he considered this. "Maybe. Maybe not. I'm thinking you're going to want your own guys to do this and come back here on a priority airlift to brief you in person. Again, I could be wrong, but whatever Shabal and Christo have planned will probably go down *after* this business in Somalia, right?"

Nolan pursed his lips and nodded slowly. "Yeah, I can see that. And we stay here, read the traffic and plan, and stand ready for a direct-action launch—if and when."

"That's it," Miller replied. "As far as a staging area, you could be here or in San Diego or at some remote location north of the Tex-Mex border, but the security is good here, and we'll be off Baja before daybreak tomorrow. And since we're in lockdown, there's probably no sense in moving until we get better information."

Engel and Nolan digested this for a long moment. The senior chief's analysis, as they expected, was linear and logical.

"So what's your move, Senior?" Engel asked.

Miller smiled. "Sooner or later, our man Christo is going to board his yacht, which, according to their last port call, is moving slowly into the Gulf of Thailand. I've asked Squadron Seven to move a Mark V detachment and to get a platoon into the area and have it standing by. Now that we're code-worded, I don't see that as a problem. If and when Christo is heloed out to his yacht, I think I'll pay a call on him."

"His boat can take a helo aboard?" Nolan asked.

"Well, it's a Westship 149 that's been modified to handle a Bell Jet Ranger. Should be easy to fast-rope aboard from an H-60. The man has sold a lot of drugs and arms, and he knows how to travel in style. And we'll need a Mark V to catch it; a big Westship can do close to twenty-four knots. But as soon as he's aboard and in international waters, we just might come calling. Any other questions?"

Engel exhaled, checking his notes. "Guess that'll do it for now. So, Chief, who do we detach for the SR mission?" He already knew the answer, but he had to ask.

"A.J. and Ray. Who else?"

"Then A.J. and Ray it is."

Suddenly Dave Nolan turned serious. "This thing is starting to heat up. Maybe our little jaunt in Costa Rica was just the beginning."

"So it would seem," Engel replied.

They rose and agreed to meet back with Miller later that evening. As they made their way to the entrance to the TOC, Nolan stopped to refill his coffee mug. The *Bonnie Dick* had more coffeepots stashed around the big ship than Starbucks had corner locations in Seattle. "Coffee, Boss?"

Engel looked over the setup. There was hot water, but he saw no tea bags. "No tea?" he inquired.

"Jesus, Boss. Why can't you just drink coffee like everyone else in the Navy?"

He gave Nolan a curious look. "Sure, why not," and he splashed some of the muddy liquid into a disposable cup. They were making their way forward toward the SEAL compartment when Engel suddenly took a stairwell up to the next deck.

Nolan paused. "Where you goin', Boss."

"Up to the flight deck for some fresh air. Why don't you join me."

Nolan hesitated a moment, then followed his lieutenant topside. It was late afternoon, still well before sunset. The sun was off their port bow as the *Bonnie Dick* shouldered her way north by northwest through the gentle Pacific swells. They exited the island superstructure on the starboard side and made their way slowly forward, walking into a twenty-knot wind. Engel tentatively sipped at his coffee, not really wanting to drink it. Then he stopped and turned to Nolan.

"Okay, Chief, let's have it."

"Sir?"

"Cut the bullshit, Chief. What's on your mind?"

Nolan just shrugged. "The op we just finished, this Christo/Shabal shit, the code-word protocols, all of it. Boss, you got a kid on the way, your first kid. Contingency deployments aren't supposed to be like this—not this active. I was hoping to break you away and get you home for a week or so. Now it looks like we're trapped. We're going to be with this for a while, probably to the end. This pisses me off. It's your first kid. You should be home with Jackie."

Engel smiled, turned, and they continued to walk. "It'd be nice, but I don't think that's in the cards."

"Maybe it'll break quickly and go smoothly, hey? Get it done and get you detached."

"Maybe, but don't count on it. If it was going to be smooth and easy, they'd send in the Marines or the Army, right?" Nolan said nothing. "You remember our last pump over in al-Anbar, when things got real slow at the end? And you wanted to cut me loose to go home with the advanced redeployment party so I could be home for our anniversary? But in the back of my mind I was thinking, 'What if something happens and we get a mission tasking? What if something goes down and I'm not there?' I just couldn't live with that."

Nolan was silent now, looking resigned.

"Well, I couldn't duck out then, and I sure as hell can't duck out now. If we get this thing resolved, then maybe I'll catch a flight back and see Jackie for a few days. But let's just focus on getting it done, which reminds me, we ought to get below and let Ray and A.J. know they're about to be detached to do the SR. They need to start getting their gear together."

"Ah, they already know, Boss. I told them to start packing just before we met with the senior chief. I've scheduled them out on the first helo tomorrow morning."

Engel stopped and faced him. "But didn't we just decide . . . I mean how did you know . . . ?"

"That's why you got the number one platoon chief at Team Seven, Boss. I'm paid to be one step ahead. It comes from drinking a lot of coffee—something," he glanced at Engel's still full cup, "you'll probably never get the hang of." He glanced at his watch. "It's almost eighteen hundred. Let's head for the mess decks and see what this tub is serving for dinner chow."

SEVEN

"Oh, miss. I'll have another ginger ale if you don't mind?"

The flight attendant scowled at him, then headed aft. A moment later she returned with a plastic cup with clear bubbly and no ice. She all but dropped the cup on the generous armrest between the two passengers, slopping a little as she did so.

"And another bag of peanuts would be nice as well."

She returned with a handful of small packets and dumped them in his lap. "If there's anything else you need," she said, "you can damn well get it yourself," and she was gone.

"You always have to push it, don't you?" A.J. said to his seatmate. He was seated by the window, thumbing through the latest edition of the special-operations quarterly magazine, *Front Sight Focus*.

"Y'know," his companion replied as he mopped up

the soft-drink spill, "you'd think that when you have your own airplane, you'd get treated with a little more respect."

"Your own airplane—yeah, right. Let me know if you're going to give the lady any more shit so I can move. The next drink order is probably going to get poured over your head, and I want no part of it."

Alfonso Joseph Markum and Ray Diamond were a study in contrast. A.J. was lean and compact, with smooth olive-colored skin and regular features. He had deep-set dark eyes that complemented thick, wavy hair, which he kept well-barbered and just slightly longer than regulation. His mixed lineage allowed him to pass for just about anything but white. There was a sense of effortless dignity to A.J. and an almost natural civility that often caused others to underestimate him. He was polite to a fault. Almost no one would take him for the capable martial artist that he was. When he moved, it was with economy and purpose, like someone with ballet training. And he could be deceptively fast.

Ray was taller and heavier, and bore the scarring of teenage acne that at best gave him a swarthy look. He had royal blue eyes and a James Coburn smile that seemed at odds with the gangland tattoos that covered both arms. He, too, was dark, but not as dark as A.J. His computer and IT skills aside, most of the Bandito SEALs, including his platoon officer and platoon chief, considered him something of a genius. He refused to speak of his past, and his service record listed his education only as a GED equivalent. Yet his military test scores were off the chart.

The two SEALs were traveling in an elevated style, at least on this leg of their journey. The analysis of the computer and cell phone they had obtained from the compound in Costa Rica had produced solid evidence of a terrorist plot. It had also yielded a date and a location in Somalia linked to the plot. This proved to be their only solid lead to what seemed to be plans for an attack on the American homeland. It was decided to send a team on a special reconnaissance mission to that location in Somalia. Since the threat appeared to be significant and credible, the operation had been assigned a code word—which greatly restricted who could be brought into the picture. It was decided to send an element from the small Bandito squad for the SR mission. Both Lieutenant Engel and Chief Nolan had officially requested that an SR team from some other SEAL or special-operations unit be tasked with the mission. For now, those up the chain of command, which reached quite high, wanted as few in on these developments as practical. So Ray and A.J. had been dispatched from the *Bonhomme Richard* for this desert rendezvous.

After Lieutenant Engel and Chief Nolan briefed them on the mission, they had launched from the *Bonhomme Richard* in a CH-53E Super Stallion. It was at the limit of the Super Stallion's range, but they had made it to the Naval Air Station in Corpus Christi, Texas, in one jump. There they had transitioned to their current ride, a Gulfstream G5. When the commander of the U.S. Special Operations Command in Tampa had been read into the code-worded operation, he had put his personal command aircraft at the disposal of the mission requirements. Now the Bandito reconnaissance team was over the Atlantic. After a refueling stop at Tenerife in the Canary Islands, they would make the final jump across

North Africa to Addis Ababa. From there, they were not yet sure of their future travel to the job site. They knew it would be interesting but most likely not so luxurious. In the rear of the Gulfstream, they had several bags of gear and they were not traveling light. Their primary mission would be that they see and not be seen, but if it came to a fight, they had to be ready for that as well. Just then, Ray's Iridium satellite phone sounded. He had it programmed to loudly play the *William Tell Overture*. The sound carried to the rear of the quiet executive jet, bringing a frown from the single flight attendant, an Air Force master sergeant who was both senior to and a little tired of her two demanding SEAL passengers. Not to mention that both cell and satellite phones were not allowed to be used on military aircraft.

"It's okay," Ray called back to her with his best killer smile, as A.J. rolled his eyes. "It's a business call." Then into the phone. "Special Operations Executive Service. Wars fought, uprisings quelled, governments toppled, and virgins converted. How may we help you today, sir or ma'am? . . . Oh, yes, sir . . . Understood, sir . . . Yes, sir . . . Absolutely, sir . . . Roger that, sir." Then after a long pause while he listened, "Just as soon as we're ready to launch . . . Understood, sir . . . Until then."

"So what's up, Mr. Executive Operator? I take it that was the boss?"

"It was," Ray replied. "He gave me the rest of our travel itinerary. Looks like we'll do it all on this trip," and he briefed A.J. on what was ahead for them.

"It seems like a lot of trouble just to cross the beach of a failed state," A.J. replied.

"I guess it has to do with the pirate thing in Somalia. It seems the Skinnies have a pretty effective coast-watching system set up, and there's a lot of traffic in the Gulf of Aden. And there are the naval vessels of several nations there on pirate patrol. They're taking no chances getting us ashore unnoticed."

"Whatever," A.J. replied. "Let's hope it's a walk in the park and not another slugfest like the last one." He sighed. "But like all our little field trips, getting there is half the fun." He went back to his magazine. Ray pushed his call button to see if maybe the master sergeant could rustle them up a couple of sandwiches.

Miles away in the Ukraine, two aging Russian pilots climbed into their ancient Albatross aircraft, which was easily five times as old as the Gulfstream that carried A.J. and Ray. They grumbled that their boss had called them at 4 A.M. and told them to get to their aircraft and start heading south. They knew it would be a rough flight, with multiple refueling stops, many of them in third-world shitholes. With each stop, they risked getting a bad load of fuel that would damage their engines—or worse.

But the money was good, and their employer had promised them a substantial bonus if they arrived precisely on time. They were flying for themselves now, not for the Russian Air Force, which had pretended to pay them decades earlier. Yet the sooner they got the mission done and got back to their adopted country, the better.

* * *

The Gulfstream set down at Bole International, just outside the Ethiopian capital, a few minutes before 1700 local time and taxied to a remote section of apron, well off the main service strip. The presence of a G5 was unusual but not unheard of. Since there were no markings, ground personnel assumed the aircraft belonged to some Saudi or Kuwaiti prince, making a refueling stop on the way to Cape Town, possibly on a diamond-buying expedition. While the fuel bowser attended to the Gulfstream, the two SEALs saw their gear off the aircraft and into a small warehouse that had been leased by the American embassy in Addis Ababa. Each had a backpack, a good-sized duffel, and a hard case for their weapon—a short hard case, as they were carrying only M4 rifles. The embassy representative who was there to meet the plane watched the two SEALs make their way inside. He waited a few moments at the bottom of the air stairs for the others. When it became apparent that there *were* no others, he followed them inside.

"Gentlemen, my name is William Leach, and I'm from the embassy. I'm to see to your needs for the short time I understand you are to be here." He proffered an envelope. "And to give you these sealed orders."

"Thank you, William," Ray replied. He took the envelope and stepped away to where A.J. waited for him. Ray broke the seal, then extracted a second envelope with yet another seal. The second envelope was marked Top Secret, Eyes Only, which meant it was not to be copied, only read.

"Concentric Russian dolls," A.J. offered.

"So it would seem."

Ray broke the second seal, removed yet another envelope, and removed the message. They read it together. The message contained little new information but did confirm the support and transportation platforms that would be available to them for this special reconnaissance. Then they turned to Leach.

"You know what's in this?" Ray said, holding up the message.

Leach had the neat look of an embassy gofer—midthirties, well turned out in chinos and a starched, open-collar shirt. He had the beginnings of mottling on his cheeks that said he was on the legation cocktail circuit. It was a known fact the embassy staffers in African capitals consumed their share of Beefeater gin and Schweppes tonic.

"Absolutely not," he replied, "and I'm told that its classification and special-handling protocols are outside my security clearance."

"So what are we supposed to do with it now?"

Leach took a step back. "Uh, I have no idea. Now that it's open, I can't handle it."

Ray looked at A.J., who just shrugged. "I guess we can eat it, or we can burn it. Probably ought to burn it."

"Yeah," A.J. concurred. He pulled a Bic lighter from his shirt pocket and fired it up. He touched the resulting tongue of flame to the corner of the message while Ray held it. Ray let the single sheet become engulfed in flames and nearly singe his fingers before he let it fall to the concrete floor. After it burned out, he scattered the blackened residue with his boot.

"Uh, I'm not sure that's an approved method for the destruction of a classified document," Leach said.

"Neither am I," Ray replied. "But I didn't want to eat it, and we sure as hell can't take it with us."

The embassy man shifted uneasily from one foot to the other. "I'll have to report this," he said, "when I get back to the embassy."

"No worries here," A.J. said, "but in the meantime, what are your instructions?"

"Ah, I'm to remain here and be of any service I can to you fellows."

"Really? Well, we have some new instructions for you. We have a long night ahead of us and some gear to prep before we leave. Why don't you see if you can rustle us up something to eat? We like to eat before we go to work, and God knows when we'll next get a decent meal."

"I, uh, well. I suppose I could do that. What do you have in mind?"

Without hesitation, Ray answered. "How about a Philly cheesesteak?"

"Exactly," A.J. chimed in. "With lots of grilled onions."

Leach stood there with his mouth open for several seconds, then said, "I'll see what I can do." He turned on his heel and left.

As he left by a side door to the warehouse, they could hear the engines of the Gulfstream begin to spool up. The Air Force master sergeant stepped past Leach as he made his way out.

"He didn't look too happy," she reported.

"Embassy business," Ray deadpanned. "We can't talk about it."

She ignored him and handed A.J. a bulky paper bag.

"There are a couple of box lunches in there that I liberated from the commander's personal larder." She paused a moment, then continued, "Look, I know you two low-lifes wouldn't be on my bird unless it was something important—and probably dangerous. You guys take care of yourselves, and good luck."

"Thank you, Master Sergeant," A.J. replied.

"Yeah, thanks," Ray echoed. "We really do appreciate it."

She threw them a casual salute and took her leave. Moments later, they heard the whine of jet engines rise an octave and then grow fainter as the Gulfstream taxied away.

"That was nice," Ray said, "but I'm holding out for a Philly cheesesteak."

"Yeah, dream on. But, yes, it was nice of her, and these, my friend," A.J. replied, sniffing the contents with approval, "are four-star box lunches. Just look at them as backup chow; it may be the only backup we have on this operation."

"Yep, looks that way," Ray agreed.

They put the box lunches aside on the floor and, under the fluorescent glow of a single suspended fixture, began to lay out their operational gear. At 2030, shortly before dusk, two Marine CH-53E Super Stallion helicopters set down a hundred yards from the warehouse. While the helos refueled, the two SEALs made ready. A.J. and Ray now wore their kits, but they were not operationally configured. They were kitted up for intermediate travel. They wore their backpacks in normal fashion, but their duffels were clipped to D-rings on the front of their harnesses. The M4s in their hard cases were strapped to their sides. As they stepped from the door of the warehouse, a Land Rover screeched to a halt in front of them. It was Leach. He handed Ray a paper sack that was well stained with large grease spots. The smell alone told them that he had accomplished his mission.

"How the hell did you find Philly cheesesteak subs in Ethiopia—in Africa at all, for that matter?" Ray asked.

"Hey, you fellows have your secrets, I have mine."

"William, old son," Ray said, putting a hand solemnly on his shoulder. "You are something else. I'm going to see that you're mentioned in our dispatches."

"Okay, thanks," he replied, not sure whether Ray was kidding or not. "You guys have a safe trip."

The two SEALs, each now armed with a grocery bag of chow, made their way to the two Super Stallions that were turning on the tarmac. Both SEALs, as directed by one of the crew chiefs, boarded the same bird—the lead helo. Both helos took off, heading southeast away from the city and then veering left to a northeasterly heading. They flew in loose formation for close to two hours approaching the Ethiopian-Somali border. The trailing helo turned away to a northerly heading for Djibouti and a clandestine refueling stop. The trail bird's mission was over; it was there only for redundancy. With its tanks topped off, it could just make it back to the USS *Bataan* LHD-5, cruising an antipiracy station off the Horn of Africa at the eastern approaches to the Gulf of Aden. The lead helo, with the two SEALs, dropped to an altitude of five hundred feet to avoid the anemic Somali coastal radars near Berbera, skimmed over the western edge of that nation, and crossed unnoticed into the Gulf of Aden. The Super Stallion's progress was carefully monitored by an Air Force E-3C Sentry airborne early-warning and control aircraft orbiting well out over the Gulf.

An hour into the flight, the two SEALs were eagerly devouring their Philly cheesesteaks, handing over their Gulfstream executive rations to a very grateful Marine Corps flight crew. Their hastily prepared box lunches from the *Bataan* were unpalatable by comparison. For all concerned, it would be a long flight, and by helicopter standards, a very long flight. The Super Stallion has a range of just over six-hundred nautical miles and a cruising speed of 170 knots. Some three hours after takeoff and eighty miles north of the Somali coast, the lead helicopter found the MC-130P Combat Shadow special-operations tanker. The Combat Shadow had launched out of Aden, Yemen, and had reached the rendezvous coordinates only minutes before the CH-53E's arrival. After taking on a full measure of JP-4, the helo continued in an easterly direction, paralleling the coast of Somalia but well out to sea.

Another two hours of flying brought it to a position some fifty miles off the Somali coastline, just north of the city of Candala. The Super Stallion descended from a cruising altitude of nine thousand to fifteen hundred feet, and there it was, right where it was supposed to be—the USS *Michigan*. The pilot made a careful approach, following the wake of the big submarine until it was matching the sub's ten knots, and hovered some fifty feet above the broad missile deck, behind the sail and just aft of the dry deck shelter—a bulbous metal lump clamped to the rear of the missile deck. It resembled a large propane tank.

"Thanks for the chow," the crew chief yelled as he hooked Ray up. The heavily loaded SEAL was sitting in the door of the helo. "I don't care what the bar girls in San Diego say about you guys, you swabbies are all right."

"You're welcome, Gyrene. Safe trip home."

He tapped Ray on the helmet, and the SEAL swung out into the night and the noisy prop wash of the 53's big seven-bladed main rotor. Because of the weight of their gear, the SEAL recon team would be winched to the deck rather than using the more expeditious fast-rope method. The sea was calm, and the Marine Corps pilot was skilled from years of training for missions such as this one. Ray and A.J., assisted by the *Michigan*'s deck crew, stepped lightly onto the metal deck of the submarine as if they were stepping down from a passenger bus. Once the two SEALs were aboard, the Super Stallion turned and continued east. It again mated with the loitering Combat Shadow, drank its fill, and continued on to the USS *Bataan*, which was steaming west to meet it. The crew of the helo had been in the air for close to eleven hours. Their only break had been two short ground refueling stops. Back at the air-sea rendezvous point, there was only empty ocean. Before the CH-53E was fifteen miles into the final leg of its journey, the *Michigan* had slipped beneath the waves.

The USS *Michigan* (SSGN-727) was originally commissioned as a fleet ballistic missile submarine and carried the most advanced versions of the Trident ICBM system. For more than two decades and sixty-six strategic deterrent patrols, this largest of U.S. submarines was converted to a new mission. The eighteen-thousand-ton *Michigan* was stripped of her ICBMs and refitted to carry cruise missiles and to support a variety of special-operations missions. During the cold war, the U.S. submarine force eschewed working with SEALs and Special Operations Forces in favor of their strategic mission of tracking Soviet-era submarines and nuclear retaliation, should the Russians and *their* ballistic submarines do the unthinkable. With the end of the cold war, the SEALs and SOF became the submariners' new best friends. They took to these new duties with great gratitude, as the SOF requirements kept their boats in the water and underway. The submarine service took on this new role with their typical high degree of professionalism and attention to detail. After they boarded the submarine, A.J. and Ray were taken to a small compartment where they dumped their gear. A ship's master-at-arms was stationed at the door. Moments later, an officer led them to the commanding officer's quarters.

"Welcome to the *Michigan*, gentlemen. I'm Captain John Toohey. Happy to have you aboard." The *Michigan*'s skipper was an affable Navy captain with an agreeable slouch and the chalky pallor of those who lived most of their working life underwater. His hair was boot-camp short, and he had kindly, highly intelligent eyes and a crooked nose over a push-broom mustache. As with the other members of the crew, he was dressed in dark blue, one-piece cotton overalls; as if they were blue-water counterparts to the SEALs desert camouflage utilities. Like the Marine Corps flight crew, Toohey was not briefed into the mission specifics of these two SEALs, but he did know it was a code-worded operation and therefore operationally significant. The *Michigan* spent much of its life boring holes in the ocean and conducting training exercises. Now they were to be a part of a classified mission. It was a break from the routine and a chance for a real-world tasking, if only in a support role. And they were prepared to play their role well. After A.J. and Ray introduced themselves to the captain, he bid them to sit at a small conference table over a chart of the coast of Somalia and the Horn of Africa. Joining them were two other blue-suits—the sub's operations officer and the *Michigan*'s COB, or chief of the boat, the senior enlisted leader.

"Here's where we are," the ops officer said, pointing to a location almost due north of the tip of the Horn, "and here is where you need to cross the coast. We can get the *Michigan* safely to a point here some twenty-three miles offshore, then it becomes a little too shallow for us. At this offshore location, the two of you will board a SEAL delivery vehicle for the rest of the trip. The SDV will get you to about a mile offshore, where it then shallows up for them. You'll have to swim the rest of the way."

The two SEALs studied the chart. "How soon will you be in position to launch the SDV?"

"We're only about thirty miles from the launch site now, so we could easily be there in a few hours." He paused to glance at his watch. "Since we have to wait until dark, or about twenty-one hundred this evening, we'll just be idling here in the Gulf of Aden, avoiding surface traffic. This will give you about sixteen hours to prep your gear, run through the launch procedures, and maybe get in a few hours' sleep."

Ray looked at A.J., then the *Michigan*'s ops boss. "Easy day, sir."

"We here on the *Michigan*," Captain Toohey intervened, "fully understand our orders. We'll get you to the launch coordinates, and we'll get you on your way. I've not been read in to the specifics of your mission ashore but I know there are issues of national security and homeland security in play here. When this all gets resolved, I'd like to be able to tell my crew of the role they played in this, if security protocols allow for it."

"Understood, sir. When this is over, we'll do what we can to see that you're included in the after-action reporting. No promises, but we'll try."

"I appreciate that. Thank you and good hunting."

They discussed the mechanics of the *Michigan*'s role in the mission, and then the COB led them back to what had been the missile compartment of the submarine, where the massive silos once housed the Trident D-5 ICBMs and enough megatonnage to create a nuclear winter. In those strategic-deterrent times, the crew referred to these closely placed silos as Sherwood Forest. Now four of the silos housed advanced cruise missile sabots, poised in the ICBM silos like the cylinders of a revolver handgun. Other silos had been converted for storage and troop-support requirements for embarked special-operations personnel. Once they reached the SDV area, Ray and A.J. were greeted with a barrage of chiding.

"Well, for Christ's sake—look what the COB dragged in."

"All this trouble for *these two*?"

"I thought this was a big, secret, high-profile mission. And here they send in the second team. Go figure."

There were six of them, SEALs from SEAL Delivery Vehicle Team One, stationed on Ford Island, in Hawaii. These SEALs specialized in the underwater launch and recovery operations associated with SEAL delivery vehicles—mini-submersibles that piggybacked on larger nuclear submarines like the *Michigan* and took SEALs into waters too shallow for the bigger boats. The boats carried by the *Michigan* for this mission were the Mk8 Mod 1 SDVs. These were "wet" submersibles, meaning that they have seawater inside the SDV as well as outside. While this subjects the occupants to ambient conditions, the simplicity of a non-pressurized fiberglass hull makes the little craft both simple and reliable.

"You know, A.J., if I knew that we had to work with these turkeys, I wouldn't have volunteered for this important and dangerous mission."

"Yeah, well y'know, Ray, we didn't exactly volunteer. We're just here following orders."

"Still, you'd think that we'd be given some better support than this bunch of misfits."

The SDV Team One SEALs each in turn greeted their brothers from Team Seven with handshakes and hugs. Meetings between SEALs from sister Teams are often accompanied by a great deal of bantering and good-natured condescension. The COB watched all this with a grin and shook his head. With close to thirty years in the Navy under his keel, he knew all about submarines and submariners. These SEALs were a different lot. After a few minutes of greetings and grab-ass, the

SDV officer in charge, a master chief petty officer, called for order. They then began to talk through the mechanics of the launch and the clandestine delivery of the two reconnaissance SEALs to a precise location on the coast of Somalia.

The USS *Makin Island* (LHD-8) was an updated, carbon copy of the *Bataan* and the *Bonhomme Richard* and the last of the eight *Wasp*-class amphibious warfare ships. Since the U.S. Navy no longer had the luxury of the huge base at Subic Bay in the Philippines, any military contingency in Southeast Asia of any size had to be addressed by an afloat presence. For this reason, the *Makin Island*, her diverse air group, her embarked Marine Expeditionary Unit of 1,400 Marines, and a SEAL task unit had been cruising the waters of the South China Sea off the island of Luzon. The SEALs and the Marines had detachments working with the Filipino military to counter Muslim secessionists in the southern archipelago in the Sulu Sea. So it was with some reluctance that the captain of the *Makin Island* recalled his disbursed SEAL elements and their combatant craft and put his ship on a course for Malaysia. After heading south for a full day with no reason given to the captain, and some harsh message traffic up his chain of command, he was granted limited code-word clearance, as it related to his ship's orders. That evening the SEAL task unit commander and Senior Chief Otto Miller, charts in hand, knocked on the door of the captain's sea cabin.

"Come in, gentlemen. My mess specialist has just

brewed a fresh pot of coffee. I only hope you have some fresh perspective as to why my ship had to abandon its duties off the Philippines and is now making best speed for Malaysia." Captain Evin McMasters, the skipper of the *Makin Island*, was easygoing, competent, and well liked by his crew. Yet it was all he could do to remain civil at having been kept in the dark while his embarked SEALs seemed to know a whole lot more than he did. When they were seated around the small conference table, the captain continued. "So, Commander," he said, pushing two mugs of coffee across the table, "what the hell's going on?"

Lieutenant Commander Todd Crandall was the embarked SEAL task unit commander. In addition to a platoon and a half of SEALs, he had an Mk5 boat detachment and two 10 meter-RHIB (rigid-hull inflatable boat) detachments. The TU also carried the associated administrative, technical, and maintenance personnel to include Senior Chief Miller's cadre of intelligence analysts. The TU commander was a short, serious former enlisted man, who had been a boatswain's mate before he was a SEAL. He knew the blue-water Navy, and he knew Special Operations. Although he did not like the tone of the *Makin Island*'s commanding officer, who was about his same age, he could well appreciate the man's irritation at being kept in the dark.

"Captain, I'm going to let Senior Chief Miller read you into this. He's been with the operation since the beginning, and he has a good handle on the situation."

"Okay, Senior, let's have it."

"Uh, it's a rather long story, sir. Before we begin," he said as he sipped appreciatively at the coffee, "let me apologize for your not being read in to this operation from the beginning. Sometimes those up the line, in the interest of security, get a little stingy with the information. So let's take this from the beginning."

Aboard the USS *Michigan*, Ray and A.J. stood off to one side in their dry suits. The previous sixteen hours had been occupied with a few hours' sleep and a lot of preparation and briefings, along with a final text message from Lieutenant Engel and Chief Nolan. They were now in the metal chamber on the deck of the *Michigan* called the dry deck shelter, a pressurized garage whose interior walls were a maze of pipes, air flasks, and fittings. In the harsh fluorescent glow of the crowded space, a single SEAL delivery vehicle rested in its cradle.

For now, there was little for the recon SEALs to do; they were merely spectators to the preparations that would see them from the *Michigan* to their drop-off point off the Somali coast. They wore only their Mk15 scuba rigs, which had been meticulously prepared earlier that afternoon. Since the depth of the dry deck shelter would be close to sixty feet, they would use the more sophisticated Mk15 mixed-gas diving rig rather than the standard Dräger rebreather. While the SDV SEALs and their diving-submersible technicians made their final checks, the speaker overhead barked out the launch countdown.

"Ten minutes to launch sequence—ten minutes to launch sequence. All nonessential personnel should now exit the shelter."

Then, "Five minutes to launch sequence initiation.

All craft personnel should be in place. All hanger handlers should be in place." The hatch that mated the dry deck shelter to the *Michigan* was now closed, and they were environmentally segregated from the mother submarine.

Ray and A.J., helped by two SDV SEALs, climbed into the rear compartment of the SDV. Up in the forward compartment, the pilot and navigator were already in place, powering up their propulsion and navigation systems. Both had done this dozens of times before in training, but given that this was an operational mission, they went through their checklists with additional attention to detail. The SDV master chief, in dry suit and traditional scuba attire, stepped to the side of the submersible and offered his hand, first to A.J., then to Ray.

"You sure that you don't need me to go along to keep you two out of trouble?"

"Thanks, Master Chief. We could probably use the help, but three's a crowd, and this one's a sneak and peek."

"Then good luck to you both. The SDV will stand offshore and surface at half-hour intervals for a comm check and in case you need an emergency extraction. They'll stay on station for about four hours before they head back to the *Michigan*."

"Thanks for everything, Master Chief. Your guys are great."

"Ditto, Master Chief," Ray echoed. "*Mahalo* and *aloha*."

The senior chief took his position along the forward bulkhead of the shelter, from where he would direct the launch. The SDV pilot and navigator signaled that their systems were up and they were ready to launch. Two SEALs and two SDV Team diving technicians stood by on either side of the SDV to assist with the launch. On the signal of one of the diving techs, Ray and A.J. began to purge their scubas, breathing in from the rig and exhaling through their nose and mask so as to replace the air in their lungs with the nitrogen-oxygen mix in their scubas. A loud buzzer sounded, and the dry deck shelter began to fill with water. As it filled, swallowing up SDVs, SEALs, and divers, the pressure inside the shelter was gradually increased to equal that of the sixty-foot depth at which the *Michigan* was moving through the Gulf of Aden. Her forward progress was about three knots, just enough to make steerageway and to hold depth. The fluorescent lights in the shelter now took on an emerald shade. Then the launch crew began the much-rehearsed and well-choreographed sequence of events that undocked the SDV, attached the bow planes, and eased the craft gently aft and out from its underwater hanger. A.J. and Ray felt rather than saw the big pressure door hinge back to open the dry deck shelter to the open ocean. They did notice the fluorescent lighting of the shelter give way to the blackness of the open sea.

The SDV was towed by a steel cable as it followed the mother sub, hovering just behind and above the shelter. When the pilot and navigator were again satisfied with their systems and instrumentation, the pilot turned on his lithium-ion-powered electric motor and began to match the speed of the *Michigan*. He then dropped the tow cable. For several minutes, the SDV matched the course and speed of the big submarine, like a small pilot fish keeping station on a whale shark. Then it veered to port and took a southerly heading for Somalia.

At the SDV's six-knot cruising speed, they had a three-hour run to their offshore insertion point. The little craft finally leveled off at its cruising depth of fifteen feet, as the four SEALs aboard shifted from their Mk15s to "boat air," or the SDV's internal supply of breathing air from the onboard compressed-air bottles. Their scubas were now backup/bailout rigs. The onboard breathing mouthpieces were modified for speech. Hearing was achieved through the use of a "bone phone," a circular transducer held to the diver's temple by his diving hood. The speech was garbled and understandable, and the bone phones transmitted sound quite well. Yet both the SEALs in the rear compartment were surprised when Rachmaninoff's Piano Concerto no. 2 in C Minor floated over the SDV's comm system. A.J. appreciated both the music and the skill of the SDV's navigator, who had found a way to hook his iPod into the underwater sound system. Ray was a little miffed that there was no salsa music on board, but he'd brought a book. He read with a waterproof mini-headlamp, and after finishing a page, he pulled it from the soaked book and jettisoned it from a crack in the canopy of the SDV. He did this because it passed the time and because he could.

EIGHT

On the *Bonhomme Richard*, Lieutenant Roark Engel and Chief Dave Nolan read message traffic and followed events as they unfolded in the Gulf of Aden and the South China Sea. Each morning they, along with Sonny and Weimy, met on the flight deck for a physical training session. The Marines aboard jogged around the perimeter of the flight deck. The four SEALs jogged bow to stern, then sprinted into the wind, stern to bow. Following forty minutes of these wind sprints, they retired to the *Bonnie Dick*'s extensive weight room for more punishment. On the third day, Nolan found Engel in the compartment assigned to the SEALs and their equipment and took him aside.

"Look, sir, we're within helo range of the beach, and you got a kid on the way. There's a good chance that this, whatever might be developing, is not going to mature into a real threat. Or if it does, some other agency or strike element is going to step in and handle it. Or the bad guys, if we just stand back and keep an eye on them, will fuck it up themselves without any interference from us. As you well know, they've been known to do just that. So go spend a few days with your wife. I can handle it, and if something breaks, I'll give you a shout and you can get right back down here. Right now it's a wait and see. Until we get more from A.J. and Ray or from Senior Chief Miller, there's not a lot we can do. Seriously, man, family is important."

Engel allowed himself to consider what Nolan was saying. As the *Bonnie Dick* steamed north, there was little for him and the others to do but await developments and more intelligence. As the Bandito Platoon commander, Roark Engel was the only one who did not have to surrender his satellite phone. He was now the sole link between his SEALs and their families back home. Jackie understood this and so when he called, he let her know all was well with the men and she passed on family news as needed. His men needed to know their families were okay, and in turn, the families wanted to know their men were fine. In her conversations with Roark she had made no demands, but he knew she would like him home if that was at all possible—he could hear it in her voice, and he knew all too well this was a challenging pregnancy. He *ached* to be there for her. It *was* possible for him to make a trip home, but not easy—at least not easy for him. First of all, there was the operation—one that could quite possibly be a big one if it did go down. And though there was little for him to do right now, if things did begin to break, they might break very quickly. What if the mission went down and for some reason he couldn't get back in time? Past the operational issues, there was the fact that he *was* on deployment. Special operators often allowed themselves privileges not normally afforded others in the military. Yes, they deployed often, and they often went in harm's way. They also spent much more time away from their families than almost anyone else in the military. But no male sailor or officer on the *Bonnie Dick* could simply have himself flown off the ship because his wife was having a baby, unless, of course, there were serious complications. Roark Engel was not someone who could easily take advantage of his position or leave what he considered his duty post. And then there was the priority of the mission. It was, after all, a code-word operation.

"Understood, Chief, and thanks. I'll think about it and get back to you."

That evening while at his small desk in the SEAL compartment, he called Jackie on his Iridium satellite phone. It was one of the few times he called his wife while on deployment when they were in the same time zone. He found her at home, folding clothes with the TV on in the background.

"Hi, darlin'. How's my favorite expectant mother?" he began.

"Roark! I'm so glad to hear your voice." She was about to ask, "Where are you?" but stopped herself in time. "How is everything wherever you are?"

"All is well here, and for the moment, things are pretty quiet." He could never discuss operational matters over the phone, but he knew that saying they were inactive would cheer her up. "The question is, how are you and the little one getting along?"

"I'm a little tired, but everything's fine. *Your* child kept me up most of last night. Wouldn't stop kicking me. Oh, and I'm as big as a house."

Engel ached to be home, to be able to hold his wife— to spoon up with her in bed and run his hand over her belly. "Listen, hon, there's a chance I may be able to break away and get home for a few days—just a chance," he quickly added.

"Oh, Roark. That would be wonderful."

"There's a project I'm working on," he said guardedly, "that could go either way. It could turn out to be nothing, in which case Dave Nolan can keep an eye on things while I'm gone. But it could be something that will keep me tied up here. I'm telling you this, as there may be a chance I can get away, but right now it's up in the air. I wish I could be more definite, but that's just the way it is."

Jackie Engel considered this and her response carefully. She sensed that her husband was torn between his duty to her and his job—more specifically his duty to his men. She'd give anything to have him with her, even for a few days. Well, almost anything. She knew that if she pressured him, he'd come, and at the expense of short-changing his strong sense of duty.

Well before the baby, before they had even talked about marriage, Roark had made it clear to her that she would have to share him with the life he'd chosen and his duties and responsibilities as a professional warrior. She'd accepted that, even thought it noble and romantic. But that was then and this was now. She always missed him when he was gone, but she'd never needed him close more than at this very moment. Yet she somehow knew that the man she loved and needed would somehow not remain the same man if she forced him to leave his post on the eve of a mission or if his men should have to go into harm's way without him. If Dave Nolan and the others needed him and he wasn't there for *them*, then something between the two of them would be lost, perhaps lost forever. *My God,* she briefly reflected, *before I met Roark, I would never have considered marriage with someone who was gone half the time and in mortal danger on the job. But that was before. I've accepted the role of the spouse of a warrior, and now I have to accept this. I love him dearly, and he's worthy of this sacrifice, but still . . .*

"Hon, you still there?"

"I'm here, Roark. Listen, if you can get here, nothing would please me more. If you're really needed there, then don't come. My mom will be here day after tomorrow, and Julia Nolan looks in on me daily. It would be wonderful to have you here, and I do miss you. But it's your call; only you know where you'll be needed most. If you can't come or even if you can't be here when the baby's born, I know it's because you're needed elsewhere, and I can deal with it. I do understand."

There was a pause before he replied, "God, I love you." Another pause. "If it's possible, I'll be there. I'll even let your mom boss me around and do what she tells me. If I can't be there, you'll know that I'm on a project and I can't leave—that it's not where I want to be; it's where I have to be."

"I know, Roark, and I know that what you decide will be the right thing for all of us." All of us, she mused—

her, the baby, and those SEALs who depended on him. "And I love you more than words can say."

They talked for another ten minutes and swapped platoon-family news, but what needed to be said had been said. And yet nothing had changed; it was as they both knew it would be, but that did not make it any easier or less painful. After Roark rang off, Jackie sat in their small Coronado living room, one hand on the cradled receiver and the other resting on her swollen belly. Tears found their way down her cheek, dripping off her chin and falling on the hand that caressed their child.

Roark Engel slipped the Iridium phone back into the cargo pocket of his trousers. He felt equal measures of relief and longing. She had made it clear that it was his call, and she supported whatever he would decide. Still, it was not an easy call. He wanted to be with her and to share in this miraculous journey they were on—this child, their first child. Yet he knew he could not leave unless this potential threat was somehow eliminated. Navy SEALs often find themselves hoping that conditions align themselves such that they are cleared for a mission. More often than not, conditions don't align and the mission is canceled. For the first time, Roark Engel found himself hoping that this one would get canceled or go down quickly, so he could somehow get home to his wife and unborn child.

He pushed himself to his feet and headed for the *Bonhomme Richard*'s communications center to see if there was any recent message traffic about Shabal and the threat. He moved with a clear head and a heavy heart. He was not the first Navy SEAL, nor the last, to find his calling in conflict with family responsibilities.

* * *

Another LHD was steaming south at best speed in the South China Sea. Senior Chief Otto Miller and his task unit commander, Todd Crandall, were again with the captain of the *Makin Island* and gathered over a chart of the coast of Malaysia.

"Sir, we are looking for a private yacht that we know from satellite imagery is somewhere off the coast of Sarawak. It was physically last seen in the Bay of Brunei, anchored several miles from the capital of Bandar. The British consulate there made some inquiries for us, but we really only know that she sailed in two nights ago, apparently coasting in Malay waters. The game here is to track her and, if possible, catch her in international waters and board her."

"What kind of a craft are we looking for?" Captain McMasters asked.

"A nice one," Miller replied. "She's a Westship Tri-Deck 149, with the ability to take a small helo aboard. Her name is the *Osrah*, which means 'family' in Arabic, and she was built in 2002 in Westport, Washington. The out-the-door price was just north of sixteen million. She has a range of twenty-five hundred nautical miles and a cruising speed of eighteen knots. Her top speed is twenty-two, which makes her about as fast as your ship . . . sir."

"And you think this Christo fellow is aboard."

"We believe so. Once we pin down her exact location and can get close enough to launch a drone, we think that we can confirm his presence by cell-phone activity. This guy has a lot of money and a lot of interests worldwide. When the owner is not aboard the luxury yacht, there's minimal cell traffic. When the owner and his party are aboard, that activity goes up dramatically. We don't necessarily need to decode his transmissions, which would be difficult, as we know he uses some very sophisticated encryption, but we can be pretty certain he's aboard by the volume of traffic."

"If this guy is just a Central American drug smuggler, tell me again why it's so important that we had to break off from our work in the Philippines and have my ship apprehend him at sea?"

Miller began in a soft, professorial tone. There's a compelling body of evidence that those linked with our friend Christo, aka Mikhail Troikawicz, are planning a 9/11–type event in our country. Christo is not a doer, but he's a supplier—an arranger, if you will. His main enterprise is the transshipment and smuggling of drugs. Yet his Chechen roots have on occasion led him to aiding and abetting terrorists. On those occasions when he has allowed his organization to support terrorism, it has been to help one Shabal Khanov Kasparian, or Moham-mad Abu Shabal, or just Shabal, as he is generally called. Christo is a capitalist—an evil, mercenary, and ruthless drug dealer, but still a capitalist. Shabal is another ani-mal. We don't know where he is, but there's every indica-tion that he's up to something big. Yet we do know where Christo is, or where we think he is. He may or may not know the whereabouts of Shabal or his plans, but it's our best lead. I, or rather we, very badly want to have a conversation with Shabal."

The *Makin Island*'s skipper digested this and slowly nodded his head. "So how do you want to play this?"

Miller looked to Lieutenant Commander Crandall,

who picked up the narrative. "Sir, once we have a good location of the *Osrah*, we shadow her at a safe distance while we observe her electronically. Given the priority of this operation, there's a Global Hawk standing by at Diego Garcia at our disposal. While the drone gets on station, we close in just out of visual and radar range, and get our Mk5 detachment and two of our RHIBs ready to launch from the well deck. If and when the Global Hawk sees a spike in cell-phone traffic, we take the yacht, and we take Christo."

"And what if the yacht is in Malaysian territorial waters?" Captain McMasters asked.

"If we have anything to say about it, we move on the *Osrah* whether it's in Malaysian or international waters, but that call will be made well above my pay grade."

"Mine, too," replied McMasters. "Okay, we make all preparations for an interdiction at sea. Let me know when there's a sighting of the yacht. That's a pretty big boat, and there are not a lot of islands off the Sarawak coast where it could hide. It shouldn't be too hard to find."

They had only their operational, desert cammies under their dry suits, but even though the water was in the low 80s, the two SEALs in the rear of the SDV were becoming chilled. Up front, the pilot and his navigator were toasty. This was their element, and they wore half-inch thermals under their dry suits. But for them, the mission would have them underwater for close to ten hours, and by that time, they also would be feeling the effects of the not-so-cold water. Suddenly the music, a superb rendition of Bach's Suite No. 2 in B Minor by the Münchener Bach-Orchester, stopped and was replaced by the burbly voice of the pilot.

"We are now approaching our destination and will soon be ascending up from our cruise depth. Please pass all drink containers and trash to the center aisle. All seats and tray tables should be in their fully upright and locked position. We ask that you check around your seats for all personal belongings, and remember, stowed baggage may have shifted in transit. We've enjoyed being of service. Next time your travel takes you to a foreign land to break things and kill people, we hope you will again book your trip with SDV Team One. Have a nice day."

Ray closed his book and pushed the remaining pages through the break in the canopy. He glanced at A.J. as he reached for the gear bag that he was sitting on and eased it forward to just under his feet. They felt the SDV begin to slow, then the canopy broke the surface, just enough for the circular GPS antenna to ride above the gentle swell.

"Very close but no cigar," came the navigator's voice. "We're about a hundred and twenty meters from the drop point. Give us another few minutes."

The SDV altered course to port and moved just below the surface at low speed. The pilot then shut down the electric motor, and the little submersible coasted slowly forward. After the continuous hum of the motor behind the music, it was now deathly quiet. It took a while for them to coast to a stop; a wet submersible full of water carries a lot of momentum. When they were dead in the water, they ballasted up to where the top ten inches of the canopy and fiberglass fairing cleared the water. Then two heads surfaced in the front compartment, followed by the two in back. The flat calm was disturbed only by a gentle, southerly swell. They were a mile off the beach, too far to hear any surf. They were also too far offshore to be heard, yet they spoke in whispers.

"We're within yards of the insertion coordinates," said the navigator. "Your point on the beach is one-eight-five magnetic."

"My watch says zero two fifty-five," offered the pilot. "We'll give you an hour to get ashore, then we'll surface and monitor your freq for five minutes every thirty minutes on the hour and the half hour. Our last check will be zero seven hundred, then we bingo for the *Michigan*."

"Thanks, guys," whispered A.J. "Safe trip home."

"Good luck to you. Kick some ass."

That was not their mission, but both Ray and A.J. understood. The two recon SEALs now had their gear bags out of the SDV with the flotation bladders inflated to where they were just positively buoyant. They would make their way ashore, towing their gear. They had not swum but a few strokes when, amid a quiet hiss of bubbles, the SDV slipped beneath the surface and drifted slowly to the sandy bottom in twenty feet of water.

"So what do you feel like?" asked the navigator.

"I dunno," replied the pilot. "I'm a little sleepy, so maybe something lively. Got any Chuck Berry?"

"Man, I got it all—even your grandfather's music." Soon they were both tapping a dry-suit boot to the strains of "Johnny Be Good."

It took the recon duo less than the hour to get to the water's edge. For five minutes they lay in a foot of water, with a gentle swell carrying them forward a few feet, then back. They listened, and Ray pulled a waterproof night-vision monocular from his kit and carefully swept the beach, the berm, and the backshore area. They heard and saw nothing. Then each eased his M4 from his rifle bag and chambered a round. There was a half moon that would not set for another two hours. It was not a time they would have chosen to cross this beach, but waiting was not an option.

"Ready?"

"Ready."

A.J. scurried across, his gear bag slung across his back and his weapon at the ready. He crossed the berm and found a stand of low beach scrub—not a particularly good place to hide, but it gave him no silhouette. Once Ray joined up, the two began to cut away their dry suits and ready their operational gear for travel. They were light on ammunition; heavy on radios, optics, and chow; and very heavy on water. They pushed through the backshore vegetation for several hundred meters; paused to bury their dry suits, swim masks, fins, and waterproof bags; and then kept going. Neither was comfortable with the footprints that followed them up from the beach, but there was little they could do about it. It was a smuggler's coast, and they'd simply have to trust that theirs was not the only clandestine beach crossing.

At 0700 they were some five miles inland. They had crossed the coast midway between Bosaso and the Horn and were making their way through a region known as the Guban, or scrub land. They contacted the SDV crew, thanked them again for their good work, and watched dawn steal across the barren wasteland that was northern Somalia. Then they turned 90 degrees from their southerly course; made another half-mile, carefully covering their tracks; and went to ground in a copse of scrub that afforded them some concealment and shade. They were carrying close to seventy pounds each, but that would get easier to manage as they depleted their water. It was a long day, and they slept most of it, but they knew the night ahead was going to be a long one.

It was their intention to be in a hide site of the mysterious landing coordinates before dawn of the following day. This was doable but not easy; it meant humping their load for close to eighteen miles. Neither had had any physical activity for close to two weeks, save the run for their lives in Costa Rica and a few days of shipboard physical training. And they had just hopscotched their way halfway around the world. It was not that they were out of shape, but they had not prepared for this trek—other than that they were Navy SEALs and when it was time to hump, they would simply just do it. At sundown they took a magnetic azimuth and set off at a steady pace. Periodically they paused for a drink, an energy bar, and a GPS fix. Otherwise, they kept moving. Neither felt the need to talk nor remind themselves of the SEAL motto, "The only easy day was yesterday." It was simply a matter of converting desert in front of them to desert behind them—no more and certainly no less.

They made it to the landing-site coordinates with thirty minutes to spare and quickly found what they were looking for—a good hide site. There was a shallow rise just north of what appeared to be a dirt road that ran straight through a dry valley wash below—almost due east and west. The ground looked as flat and smooth as the Bonneville Salt Flats. They found a crag just below a series of rock outcrops that allowed them to see out without being seen from below. And with the sun moving left to right of their position, there was little chance of a reflection from the lenses of their surveillance equipment. Once they had stowed their equipment well into the recess of the crag, and had a ghillie blanket set in place to break up any outline made by their person or gear, A.J. rigged their AN/PSC-5 satellite radio. With the PSC-5 in place, mated to the keyboard of a small Toughbook computer, they quickly established a secure, real-time voice link with the task unit embarked on the *Makin Island* and Roark Engel on the *Bonhomme Richard*. The latest generation of encrypted Iridium satellite phones had almost done away with the need for a man-pack portable satellite radio—almost. The Iridium could not handle imagery and data transmission. The PSC-5 was bulky but still needed.

Once finished with the housekeeping chores, Ray took the first watch while A.J. curled up on his poncho liner and was soon asleep. It was all done but the waiting; they were well hidden and no more than two hundred yards from the target GPS coordinates.

There was nothing the first day, or that night—not that they expected anything at night. The two recon SEALs fell into a routine of sleeping, eating, and communicating, even though there was nothing to report. That first afternoon, the temperature climbed to 105 degrees in their shady, rocky hideout, and they moved little in deference to the heat. They drank into their precious supply of water in proscribed amounts at prescribed intervals.

"Y'know, A.J.," Ray offered during a mid-afternoon watch change, "We've spent about a gazillion dollars on drones that can do what we're doing out here. Think about it. We could be in some air-conditioned space on some cushy Air Force base, sitting in a padded swivel, drinking an Arnold Palmer, and watching an LED screen. We could see everything we can see right now. And then when we're not on duty, we could be out on the golf course. Air Force bases are all about nice golf courses."

"You got a point," replied A.J. as he settled in behind a tripod-mounted pair of Zeiss 20x60 mm image-stabilized binoculars. He adjusted them to his eyes, but they would not be needed unless there was activity. "But there's no substitute for eyes on. And a drone can't see eye level like we can. By seeing it from here on the ground, we can determine intent and purpose by observing movement, procedures, interactions, and the handling of equipment. A drone can't do that stuff. And besides, there are Russian ships on piracy patrol in the Gulf of Aden. Their radars would pick up any drone activity."

"So then," Ray reasoned, "we ought to be paid a gazillion dollars for doing this, since the drones can't."

A.J. started to respond, thought better of it, and turned to survey the vacant sandlot below. "When did you last call in?"

"Fourteen hundred, right on schedule. No new word for us."

They maintained their vigil into the night, swapping the Zeiss binoculars for a set of Pulsar Edge GS2 2.7x50 night-vision binos with an IR capability. They were only just a little better than their helmet-mounted NODs, but with the advantage of convenience and magnification. Yet nothing moved that first day and night.

Dawn broke, and Ray and A.J. switched their night gear out for their day equipment and maintained their watch. But miles away, much was happening.

The two Russian pilots sat in the cockpit of their ancient Albatross aircraft, waiting.

It had been a long flight from the Ukraine, punctuated by multiple refueling stops. The relic they were flying had a cruising range of barely a thousand miles and had to stop at every godforsaken airfield in Turkey, Syria, Egypt, Sudan, Ethiopia, or wherever they happened to be. On this job, each time they stopped for fuel they had to check in with Shabal.

Now they sat on the tarmac of Yemen's Aden, International Airport, the searing heat draining what little energy they had left. There was no auxiliary power unit here to push in air-conditioning, nor was the old amphibian equipped for that anyway. They had spent the night there, and Shabal had ordered them to be in their aircraft first thing in the morning, ready to take off.

"Yes, yes, we have been told to just wait a few more minutes," the first pilot said into his satellite phone. "The vans with our passengers are coming from the port. And, yes, we will call when they are aboard, and we are on the final leg of our journey." After a further exchange, he ended the call.

"I'm glad you were talking to him," the second pilot said, scowling. "If you let me talk to him, I'd just tell him to leave us the hell alone and let us do our fucking jobs."

"That's exactly why I don't let you talk to him," replied Vitaly, the first Russian. Both of them had been mercenary pilots for years, and both had earned more money in their current job than they had ever earned flying bombers for the Soviet Union. Back then, they were young men flying new airplanes. Now they were older men flying museum pieces, but it paid well. Usually they were employed by the Russian mafia to smuggle all manner of contraband around Russia, the former Soviet Republics, and Central Asia. When Shabal approached them and offered them twice what the Russian mafia was paying, they had been more than willing. It had intrigued them that somehow this rough-looking Chechen knew exactly what they were earning from their former employers.

"Yeah, I know I'd probably piss the guy off, and sure, the money's good, but this guy scares me. I heard he's some kind of fanatical Muslim, and who knows who's on his tail. We don't want to get caught in the crossfire if he decides it's time for paradise or some other goddamned thing. I don't like it. I like the money, but I don't like him. I don't like any of them."

"You're right. These Chechens are all the same, whining about how we raped their country and all that bullshit. And when they get the chance to get it over on us, they take every advantage. But it's a payday and a good one."

The second pilot didn't reply, just shook his head. Even more than two decades after the dissolution of the Soviet Union, ethnic Russians still had a condescending attitude toward anyone from any of their former Republics.

They continued to sit and wait, mopping sweat from their brows and bodies with ragged towels, hoping their passengers arrived before the sat phone jangled again and Shabal continued to micro-manage them.

"Look, Vitaly, here come the two vans," said the second pilot. "Now maybe we can get going and get out of this fucking heat. I wonder how many of these guys we're going to have to haul."

"I dunno, Sergei. Shabal said it was high priority. Maybe three or four; maybe a half dozen." The Russians watched as the two vans drove right up to the Albatross. There was no airport or tarmac security, or if there was, it had been bought off. A tall, stocky Yemeni alighted from the first van.

"You stay here and get all our takeoff checks done, Sergei. I'll go meet them and get them aboard."

"Better you than me," Sergei replied, as he began to run his hands over the Grumman's switches, a well-rehearsed routine he'd done hundreds of times since they'd bought this Korean-War-vintage relic on the black market a decade ago.

Sergei allowed his hands to brush across the switches; he no longer needed to look at them. As he did so, he watched Vitaly and the Yemeni engage in an animated conversation. The conversation got more and more animated until he saw Vitaly throw up his hands in a gesture of resignation. What now?

He soon found out. The Yemini opened the cargo door of each van, and eight dark-skinned Asians alighted from each one. Half were women, and all of them carried something rolled up under their arm—nothing else. The Albatross barely had seats for half that many.

Vitaly and the Yemini quickly crowded them into the Albatross's cargo door. The Yemini got back into the first van, and as quickly as the vans had appeared, they headed back the way they had come.

Sergei twisted around and saw Vitaly getting the sixteen Asians situated in the back of the aircraft. Shabal! He knew damn well the Albatross usually carried a max of ten passengers in back. Now he was really taking advantage of them.

When Vitaly finally climbed back into his seat beside his copilot, Sergei exploded.

"Are you kidding me? Sixteen of these assholes? What the hell is Shabal thinking?"

"Yeah, but they're all skinny fuckers. We're still only slightly over our takeoff weight. We'll have no problem hauling them all to our final stop in Somalia."

"Still . . ." Sergei countered, but he didn't want to unload on his pilot. Yet he didn't like surprises, either.

"I know, I know," Vitaly replied. "It seems this Yemini guy works directly for Shabal, or that's what he said. He says this bunch started out in Indonesia and that he was contracted to bring them here. They're all Filipinos, and he says Shabal's been training them for almost a year."

"But how the hell did they get here?" Sergei interrupted.

"I was getting to that. He says they crossed the Indian Ocean on a tramp steamer, and they've been cooped up in that hulk for weeks. The steamer just docked in the port a few hours ago. Now they're ours or at least ours for a while."

"Yeah, but sixteen of them!"

"Be patient my friend. Shabal himself will be at our destination. We'll trade this lot for our usual load and be out of there before nightfall."

Sergei didn't respond but started flicking switches with a purpose. He then moved to the engine levers, then more switches. Within seconds the first of the two Wright R-1820-76 Cyclone nine-cylinder, air-cooled radial engines coughed to life, spewing white smoke as it did. Then the second Wright coughed to life in a similar fashion. While Sergei monitored the cockpit gauges, Vitaly keyed the radio.

"Aden tower, this is Albatross Two Seven ready to taxi for takeoff."

"Roger, Two Seven. You're cleared to taxi and take-off. Stay with me on this frequency until five miles clear."

"Roger, Aden. Thank you and good day."

"I cannot wait to unload these cattle," his copilot groused.

"Remember, Sergei, patience. Patience and a payday," the other Russian replied as the Albatross lumbered down the active runway, climbed into the morning sky, and turned south.

Eight hundred miles away, as he sat in the back of the Tupolev Tu-134 parked at Nairobi's International Airport in south-central Kenya, Shabal was anything *but* patient.

"So you've finally taken off with my cargo. Good. Are you sure you know the exact coordinates of where we will meet in the desert?" Shabal all but shouted into his satellite phone.

"Yes," he continued, after hearing Vitaly's reply. "But this is too important to leave anything to chance. Read the coordinates back to me."

Shabal nodded as he absorbed the Russian's transmission.

"Good. Be sure you are on the ground as planned. I want you there before I arrive. We'll make the transfer then."

With that, Shabal ended the call, and walked up the aisle and into the cockpit of the Tupolev—the Russian version of the venerable DC-9—and barked his orders to yet another two Russian pilots.

"Call for takeoff. We begin the final leg of this part of our journey now."

The Tupolev pilot glanced at his copilot, trying to mask his annoyance, and began his pre-engine-start checklist.

A.J. and Ray had watched the sun continue to rise in the desert sky, boredom setting in. That all changed at about 1000. A.J. had the 0800–1200 shift and picked up a faint rooster-tail of dust in the distance. He watched it for close to fifteen minutes before rousing Ray.

"Yo, sleeping beauty, wake up. Looks like we might have some company."

Ray was soon by his side with a small pair of Leica Silverline 10x42s and began to track the running line of dust. Soon they were able to discern a file of four vehicles. The two in the front were pickup trucks, followed by a panel truck and a tank truck. As they got closer, the pickups became Toyotas with mounted automatic weapons in their beds and each with a half dozen armed men. They were technicals and the face of insurgent Africa— teens with headbands, designer sunglasses, blue jeans, and AK-47s in armed Toyotas. Young black men with no prospects and nothing to lose. The panel truck seemed to be in better shape than the battered Toyotas and the tank truck and, by African standards, quite modern. It had just been stolen from the airstrip at Botiala. The four vehicles came to a stop just below and to the southeast of their position. It seemed that they, too, had GPS receivers. After a few moments, the armed men in the back of the pickups dismounted. Some looked to seek the limited shade afforded by the vehicles. A few of them crawled under the tank truck. The others stood about talking, posturing, and smoking cigarettes. These were wild young men, equally immune to the sun and to matters of conscience. They, too, were waiting.

Up in the rocks, the two SEALs moved without speaking. Ray came up on the PSC-5 to report the activity while A.J. began to assemble the camera—a Nikon D3X SLR body mated with a custom lens that amounted to a variable-power spotting scope. While Ray was the IT SEAL and a genius with radios and comm gear, A.J. was the team cameraman, and he knew his cameras. When he had assembled his gear, he began to photograph each of the new arrivals on the desert floor. It took a while, but soon each was recorded with a high-resolution, full-on head shot, one perfectly compatible with face-recognition software—something else no drone could do. Ray quickly took the digital images and sent them over the PSC-5 data link to the task unit and the SEALs on the *Bonnie Dick*. If any of these guys were on someone's terrorist watch list, they would soon know it. As they watched the small assembly of vehicles on the desert floor below them, they heard the faint drone of an aircraft engine, a sound that momentarily puzzled them both. It was the sound of radial piston engines, gasoline powered, and it was growing louder.

"Over there," said A.J. as they scanned the horizon, "coming from the east."

"Got him," Ray replied as he caged the aircraft with his binoculars.

They both watched as the dot sprouted a high wing, engine nacelles, and finally a tail section. The aircraft lowered its landing gear and made a straight-in approach, raising its own rooster tail of dust as it touched down. It was an old Albatross. Neither of the SEALs had seen one before, except possibly in an old movie, nor was there any reason they should have. It was made in the USA but had left active Navy and Coast Guard service before either of the SEALs was born. And yet here it was in a remote piece of desert in Somalia. Both knew it was an old amphibian, but that was all.

Once on the ground, the Albatross taxied to a stop and shut down. One of the pickup trucks drove over to the aircraft, close but not too close. After several moments, the rear door opened, and a white man in shorts and a dirty, open-collar short-sleeved shirt stepped out. He had dark hair and several days' growth of facial hair. He ignored the technicals in the pickup and went about placing a small metal step under the door of the aircraft. He then helped a woman in peasant's clothes to deplane from the flying boat. Then another, and another. The two SEALS watched in silence as a total of sixteen passengers disembarked—eight women and eight men. They were not large people, nor were they imposing like the Somalis who looked on. They carried no baggage, save for a roll of cloth each carried under one arm. Once clear of the aircraft, they began to unroll their cloths, kneel on them, and lower their foreheads to the desert floor. The cloths were prayer rugs. Within minutes, the amphibian's passengers were lined up in neat rows, facing east, and chanting prayers. All the while, Ray scanned the new arrivals with his binoculars while A.J. captured high-resolution images. It was hard to catalog their faces, as they prayed to the east and the two recon SEALs were north of them.

"Whadda you make of all that?" Ray finally asked.

A.J. did not immediately respond. Finally he took his eye away from his camera. "I haven't a clue, but they're not Skinnies."

"Not Somalis—you're kidding me."

"Nope. I think they're Filipino. Maybe Indonesian, but probably Filipino."

Ray did not question him. A.J.'s background in Thai boxing made him something of an expert on subtle Asian differences—variations that would escape most Western eyes. And though he himself could not put his finger on it, they *seemed* to move and act like those he had known from the Philippines. And that was how they would report it; they appeared to be Filipinos—Filipino Muslims praying in the desert in Somalia not far from the Horn of Africa.

"Y'know, A.J., this whole business is starting to get weird."

"Weird is the new normal," A.J. replied. "We just

need to separate the weirdness from the violence if we can. Or the boss and the chief need to."

The scene before them was about to become strange as well as weird. While the contingent on the prayer rugs continued their devotions, the two SEALs heard the sound of another aircraft approaching. They heard it, but they could not yet see it; it was coming from the north, behind them. The whine of the jet engines was nearly overpowering when it flashed overhead about four hundred feet. It was a twin-engine, commercial-looking passenger jet, with two tail-mounted rear engines. This one looked familiar. The aircraft banked to the east, executed a 270-degree turn, and lined up for an east-to-west approach. Only after it had neatly set down and taxied up close to the Albatross was A.J. able to confirm what he suspected when the aircraft had turned on final. It was a Soviet-era Tupolev Tu-134—almost like a McDonnell Douglas DC-9, but not quite. This pilot did not shut down nor did he leave the aircraft. The Tupolev sat parked on the desert floor, engines at idle. When the rear door opened and an internal ladder dropped into place, a single individual stepped to the door and gazed out. He had an automatic pistol in his hand and a hard look on his face. The recon SEALs were in luck in that the Tupolev presented its starboard side with a clear view of the passenger door. A.J. was able to get a high-res close-up of the man. Seemingly satisfied with what he saw, the man cached the pistol in the waistband at the small of his back and climbed down the ladder. The man was tall with a rakish look and a scar down the side of his face. He was clearly a figure of authority and clearly the man in charge. He was Shabal.

A particularly large, brutish-looking Somali approached Shabal, and they spoke quietly for a few moments. Then under the big man's direction, the Somalis formed a human chain and began to move bags of cargo from the Tupolev to the Albatross. After a dozen or more bags were put aboard the aircraft, the men shifted to the panel truck and loaded the remaining bags into the back—close to two dozen of them. The bags seemed to weigh on the order of fifty pounds each, and the young men had no difficulty with them, laughing as they tossed them from one man to the next. The big man admonished them and they began to handle the bags with more care. While the cargo was being shifted, the tank truck backed up to the jet, and fuel hoses were passed up to the pilot, who now stood atop the wing to supervise the refueling. Those on the prayer rugs continued to pray, as if the activity taking place around them was none of their concern. When the handling of cargo was complete, a man stepped tentatively from the cab of the panel truck. He wore a broad-brimmed sun hat and dark sunglasses. When he removed his hat and glasses to mop his brow, A.J. quickly captured his image with his Nikon and entered him into the system. He was definitely Slavic, and a big man with coarse, rough features, but one who moved with a bit of grace.

From his dress and mannerisms he appeared to be Western, or at least eastern European, and he and Shabal immediately fell into conversation. Shabal remained stoic, but the other man began to grow animated. He seemed to be shouting as he spoke with his hands. Even at this distance, and not being able to hear a word of the conversation, A.J. and Ray could tell who the alpha dog was—it was the man who had arrived in the Tupolev. The other man seemed to be bargaining or pleading. He was clearly unhappy with what was taking place.

Only when Shabal pulled the automatic from his waistband did the other man settle down. He never threatened him with the pistol, but their conversation seemed to become less spirited while Shabal held the weapon at his side. Finally, the man shrugged and turned to the large Somali now standing off to one side. The big man then turned to give a few short commands, and the Skinnies took what appeared to be two large steamer trunks from the panel truck and passed them up and through the door of the Tupolev. Shabal, the man from the panel truck, and the big Somali huddled for a short while, and then broke away. Shabal and the sixteen Filipinos boarded the Tupolev. The big Somali returned to the cab of one of his pickups and the little European climbed into the Albatross.

It was the flying boat that was the first to leave. The pilot cranked one of the old radials for what seemed to be a long while before it exploded with a burst of smoke and noise, followed by the second. The little amphibian then pirouetted to an easterly heading and began to crawl across the desert. It slowly gathered speed and finally clawed its way into the air, turning north for the Gulf of Aden. The Tupolev was next. This pilot brought the jet engines up to takeoff power and then released the brakes. The long fuselage darted across the desert floor and pulled up steeply, then quickly leveled off. The SEALs watched as it banked to the south and banked again to a westerly heading.

The driver of the tank truck jumped onto one of the

pickup trucks, and with the other pickup and the panel truck, they headed back the way they had come. The two SEALs watched them go, noting that there was a carefully hidden bag of product in the back of each truck. The Skinnies were all smiles as they each in turn took a peak at their generous payment for service.

"What the hell just happened?" A.J. said to Ray as he clicked off one last frame of the retreating convoy.

"Ours is not to reason why; ours is but to catalog what we see and call it in." Ray then took up the handset of the PSC-5. "Bulldog, Bulldog, this is Redrum, how copy, over?"

"This is Bulldog, hear you, lima charlie. Do you have traffic for us?" The speaker was an Air Force controller at the console of an E-3C Sentry Airborne Warning and Control System, or AWACS, aircraft. The Sentry's Boeing 707 airframe had entered into service in 1977, making it older than most of the eighteen-person crew who were flying this mission. They had been on runway standby at Al Ta'if Air Force Base, a hundred miles west of Jiddah and the Red Sea in Saudi Arabia. The Sentry had been launched immediately after the recon SEALs had spotted the inbound Somali convoy and was now orbiting over the Gulf of Aden.

"Roger that, Bulldog, and good to have you with us. We have two aircraft outbound from location Ten Hopper Lima Sierra 53260089. One is a slow mover headed northbound, the other is a commercial fast mover headed west, over."

"Thank you, Redrum. We have them, and we are tracking them both. Did you have eyes on those aircraft, over?"

"Affirmative. One was an old, two-engine amphibian flying boat. The other was a Russian Tango Uniform One-Three-Four. Neither had tail numbers nor any other identifying markings, over."

"Understand an old amphibian and a Tupolev 134 with no markings, over."

"You got it, Bulldog, over."

"Roger, Redrum. We'll take it from here. Bulldog, out."

While Ray made a final radio contact and data download to Lieutenant Engel on the *Bonhomme Richard* and to Senior Chief Miller and their task unit on the *Makin Island*, A.J. began to pack up their gear. Their orders were to leave the hide site and make their way north to the coast for a dawn pickup by helo. It would not be as stealthy as their arrival in Somalia, but then it didn't need to be. The job was done. They would be traveling lighter than when they made their way inland two nights ago, but they would have to cover close to twenty-three miles to get to the coast before dawn. They knew they could do it, but they also knew they'd have to bust their balls to get there before sunup.

"Well," A.J. said stoically, "I guess we better get some rest while we can. That's one helluva hump we have to make."

"I got a better idea," Ray said, taking his binoculars from his eyes and handing them to A.J. "See what it says on the door of that tanker?"

"Uh, Botiala Municipal Airport," A.J. replied, adjusting the focus. English was the language of aviation worldwide, and that convenience extended to aviation service providers.

"And Botiala," Ray said, moving his Toughbook

computer screen so that A.J. could see it, "is only about seven miles up the coast from our pickup coordinates— practically on the way."

"You're not suggesting that we take the truck . . ."

"And only drive it part of the way," Ray cut in. "We can drop off the truck on a side road and hoof it back along the coast to our pickup point. Besides, the cover is better just inland from the coastline, and it's a lot easier than busting our ass for twenty-some miles over land. And it'd be a nice gesture to return the truck or at least leave it closer to the airport."

"I don't know about this, Ray. I'm not so sure."

A half hour after sundown, they were in the tanker and traveling on secondary roads, with an enhanced version of Google Maps as their guide. A.J. drove and Ray navigated. They drove at twenty miles per hour, both SEALs continually scanned the barren terrain with their night-vision devices. Both had their M4s at the ready. The truck ran out of gasoline six miles from the location for their pickup. As Ray had predicted, it was an easy six miles with good cover. They arrived at the coastal rendezvous site just after 0100 in the morning. At 0530, a pair of Navy H-60s came in low over the water, homing in on the SEALs' IR beacon. Moments later, they were aboard and over the Gulf of Aden, headed outbound from the Horn for the USS *Bataan*.

NINE

Thirty-six hours later, they were on the flight deck of the *Bonhomme Richard*—Chief Nolan, A.J., and Ray. The ship was steaming at a leisurely six knots some seventy miles off the coast of Baja California. The three had been in deep conversation for some time; now they were silent. After a long pause, it was Nolan who finally broke the silence.

"I still don't get it. What the hell were you thinking when you stole a Somali tank truck?" His voice was low and controlled, but he was seething. "What if you'd been stopped by the local *gendarmes*? What were you going to do, shoot it out with them?"

Ray shrugged his shoulders sheepishly and gave the standard SEAL-called-on-the-carpet reply: "Well, y'see, Chief, it seemed like a good idea at the time."

"And you," Nolan said sharply, turning to A.J., "I could expect this from Ray, but not you. Part of your job was to keep an eye on him. That was a dumb stunt—really dumb. It could have jeopardized the entire mission."

"Sorry, Chief." A.J. was contrite, but not as overtly submissive as Ray. "I guess we did it because we could. We're SEALs, and SEALs are opportunists. I could have said no, and I probably should have, but I didn't. Chief, I'm sorry I let you down."

"It's not about me or you; it's about the mission and the Team. And to save yourself a long walk, you put yourselves first and the mission and your teammates second." Nolan paused, looking from one to the other, letting his words sink in. "Okay," he continued, "it's done and over with. Let's move on. For now, this will stay between the three of us, okay?" Both nodded. "Now get below and see to your gear."

Nolan then made his way inside the ship's superstructure and down one deck, heading for the *Bonnie Dick*'s combat information center, or CIC. He was still not sure whether or not he wanted to tell his officer about the caper with the tanker truck. They were a leadership team, and keeping information from each other was not how the two of them worked. It was an issue of trust. Nothing could be done about it now, he reasoned, and it was just one more thing for Roark Engel to worry about. God knew he had enough on his plate. Nolan was still turning the matter over in his mind when he arrived at the CIC. One corner of the center had been sectioned off and converted to a small tactical operations center for the SEALs and those read into the operation. A marine sentry stood guard at the partitioned entrance. The guard knew Nolan by sight but still asked to see his ID. The marine matched the face on the ID with Nolan's and let him pass, logging in his arrival. When Nolan saw Engel, he immediately knew something was up. That knowledge seemed to be confirmed as he felt the *Bonnie Dick* heel into a port turn and shudder imperceptibly as she gathered speed.

"Hey, Chief. I was just about to have you paged. You know that Russian passenger jet Ray and A.J. tracked in and out of the Somali desert rendezvous?"

"Yes, sir."

"Well, the guys at NRO and NSA managed to follow its movements. It flew into Lagos, refueled, made the jump across the Atlantic, and landed at Rio. There it took on more fuel, flew to a remote airfield in Colombia, probably a strip controlled by the cartel, and then made the jump up to guess where?"

"Uh, lemme guess: Cedros Island," Nolan deadpanned.

"Give the man a cigar—Cedros Island. It landed at night, so we don't know who got on or off, but it would seem likely that at least some of the sixteen Filipino pilgrims put down there."

"Where's the plane now?"

Engel grimaced. "That's a problem. It immediately returned to the airstrip in Colombia and is still there. If it leaves and returns to Rio or some other commercial destination, then there's a chance we can detain the aircraft and maybe even interrogate the flight crew. But there's not much we can do as long as it's sitting on that strip in Colombia."

Nolan considered this. "This operation has top priority. Couldn't we whistle up a Ranger battalion and have them take that airfield down?"

"That's been considered, Chief, believe me it has. But the Colombians probably wouldn't sit still for it, and it probably couldn't be kept quiet. And it would also tip our hand that we're on to them."

"So what?" Nolan offered. "Wouldn't that be better than letting whatever they're planning go forward?"

Engel considered this. "Maybe, maybe not. But that's not our call. For now we're headed for Cedros Island to stand by for an over-the-beach operation. I don't think much else will happen until we get more intelligence."

"Any chance of that?"

"Good chance. Senior Chief Miller and the task unit are tracking a yacht in the South China Sea that may have Christo aboard. If they can verify he's on the yacht, they'll board it and have a chat with Mr. Christo."

With that, Dave Nolan smiled. "If the senior chief can go eyeball-to-eyeball with that bastard, then maybe we can get to the bottom of this."

"Just maybe. Meanwhile, get the guys ready to go ashore tonight. It might be by CRRC, or it might be by helo. We'll just have to wait and see."

"On it, Boss, and whatever happened to those drugs that were flown into the desert, the ones loaded into that panel truck and put aboard that old flying boat?"

"I wondered about that myself," Engel replied. "I thought it might lead to a big drug bust, as that seemed to be a large shipment of cocaine. From reading the traffic, the powers that be let the shipment go through. The priority is finding out what Shabal is up to and stopping him. So the druggies get a pass on this one."

Nolan just shook his head. "I'll go check on the guys. We'll be ready, if and when."

* * *

In the South China Sea, it was half past midnight, and the *Makin Island* was just over the radar horizon from the *Osrah* and matching her course and speed. Senior Chief Otto Miller was pacing *his* task unit's small TOC in *that* ship's combat information center. They were waiting for the Global Hawk from Diego Garcia to arrive on station. Meanwhile, the rest of the task unit was busy getting their boats ready. The SWCCs and SEALs assigned to the two Mark V patrol craft crawled over them, checking and rechecking everything—engines, fuel cells, radios, weapons stations, and ammunition. The same thing was happening with the SWCC crews on the two 11-meter rigid-hull inflatable boats, or RHIBs. Up on the flight deck, two MH-60S Navy Knighthawk helos were being readied and armed. The Knighthawks would carry a pair of Hellfire missiles each, but their real cargo would be SEALs—eight SEALs from the *other* Bandito squad, four in one helo and four in the other. Additionally, there would be a task unit sniper in each bird. While the *Osrah* was ostensibly a pleasure yacht, it could prove to be a wolf in sheep's clothing. Quite often, world-class cruising yachts were armed against pirates, and sometimes that armament included heavy-caliber weapons. And given the background of the yacht's owner, they were taking no chances.

The Mark V Special Operations Craft was an eighty-two-foot patrol craft that could carry up to a platoon of SEALs, and like its freshwater little brother, the SOC-R, it was armed with mini-guns and .50-caliber machine guns. And it was scalded-dog fast. The twin 2285-horsepower turbo-blown MTU diesels could push the Mark V over a flat sea at close to seventy miles an hour. The 11-meter Special Warfare RHIBs were both smaller and more lightly armed. Their main gun was a center-mounted .50-caliber supported by a 7.62 machine gun and a Mk19 grenade launcher. Its dual 6-cylinder Cat turbo-diesels gave it a top speed of 50 mph. The value of the Special Warfare RHIBs, especially when working with the Mark Vs, was that they were agile crafts, and because of their soft-sided tubes, they could hold themselves against the side of a larger craft, like the *Osrah*, and quickly put SEALS aboard. The boats themselves were carried in the well deck of the *Makin Island*. This well deck occupied the stern one-third of the ship's 850-foot length and could be flooded so that small craft could become waterborne while in the well-deck bay and leave the ship by way of the stern gate that opened to the sea. The *Makin Island* could carry a mix of watercraft, but the two Mark Vs and the two RHIBs assigned to the embarked SEAL task unit left only a little space for the single Marine RHIB detachment. But the ship's current mission was all about SEAL support.

Up in the TOC, a shipboard controller had just taken command of the Global Hawk and brought it down from its cruise altitude of fifty-five thousand feet to a lazy orbit over the *Osrah* at a comfortable twenty-five thousand feet. It could neither be seen nor heard, and the big yacht hadn't the radar to find it. There it orbited and listened while Senior Chief Otto Miller hovered over the controller, making him more than a little anxious.

"You got anything yet?"

"Relax, Senior. We're still running a bandwidth search to see if there's any traffic. They have to be using satellite phones out here, as there's no cell coverage. It'll take a minute to see if they are, in fact, transmitting and then to see if there's any volume. If they're talking, I'll know about it."

Miller prowled the small space, periodically pausing to look over the controller's shoulder, then continuing his pacing of the TOC.

"Hello there," the controller said, barely audible, but Miller was instantly at his elbow. "Here they are at 1620 megahertz."

"What?" Miller asked.

The controller turned with a grin. "Coded chatter—and a lot of it. We have incoming calls and outgoing calls. Have no idea what's in the transmissions, but it's active. We're recording them, though. If you can get aboard and get their phones, maybe the guys at NSA can go back and unscramble the text. But for now, it's my guess that there's more going on than some crewman calling his girlfriend in the next port."

"Good work," Miller said, clapping the controller on the shoulder. "Let me know if anything changes."

Moments later the little TOC became more populated as both the task unit commander and the captain of the *Makin Island* crowded in. Miller quickly briefed them on the cell-phone activity; everything was pointing to the presence of Christo aboard the yacht. Captain McMasters stepped away and made his way to one of the CIC's radar repeaters. It was a sophisticated display that featured data from the *Makin Island*'s powerful surface-search radar and imagery from both the Global Hawk and any passing naval ocean surveillance satellite that might be prowling the skies in low-earth orbit.

"Where is she now?" he asked the technician at the scope.

"Right here, sir—designated skunk Bravo Delta. She crossed into international water about twenty minutes ago. I hold her about fifty-five miles from us on a bearing of two six five. She's on a course of three one seven and making about twenty-two knots. We're closing on her, but it's a stern chase, and it'll take a while."

"Good job, Sullivan. Stay on it." McMasters returned to the TOC, where Miller and Lieutenant Commander Crandall were huddled with two other SEALs. One was the Bandito Platoon AOIC, or assistant officer in charge—a junior grade lieutenant and Roark Engel's number two in the platoon. The other was a first-class petty officer and the Bandito Platoon leading petty officer. Since it had been the detached Bandito squad that had begun all this, it had been Crandall's decision to read the other Bandito squad into this portion of the operation and assign them to take down the yacht. SEALs from the other task unit platoon would be on the Mark Vs and RHIBs in a support role. They would do as ordered, but they were disappointed not to have been assigned a more active participation. The Bandito SEALs were in black one-piece coveralls, with assault vests over body armor. The platoon officer's helmet and weapon were already aboard one of the helos, the leading petty officer's on the other. The task unit commander was in like coveralls but no kit.

"How soon can you go?" McMasters asked.

"Sir, we can have boats away within the hour depending on the well-deck flooding. The helos are standing by.

I'll be on one of the Mark Vs as the surface-force commander."

Captain McMasters paused a moment in contemplation. "Okay, gentlemen, get to your stations and stand by. Commander, a word."

Everyone left but McMasters and Todd Crandall. "I've been authorized to proceed at my discretion when this yacht leaves Malay territorial waters," McMasters told his embarked SEAL commander. "That's already happened. You are clear to launch as soon as you're ready. I'll alert those up the chain of the pending action. Go do what has to be done. I'll not tell you how to do your job, but those are my aircrews that will be supporting you. They are your SEALs, but since it's my ship, you are also my SEALs. I take this personally. Get this job done—swiftly, professionally, safely, and, if you can, bloodlessly. If not, kick some ass. In any event, good luck." He held out his hand and Crandall took it.

"Roger that, sir," Crandall replied. "And thanks—for everything. For us it's always personal." With that he took his leave and made his way down to the well deck, where his Mark V waited in its cradles on the bottom.

In the task unit spaces belowdecks and on the well deck, the SEALs were making their final preparations, which amounted to a rechecking of everything, from their weapons loading to their tactical radios. Then they made their way up to the flight deck to the helos or down to the well deck to the boats. One of those who was making ready did so a little differently from the others. Senior Chief Otto Miller looked as if he were going nightclubbing rather than embarking on a special operation. His hair and beard were freshly barbered and combed into place. He was dressed in a cream-colored linen suit, a blue oxford-cloth shirt, and a tasteful, paisley ascot. Tasseled loafers and Norte wire-rimmed aviator sunglasses completed the look. His only concession to anything military was a Glock 9mm he kept well concealed in a shoulder holster and an MBITR tactical radio and headset that he would hand-carry.

"Well, how do I look?" he asked one of his intelligence specialists.

"To be honest, Senior, like you're trolling for boy toys in Venice."

This brought a frown, immediately followed by a chuckle. "Then I guess I'm good to go," he said, and he made his way up to the flight deck.

Jackie Engel was in the middle of organized chaos, surrounded by boxes, wrapping paper, and "neutral" baby things—toddler toys and support items that were non-gender-specific. She was sitting in the recliner of her small living room, and the space was crowded with close to a dozen other women. Her mother had arrived the day before, and she and Julia Nolan had organized a surprise, impromptu shower. There were several other SEAL wives, two of her friends from work, and three neighbors. All was gaiety and laughter. When the phone rang, her mother rose quickly with an, "I'll get it, dear," and stepped down the hall to take the call on a wireless handset.

"Hello."

After a short pause, "Hello, Mom, is that you?"

"Roark?"

"It's me, Mom. Sounds like you're having a party there. I hope I'm not interrupting anything."

"Roark, how nice to hear your voice. No, no—we're just having a little shower for Jackie. Where *are* you?" She was the mother of a Navy wife; she could ask those questions.

"I'm on deployment," he replied, allowing just a trace of humor in his voice, "over there or over here, depending on your prospective. Hey, I'm really glad you're there with Jackie. I know it means a lot to her, and it sure means a lot to me. Thanks for making the trip out."

"Roark, I'm only too happy to be here, and Coronado is such a delightful place. And there's snow on the ground in Indianapolis. This is much nicer. Now, I know you didn't call to talk to me. Let me get herself. Take care of yourself, Roark. Jackie misses you—we all miss you."

"Thanks, Mom, thanks for everything."

Moments later, "Roark?"

"Hi, hon. Just calling to check in, and I hear you are having a party."

"Oh, Mom, Julia, and some of the girls sprang a surprise shower on me. We're having fun, and we got some great things for the kid."

"Catcher's mitts and hockey skates, right?"

"Maybe. They work for girls, too, you know."

"I know, I know. Listen, all the guys here are doing just fine. Update me on the families, will you?"

"Oh, yes," Jackie replied, organizing her thoughts. "Everybody here is A-okay . . . We all get together fairly frequently, and you'd be proud how the wives and girl-friends are all supporting one another . . ."

"So . . . no problems?" Roark probed.

"Nothing we can't handle. Tell Diego that Anna's mom is finally having that hip replacement that she's been putting off for so long. Anna's taking their son and flying to Jacksonville for two weeks to see her through the surgery and the beginning of her recovery. Oh, and Sonny's older daughter, Becky, took a nasty spill playing soccer. Carla took her to the Balboa ER, but the docs cleared her. She has a shiner, and she's bragging about how the other girl looks worse. She's one tough kid, just like her dad."

"I hear that," Roark replied.

There was a moment of silence as Roark thought about how to phrase what he was about to say. "Hey, hon, I just wanted to check on the families and to hear the sound of your voice, but I also needed to let you know that this project I'm working on seems to be a little bigger than I'd first thought. It looks like I'll have to stay with it. I'd rather be shot at than to tell you this, but it doesn't look good for me being back there anytime soon. I wish it were otherwise, but that's as it stands right now."

"Oh, Roark, I am disappointed, yet . . . yet I do understand, believe me, I do."

"But, hey, the good news is that once we finish up with this, there's a good chance I can get back for a few days."

"That would be great. But," she replied, trying for some levity, "are you sure you're not just trying to duck my mom? She's very sensitive about those things, you know."

That got a chuckle. "I'd brave your mother and any

other mortal danger to be with you right now. And you tell her for me that I am really glad that she can be there with you. Tell me, how are you and the little one doing? Are you feeling well?"

"We are both doing just fine. We just want you to take good care of yourself."

"No sweat, hon," he assured her. "But listen, I have to run for now. So I'll let you get back to the ladies and the Chippendales and whatever else you may have going on there."

"Listen to you! You are my one and only Chippendale. Never forget that."

They traded I-love-you's and shared another laugh, then she returned to the girls.

"That was Roark," she announced, feeling the need to comment, "checking up on me. He says hello to all of you and to thank you for the wonderful gifts. He and I both appreciate this so very much. Now, who needs another cup of tea?"

She continued to be the picture of graciousness and good humor to most in the room, but her happy facade did not get past Julia Nolan or her mother.

It was shortly after dawn when the *Makin Island* slowed to a barely discernable three knots and began to ballast down. The process of venting some fifteen thousand tons of seawater into the well deck of the ship took close to an hour. The RHIBs motored out ready to run. Once clear of the mother ship's stern gate, the Mark Vs took another ten minutes to hinge into place and secure their radar and communications masts. During this time, the

Osrah was able to gain another thirty miles on them, but that was about to change. There was a light chop on the surface with a wind out of the south, so the four-boat flotilla was able to make best speed across the water. With a twenty-five-knot speed advantage, they could overtake the yacht in just under four hours. The *Makin Island*, after dewatering her well deck, took up the pursuit at her best speed of twenty-two knots. Three hours after the two Mark Vs and the two RHIBs had sortied, the two MH-60Ss lifted off and followed their waterborne brothers.

Lieutenant Commander Crandall stood alongside the SWCC officer in charge. As task unit commander, he was in charge of the overall operation, but the swick officer, also a SEAL, would coordinate the approach. It would be impossible to achieve total surprise, but they would do what they could to delay the detection of their approach. Both the Mark Vs and the RHIBs carried good radars, but they were turned off. There was the very real possibility that the *Osrah* had the ability to detect surface-search radars in the area. Some of the larger yachts were so equipped as an antipiracy measure. The boats relied on a data link from the Global Hawk for a bearing and distance to their target. When they were ten miles from the *Osrah*, just below the visual horizon, the swick OIC signaled his coxswains to fall in astern of him, so the four boats continued at high speed in a file. Cruising yachts, and indeed many warships, had their radars mounted on masts forward of their exhaust stacks. This gave them an unobstructed radar picture in their direction of travel but sometimes left them a blind spot directly astern, or, in Navy speak, in their baffles. And since there were no other craft in the area and it was a clear day, the helmsman on the yacht, or bridge crew if there were two of them, might not be paying close attention to the radar. At eight miles out, the SWCC boats were joined by the Knighthawks, flying in a loose combat spread at six thousand feet and slowing to match the speed of the flotilla.

On the *Osrah*, Christo was enjoying a light breakfast of fruit and yogurt, fresh-squeezed pomegranate juice, and black coffee. He was at his desk in the yacht's spacious solarium, dressed comfortably in white cotton slacks, a turquoise long-sleeve pullover, and sandals. His long hair was pulled into a ponytail out of his way. He wore no jewelry but for a gold Rolex President and a gold baht chain. His role in arranging for the shipment of cocaine and assisting the little Russian bomb-vest maker with his wares was over. Now that what was about to happen was soon approaching, he wanted to be as far away from America—North, Central, or South—as possible. His wife and daughter, along with his mother-in-law and a small contingent of extended family, were in Rome. They were being guarded by a handpicked security detachment. There would be far-reaching repercussions for what Shabal had planned, and should any blowback reach him, he wanted his family somewhere safe and well away from him. He did not expect to be linked to Shabal's plans, but regarding issues of family, one could not be too careful. Plus, he had work to do, and the yacht was one of his better offices.

While Shabal planned his attack, Christo had been planning how to capitalize on it. He had mobilized as much cash as he dared, something on the order of

$300 million. He had carefully analyzed what would take place if Shabal succeeded—the companies that would plummet in value and those that would rise in value. Using intermediaries and discreet brokerage firms around the globe, he had bet on chaos in the U.S. and European economies. As a result, he found himself shorting airline and entertainment stocks and going long on energy and U.S. defense stocks. Of all his holdings, he thought grimly, the U.S. defense stocks would fare the best.

His desk was a spartan place of work, with several multiline telephones and a neat but well-ordered stack of file folders. The only thing seemingly out of place was a Newton's Cradle. This suspended rack of steel balls was normally viewed as a senior executive's play toy. It had come with the boat and was normally a device that would be ill-served on a pleasure craft. But this version of the Westship 149 had a sophisticated, gyro-stabilization system that took nearly all the roll and most of the pitch out of the motion of the yacht. It was an extremely stable craft. Several feet below the waterline on the *Osrah*, gimbaled fins extended from the hull, which sensed certain hull movements and gave immediate correction. That the Newton's Cradle could smoothly transmit action and reaction in almost any weather was a tribute to the *Osrah*'s stabilizers.

This morning, as the sun climbed into the sky, Christo was at his desk and his ten-person crew was about their duties. His captain was on the bridge with his helmsman. The yacht was on autopilot, and the two were performing routine maintenance checks, most of them with the help of the engineer, who was presently at his station in the engine room. There were two women on board whose duties involved cooking and cleaning. They both had supermodel good looks and, when necessary, could dress in skimpy bikinis and drape themselves conspicuously on the bow or the afterdeck when entering or leaving port, thus portraying the *Osrah* as the vessel of a rich playboy. But they were only for show; Christo was a family man, monogamous, and he insisted on the same from those who worked around him. Many men of wealth paid for lewd conduct; Christo paid, and paid well, for the absence of it. The other five members of his crew were dedicated to security—a security chief and four others. At this point in time, two of them were close by in their own craft, a six-meter RHIB that raced over the sea, keeping station on the *Osrah*. Every few days, Christo's security-detail chief asked that the yacht's tender be put in the water for testing and crew training—and also as an anti-piracy measure. One member of the security team had had the night watch and was below, sound asleep; the other was in the small crew's galley having breakfast. It was the security chief, a former Spetsnaz major, who first noticed the fast-closing lead Mark V and what seemed to be several small craft in its wake. He studied them for a moment, then raced to the pilothouse to get a pair of binoculars. From the pilothouse wing, he studied them for a long moment, then stepped back inside, pausing to speak to the *Osrah*'s captain.

"We are being followed and may soon be boarded. Make all preparations to resist a boarding, and send someone to wake Dmitri and notify Mikhail." He didn't wait for an answer but headed aft to the solarium. Christo glanced up with some irritation at his hurried entrance.

"What is it, Vladimir?"

"Sir, we are being followed and overtaken by several military small craft."

"Pirates? Here?"

"I don't think they are pirates. If I had to guess, they are an American special boat unit. And they are coming very fast."

Christo considered this a moment. "Very well. Has the captain been notified?"

"Yes, sir, he has."

"And how soon will they overtake us?"

"Quickly, sir. Five minutes, maybe less."

Christo frowned, as if this were but a minor annoyance. "Any chance we can repel them?"

"No, sir. There are at least three boats, and they are heavily gunned."

"Very well." He sighed. "These are your instructions: Delay them as long as you can, however you can. I have matters to attend to here."

Vladimir was immediately on his handheld Motorola radio. He was no sooner out the door than Christo began feeding documents into the shredder and deleting files from the laptop computer on his desk.

"Think they know we're here?" Crandall shouted over the engine's roar.

His Mark V detachment (Det) OIC was studying the *Osrah* through a pair of stabilized binoculars. "There's no way to be sure, but I don't think so. They have a tender in the water, and it seems to be keeping station on the yacht. But it can't be too much longer before they see us. I recommend we go to a combat spread."

Crandall nodded. "Make it happen."

The Det OIC spoke a few words into his lip mic, and the four boats broke from their line-astern formation. Immediately, the two Mark Vs accelerated up to their top speed and to headings that would have them flanking the yacht, a hundred yards to either side. The two RHIBs continued along the wake of the *Osrah*, now on side-by-side and on parallel courses that would bring them up to the port and starboard quarters of the big yacht. Above, the two Knighthawks moved into position to support the waterborne assault.

According to the plan, the two Mark Vs were to stand off to either side of the *Osrah*, hail her, and order her to stop for boarding. The RHIBs would then move up to a close-in support position near the stern sheets. One helo would serve as a platform for the SEAL sniper overwatch while the other would touch down on the *Osrah*'s helo platform to insert the initial fire team. The helo deck would save them from the exposure and danger of a fast-rope boarding. After depositing the first team of boarders, the first helo would then take up the overwatch while the second helo inserted the second fire team. The yacht and Christo were being surrounded; it was now only a matter of time and the level of force involved.

Vladimir was standing on the main afterdeck of the yacht, watching the four boats flank and close in on the *Osrah*. He and his four Spetsnaz commandos could at best only conduct a holding action, and Vladimir knew this. He sent the tender and his two men off on a heading of 45 degrees to port from that of the *Osrah*. The tender had twin 250 horsepower Mercury outboards; it was fast but not quite as fast as the Mark V. It quickly began to put distance between itself and the *Osrah*, and one of the Mark Vs followed, which was what Vladimir had in mind. One less boat for him to deal with.

The Russian security chief now knew they were American boats and correctly assumed they would soon be boarded by Navy SEALs. The only issue was how long he could delay that boarding before things got nasty. He was a security consultant, not a criminal, and he would honor his employer's wishes—up to a point. Then Mikhail, the youngest of his security team, stepped out topside onto the helo deck, brandishing an AK-47. It was a mistake—and a fatal one.

The pilot of the lead helo was a skillful one. He had closed on the *Osrah* carefully, keeping his Knighthawk between the sun and the yacht. He was, in effect, coming out of the sun. With the noise of the yacht's engines and the distraction of the closing surface craft, he was able to crab down a thousand feet and to a position some 150 yards on the starboard beam of the *Osrah*. The SEAL sniper in the port door of the helo had a clear field of fire, and his Winmag 300 dialed in for the range and altitude.

"I have a Tango armed with an AK on the helo deck, and a shot," the sniper calmly reported on the tactical net.

It was Crandall's call, and he made it quickly. "Take him."

The sniper elected a head shot, which was not easy

from a moving helo to that small of a target in a moving boat. But again, the *Osrah* was a highly stabilized yacht, and the helo pilot was very good. The big 190-grain, boat-tailed, special-purpose round went through Mikhail's head like it was passing through a melon and buried itself into the reinforced helo-pad decking. Mikhail collapsed to the deck like a wet rag. A red-gray cloud of blood and brain tissue hung in the air over him for but an instant, then was snatched away by the wind.

Well off to port and now north of the main sea chase, the trailing Mark V was slowly closing on the *Osrah*'s tender. At the beginning, the two security men felt they could outrun their pursuer. They knew they were making something close to sixty miles per hour, but the sleek gray shape gradually closed the distance. Now it was nearly off their beam and working its way closer.

"What do you think?" the Russian at the helm yelled to his companion.

"We can't outrun them, but maybe I can slow them down a little."

With that he took his Kalashnikov and sprayed a long burst at the speeding Mark V. He could see waterspouts between the two vessels, and he knew at least a few of his rounds had hit their pursuer. It was his last conscious thought.

On the Mark V, the port-side .50-caliber swick gunner did not have to request permission to fire; the gunman on the tender had just done that for him. He saw the muzzle flashes from the AK-47, and even felt a round ping off his gun's armored fairing. Then he pressed the butterfly trigger of the big machine gun. He swept the little RHIB bow to stern and back again, shredding the spray tubes, the two outboards, and the two men. Several rounds ripped into the onboard fuel tanks that were under pressure, creating an atomized cloud of gasoline vapor and liquid. A tracer round did the rest. The RHIB mushroomed into a fireball, as only a gasoline-powered watercraft at high speed can. The Mark V slowed and circled once, then twice. There was nothing but burning debris on the water, a few charred life jackets, and no sign of life. The Mark V OIC, a senior chief petty officer, marked the debris field with eight-digit GPS coordinates on his Garmin navigation system and headed back toward the *Osrah* at maximum RPMs—back to the fight, if there was to be more of a fight. They could return to the site of burned wreckage later if necessary.

Vladimir watched as the two RHIBs climbed up his wake. On each RHIB there were two men, SEALs he rightly guessed, laying on the spray tubes with automatic weapons. The bow .50-caliber was trained on him.

"On the motor-yacht, this is the United States Navy," came the voice on the bullhorn from the single Mark V now no more than fifty yards away. "Heave to and prepare to be boarded! I say again, heave to and prepare to be boarded! This is your final warning!"

Vladimir held the Motorola handset to his mouth with one hand and kept the other in plain sight. "Okay, Captain, we have no choice. Slowly bring down your speed and come to a complete stop." Then he stood along the starboard rail in full view of the Mark V, his hands spread wide in a crucifixion gesture.

The *Osrah*'s captain did not answer, but he immediately complied and the yacht began to lose way. From the pilothouse he had watched the gray speedboat chase after their tender and destroy it. He was all too willing to resist no further. In the solarium, Christo completed his shredding and the deletion of the most sensitive files from his laptop. He thought about stepping onto a weather deck and dropping it over the side, but he too had seen the tender leave the *Osrah* and watched as it was run down and destroyed. He sighed, closed the lid of the laptop, and picked up his Iridium satellite phone. He hit a number on the speed dialer and waited for the connection to go through. It was answered immediately by a trusted retainer.

"Please let me talk to my wife," Christo said without preamble, and he waited. A moment later, "*Cherie*, it is good to hear your voice this day," he said warmly. "I am fine, could not be better. And how are you and the little one?" The sat phone was encrypted, but he still never mentioned their names on the phone. "Excellent. I am happy for you both . . . No, I am not sure when I can join you, and that is why I am calling. I may be tied up for a period of time and perhaps hard to reach . . . No, no, nothing's amiss . . . just business." Christo then heard the thumping of an approaching helicopter. "Listen, *Cherie*, I really must go now . . . I know, and I miss you as well. My best to the little one . . . Yes, all my love as well."

Christo pulled back on a heavy sliding window near his desk and, with a penknife, cut a long slit into the window screening. He tossed the sat phone through the opening, over the rail, and into the water. Then he lifted one of the balls of his Newton's Cradle and let it go. When the first SEAL exploded through the door, he was sitting back comfortably and listening to the *klack-klack-*

klack of the steel-ball interaction. The *Osrah* was now almost dead in the water and beginning to wallow in the gentle seaway. He noted, and not for the first time, that the inertial interaction of the steel balls was not as smooth or precise as when the yacht was up and running and the gyro-stabilization system deployed to full advantage. Like many who engaged in complex and dangerous enterprises, when things became stressful, he noticed the little things.

The second helo touched down to deposit the second fire team and Senior Chief Otto Miller without incident. This insertion helo did not actually land, as the *Osrah* could not take a helo as large as the Knighthawk fully aboard, so the pilots simply put the tip of a single skid to the deck and held a semi-hover while the SEALs scrambled aboard. The RHIBs were now close aboard on either stern quarter, but remained abaft the beam so as not to put themselves in a crossfire if the shooting started. As it turned out, there were only two more shots fired. Dmitri had not heard the call from the captain of the *Osrah*. He had been awakened from a sound sleep by the approach of the helicopters and raced topside. He bolted from a port-side door to the main deck with a pistol in each hand. It was a theatrical move, and his last. The lead SEAL of the port clearing team saw him, saw the pistols, and center-punched him twice. He was dead before he hit the deck.

Miller waited patiently on the helo deck, with a single armed SEAL there for his security. The *Osrah* was now fully stopped and rolling gently in a modest swell. He could hear the SEALs calling out with room-clearing chatter: "Pilothouse clear! . . . Salon secure! . . . Moving forward! . . . Entering port forward stateroom!" and so on. As they moved deeper into the boat, he listened to them on the tactical radio circuit. When the platoon leader declared the yacht secure, the two RHIBs came alongside and disgorged more SEALs. Miller pulled off his headset and handed it, along with the MBITR, to the SEAL at his side. Then he made his way aft and down to the main afterdeck. There he met Vladimir, who was now on the deck facedown, with his hands slip-tied tightly behind his back and a SEAL standing over him. There was a nasty bruise on his cheekbone; he was going to have quite a shiner. Miller squatted beside him, tilting his head to one side to better bring him into view.

"Dobraye utro. Kak pazhivayte?"

"I'm fine, you Yank bastard," Vladimir spat in English. "And fuck you, too, you son of a bitch."

Miller regarded him a moment, then, *"Kak vas zafut?"*

"It's Vladimir, and that's all you need to know."

"Very well, Vladimir," Miller continued in a reasonable tone and in English, "we have accounted for four of your men. Are there any more? I ask for a truthful reply, for their sake as well as your own."

"There are four besides myself, and we are a lawful contract security team employed by the owner of this boat. You have no right to board this vessel and threaten us."

"Perhaps not," Miller conceded, "but all four of your men are dead. And should we find a fifth or a sixth, then I will be back to speak to you, and you do not want that."

Vladimir started to protest, but Miller nodded to the guarding SEAL. He put a foot into his back and a strip of duct tape over his mouth. Miller rose and stepped to the Bandito Platoon assault leader standing by the door

to the solarium. The other SEALs were carefully search-
ing the *Osrah* except for the solarium, which they carefully avoided.

"Have the rest of the crew been restrained and segregated, sir?"

"Roger that, Senior Chief."

"And the owner has been confined to his desk, as I
instructed?"

"Roger that, as well. Billy and Walt are guarding him,
and everything is in place. We'll be standing by close at
hand and observing from where he can't see us. He's all
yours, Senior."

"Thank you, sir," and he stepped into the solarium.

Half a world away on the *Bonhomme Richard* another
group of Navy SEALs were preparing for an entirely different kind of mission. They were going ashore to conduct a raid on a small village on Cedros Island. Earlier
that afternoon, a platoon of SEALs from SEAL Team
One had been flown aboard by VS-22 Osprey. SEAL
Team One was the next team from the West Coast in
deployment rotation, so the Team One SEALs were the
most combat ready of the West Coast platoons. The
Team One platoon, together with the Bandito squad already aboard, gave Roark Engel three SEAL squads to
conduct the assault. It would be an over-the-beach operation conducted in CRRCs, or combat rubber raiding
craft—Zodiac-type boats with powerful outboards that
could carry a squad of armed SEALs into and through a
line of surf.

Earlier the previous evening, Lieutenant Engel and

Chief Nolan had conducted their warning order, a three-hour-long briefing that covered every aspect of the raid. The warning order was attended by the SEALs, the SWCC coxswains, and the helicopter pilots that would support the operation. It was now just after midnight. The SEALs were either below in the *Bonnie Dick*'s well deck preparing their gear and the CRRCs, or on the flight deck preparing to board the Knighthawk helos for their insertion role. Lieutenant Engel was conducting a final briefing for his squad leaders and boat coxswains. They were crowded into the little TOC around a large flat-screen monitor. Everyone was in black night-assault uniforms.

"Nothing has changed since the warning order," he began. "If anything, the cell-phone chatter and thermal activity in the village has increased. Too much so. This is a very small village and a very poor one. And it's isolated. Most of the population on Cedros lives along the southern coast of the island. Here we are some forty miles from Cedros." On the monitor, the island was shown as a green land mass with a blip to the west that was the *Bonnie Dick*. "We're still scheduled for a zero two zero zero launch in the two CRRCs. The Bandito squad will be in the lead boat, and the Team One alpha squad, Tom's squad, in the trail boat. A third CRRC will follow us in case one of our boats has a problem. We'll skirt the northern tip of the island and come in from the east. Two miles offshore, we'll throttle back to idle and make our way in as quietly as possible." The monitor expanded to show the northeast coast of Cedros Island and a small fishing village. "Once we're on the beach, the boats will pull back out and wait offshore. The weather guys are still calling for less than three feet of surf, so you should be able to deal with that." The three SWCC coxswains all nodded. "After we're ashore, we'll go into a security perimeter and wait until just before first light."

The presentation again altered, and enhanced, to show just the village, a small harbor, and a portion of the beach. There were several fishing boats anchored in the harbor and several more hauled up on the shore of the small inlet. The SEALs would come across the beach just south of the town. Engel pointed to the section of beach where they would come ashore.

"Tom, you and your squad will move out and set up two support-by-fire positions here and here, and a sniper overwatch here." The platoon officer from Team One acknowledged. "My squad will assault only after you are in place. When and if—more than likely this will be *when*— the first shot is fired, Gerry and his squad will insert by helo here and set up a blocking force, okay?" The other SEAL officer gave him a thumbs-up. "Nothing fancy here, gentlemen, just rifles, radios, and basic infantry tactics. Any questions?" There were none, nor did Engel expect any. The details had been covered in the warning order. "Chief Nolan."

"I've nothing to add, sir. Just remember the basics— the element of surprise for as long as possible, then violence of action when it goes down."

"One last thing," Engel added. "This is a friendly foreign country, and there are civilians and noncombatants in the mix. Believe me, the State Department is holding its breath on this one. So remember your rules of engagement and make sure of your targets." He looked at his watch. "Okay, I have zero zero twenty-seven . . . and four, three, two, one, mark: zero zero twenty-seven. We leave the well deck of the *Bonnie Dick* at zero two hundred. Good luck."

Minutes later Engel and Nolan were back in their squad bay, donning their body armor and combat vests. The rest of the Banditos—Ray, A.J., Sonny, and Weimy—were already below in the flooded well deck helping to make ready their CRRC. Earlier, Chief Nolan had inspected them, checking their weapons, radios, and equipment. When they were ready to go, Nolan inspected Engel, and Engel inspected Nolan. SEALs always inspect each other before going to combat. As he was going over his chief, Engel fingered a dark, olive-drab patch on Nolan's shoulder. It blended in with the dark black fiber of the assault clothing, but it was still readable. It read: ENGINE COMPANY NO. EIGHT.

"I thought you were going to get me one of those," Engel said.

"Are you still busting my balls about that patch? Like I said, I got them from my uncle right after 9/11, and I gave 'em all out. Tell you what, when we get back, I'll give you this one."

"No, it's no big deal, and I don't want to rob you of your family memorabilia." Engel finished and stepped back to allow Nolan to inspect him and his gear. As Nolan watched, Engel chambered a round into his M4 and turned the weapon over so that Nolan could see him put it on safe.

"No big deal, huh. Well, what about this?" as he patted a cargo pocket on Engel's right thigh.

"What?"

"This. What you got in there?"

Engel drew out a very tightly folded, forty-eight star

American flag. "It was my grandfather's flag. Dad gave it to me, and someday I'll give it to my boy."

"I like that, Lieutenant. I like that a lot."

"And while we're at it," Engel continued fishing a square-folded, letter-sized sheet from a pocket on his shoulder, "I want you to hold on to this. Just in case."

Nolan stared at the folded paper, then at his officer. "What's this supposed to be?"

"It's, well, it's just in case."

Nolan stuffed it absently into a pocket and continued with his inspection of Engel. "When we get back from this op, I'm going to make that into a paper airplane. Or maybe I'll just wipe my ass with it."

"Y'know, Chief," Engel replied with a grim smile, "that's why you're such a damn fine platoon chief. I know I can count on you to do the right thing."

"You're good to go, Boss. Let's go to war."

"Let's," Engel echoed, and they headed for the well deck.

Miller gently closed the solarium door behind him and regarded Christo for several moments as Christo, in turn, regarded him. Miller glanced from side to side, as if he were not sure just how to proceed. He carefully removed his sunglasses, put them in a folding hard-case, and filed them in an inside jacket pocket. Tentatively, he made his way over to the desk and pulled back one of the chairs in front of it but stopped abruptly, raising his eyebrows to ask permission. Christo, now considering Miller with some disdain, inclined his head in approval.

Miller cleared his throat to address the two SEALs standing guard.

"Ah, would you two please excuse us."

"Sir, I'm not so sure about that," one of them protested, but Miller raised a hand to silence him.

"Please, it will be all right. And before you leave, would you also please cut his bonds."

One SEAL started to protest but merely shrugged and took a set of side cutters from his combat vest. He cut the snap tie that bound Christo's wrists behind him and, together with the other SEAL, left the room. Christo, now able to sit up straighter, did so. He wanted to rub his wrists where the nylon had bit into them, but he consciously refrained. Miller took a seat across from him and again cleared his throat.

"*Zdra-stvu-eetee. Minya zavoot* Otto. *Kak pazhivayete?*"

Christo smiled. "Your accent is not bad, Otto, but I sense you would be more comfortable in English, no?"

"Quite so," Miller replied. "And you are?"

"I am Christo."

"Not 'Mikhail Troikawicz'?"

This brought another smile. "Just Christo will do. And how am I, you ask? Well," he looked around, "as you might imagine, I've had better days."

"Indeed." Miller looked around as well. "This is quite a boat. The Westport Shipyard makes an excellent yacht. You seem to enjoy things of quality, Christo."

He paused to again regard the man across from him; he appeared to be a little more sure of himself now than when he had entered. "I have worked hard, and my business interests have prospered. You might say I have been fortunate."

Miller nodded. "I would agree with you, Christo—you have become a very wealthy man. Or at least you were. The many material things that you have worked so hard for are no longer yours. Not the estate in Costa Rico, not the compounds in Kuala Lumpur, in Rio, and on the Black Sea, and not your penthouse condominium in Rome. And certainly not this fine boat." At the mention of the Rome penthouse, Miller thought he detected an almost imperceptible fracture on Christo's bland features.

When they were being overtaken by the American boats, Christo knew he was in for some trouble. He would have to wait and see how much trouble. But, thanks to Shabal and his plotting, he had never before been in such a liquid position. He would survive this and with a good deal of his wealth intact. Personally, he knew the Americans were great proponents of due process, and he knew they would have a great deal of trouble making a case against him—at least a legal one. If he had learned nothing else in his business dealings, it was how to cover his tracks. The Western legal systems, and the American system in particular, were a joke. But, for now, he needed to get past this increasingly disturbing man and the scrutiny of his now-steady green eyes.

"Otto, here we are in the middle of the ocean, clearly in international waters. You may seize and impound my vessel, but you have no claim to it or to my other assets. What makes you think you can just take what is mine?"

Miller seemed to hesitate and consider his question. "I think the best and only answer is simply, because we can. Your properties are being seized for tax liens in their respective locations by government officials only too willing to enjoy what you've worked so hard for. Our government has a way of rewarding and indemnifying those who help us. As for your other assets, well, perhaps you should take a look at this."

Miller took a single sheet of paper from his inner jacket pocket. It was folded lengthwise. Miller carefully smoothed the crease from the fold and placed it in front of Christo. As he read it, the blood began to drain from his face. Listed on the paper were *all* of his foreign bank accounts, complete with account numbers, access codes, and passwords.

"It's our obsession with terrorists," Miller continued in a gentle voice. "We Americans have ceded much to the Chinese, Germans, and Koreans in the way of technology and manufacturing. But when it comes to banking, finance, and money transfer, no one knows more about it or does it better than we do. We simply put our best minds and brightest hackers to work on this particular project."

Miller sat forward with his elbows on the desk. When Christo looked up, the green eyes had suddenly become intense and predatory. This was definitely not the same timid man who had entered the solarium only a short while ago. Without looking away, Miller took an iPad from his outside jacket pocket and set it down on top of the paper.

"But as we both know, there are things that are more precious than houses, boats, and money." He tapped on the iPad, and an image came into focus. It was Christo, waist deep in the pool of their Costa Rican estate, with his daughter, Solana, on his shoulders. In the background, fully in focus, Dominga looked on. Miller reached over and moved his finger across the screen from Christo's left to his right. A second image showed the three of them eating at poolside. Another swipe of the finger, another image. This one was of mother and daughter walking on the streets of Rome, hand-in-hand, with retainers in dark glasses walking a few steps behind. Then an aerial image taken from above the level of the penthouse showing Dominga in a lounge chair reading a magazine and Solana playing with her dolls. After several more images, Miller turned off the iPad.

"You may keep this and leave here with it. It's nice to have pictures of your loved ones with you, especially when you are in confinement."

For several minutes, neither man spoke. It was Christo who broke the silence.

"You . . . you would hurt my family?"

Miller held him with those intense green eyes for only a moment, then replied, "I would never hurt your family." Christo believed him; he was not sure why he believed this man, but he did. "But as you might imagine," Miller continued in that soft, steady voice, "there are conditions. While I can promise that no harm will come to them, the quality of their life and any future contact you may have with them will depend on your cooperation." He sat back and exhaled. "Life as you knew it, as a businessman and as a family man, is over. We can and will take all your assets. But your wife, daughter, and extended family will have money to live on—reasonably, if not elegantly. Your wife will not have to take work; your daughter, who we understand is gifted, will be able to go to college. Perhaps even to the University of Virginia if she chooses."

As Miller exerted his influence and control over Christo, Christo himself seemed to shrink. He had gone from condescension to curiosity to uncertainty. Now a cold fear gripped him, such a fear as he had never known. "And what of myself?" he asked, barely audible.

"I can promise only detention and humane treatment. Will you ever see your family again? That I cannot promise, but who knows what the future may bring. However, you do have information about Shabal and what he might be planning. This is information we would very much like to have. So cooperate—by telling all that you know—and you will be kept informed about your family and given proof of their continued safety. On that, you have my word. It all depends on you and your desire to help us."

Christo was now slumped in his chair with his eyes pressed tightly closed, as he pinched the bridge of his nose with a thumb and forefinger. He was desperately trying to come to grips with a world that was quickly collapsing around him. Christo gathered himself up in his chair to again face Otto's relentless green eyes, which were still upon him. A small audio recorder had now appeared on the desk in front of him.

"Very well," he managed, "what do you wish to know?"

Miller knew he had broken Christo, but that was just the first step. He wanted everything from Christo, not just what the man thought he wanted to hear. So gently, quietly, professionally, and persistently Otto Miller began to extract every bit of worthwhile information from Christo. This would be a marathon, not a sprint.

As Miller prompted him, Christo guided the senior chief through the details of the explosive vests with the ceramic balls, the Filipino Muslims who had been recruited to carry out the plan, and how Shabal planned to get them across the border and into the United States. The device on the desk was in fact a recorder, but it was also a radio with limited range. A communications technician had been ferried over to the *Osrah* from one of the Mark Vs. He and his radio relay equipment were now on the helo deck. A running encryption of Miller's interrogation of Christo was being beamed by satellite relay simultaneously to NSA headquarters at Fort Meade, Maryland, and to the Nebraska Avenue Complex of the Department of Homeland Security. NSA, being far more entrenched and nimble than DHS, quickly decrypted and collated the information and disseminated it by flash precedence to those recipients with code-word authorization.

TEN

It was an excellent night for an over-the-beach operation, as there was no moon, and a spotty cloud cover blocked much of the starlight. But the sea was a problem. Four-foot waves rode atop the long Pacific swells coming out of the southwest, and their initial course for Cedros Island had the three CRRCs running on a due easterly heading. With the swells on their starboard quarter, the CRRCs slid down them in a wrenching, corkscrew motion while they pounded across and through the waves. The SEALs, with their gear tied down, clung to the spray and cross tubes and endured the misery. The fact was that the boats could take more than those riding in them. The SWCC coxswains had wedged themselves in the rear of their craft. They wore night-vision devices and, with one hand on the big outboard tiller and the other on a handheld GPS, guided their craft through the night. The swicks brought two more of their own along for security and to ride in the front of the third CRRC to hold down the bow. After an hour and a half of the continuous, uneven pounding, they skirted past the uninhabited Islas San Benito and rounded the northern tip of Cedros. Turning south, they came into the lee of the island and some relief from the sea conditions. They were well offshore, but they could see the lights of the village.

The tumultuous ride afforded Engel some time to think. Though he was being physically punished by the pounding of the CRRC, he could still think—and think clearly. Like most SEALs, he could detach mental activity from physical discomfort. So while he was being jerked this way and pulled that way without warning, he carefully reviewed the information Senior Chief Miller had sent to them from his interrogation of Christo. Although Christo had confirmed the nature of the threat and the methods of the attackers, he had few operational details; they knew the how but not the all-important where and when. Christo had known nothing of Cedros Island, but on one thing he had been most specific. The explosive vests that Shabal now had in his possession were virtually undetectable by current screening technologies, and those recruited to carry the vests were from a Muslim sect in the southern Philippines who were completely dedicated. And the explosives were of a new and more powerful design—so new that dogs trained to find explosive materials would not have been trained to detect them. It was a formula for mass casualties and panic. This threat, and the knowledge of casualties these vests could inflict, occupied him as they bounded through the night for Cedros Island. Yet on occasion, his thoughts drifted to Jackie and their new baby. These thoughts were mixed with a longing and a regret that he could not be with her, but with some effort he pushed them aside and focused on the task ahead.

Cedros Island, or Isla de Cedros, "isle of cedars," is close to twenty-five miles long and five miles wide, with a population of some fifteen hundred souls—most of whom live along the southern coast. Located sixty miles off Baja California in the Pacific, it was misnamed by early Spanish explorers who took the pine trees on Cedros for cedars. There had not been much activity or anything of real importance in the past two centuries to add to Cedros's recorded history. Copper and gold were mined on Cedros at the turn of the last century, but the ore was marginal at best. The mining gave way to fishing, and the fishing gave way to ecotourism and smuggling. The small target village on the northern coast of this island was a hotbed of the latter. The village, if it could even be called that, had no name. It was a mile north of the old mining town of Punta Norte and consisted of a few shacks, some trailers, and a cantina. Those who lived there made a poor living from fishing, smuggling, and the transshipment of drugs, and the island authorities from the borough seat of Pueblo Cedros made it a point not to go there.

The lead CRRC with the Bandito squad aboard finally throttled back, and the other CRRCs followed suit. They drifted forward at idle, swicks and SEALs alike watching and listening. Engel's coxswain leaned toward him with an iPad in a clear, waterproof housing.

"Sir, here's the village," he said in a low voice, "and here's the insertion point some eighteen hundred yards due west. We'll have an offshore breeze, so they shouldn't hear us coming. I got zero-four-thirty-two. How do you want to handle it?"

Engel considered this. Not much could be gained by waiting out here; even this mild seaway would wear on his SEALs and make them less combat ready. And the sooner he could get his ground force ashore, the more time they would have with their approach to the target.

"We're a little early, but not that early. Let's stand in."

"Roger that, sir."

The swick coxswain turned the lead CRRC toward the beach, and they began to idle toward the island. Engel had neither to pass word for the other CRRC to follow, nor to alert those in the raiding force that they were heading for the insertion point. When the boats had come off step and gone to idle speed, the SEALs on both boats began to prepare for going ashore. They snapped their NODs onto their helmets and began to cinch down their body armor and combat vests. Ray, as the lead communicator, quietly began a radio check with the SEALs in both squads and the boat coxswains. They had done this just as they were leaving the *Bonhomme Richard*, but that was several hours ago and a kidney-pounding ride across forty miles of open ocean. All the SEALs in both squads were up and alert. Ray then shifted channels on his MBITR radio, the one that linked him to the TOC on the *Bonnie Dick*. He had a light, continuous wire cross-hatched on his combat vest, making himself a human antenna, and the LHD had a helo aloft—shadowing them but well out to sea, to serve as an airborne communications relay.

"Home Plate, this is Blackbeard, over."

"Roger, Blackbeard, this is Home Plate, over."

"Blackbeard here, we are at Point Alpha, over."

"Roger, Blackbeard, hold you at Point Alpha. Rat Pack turning on deck, over."

"Blackbeard, roger, out."

Ray, who would never be far from Engel during the raid, touched his elbow. "Comm check good, Boss," he whispered, "and the Rat Pack is turning on deck." Rat Pack was the helo support team—two armed Knight-hawks with the third squad of SEALs.

Two of the three CRRCs were now headed toward the shoreline at idle speed. The third CRRC would wait offshore. It was still dark, yet the SEALs now hugged the main and cross tubes of the boats to lower their sil-houette. The odd splash of wave against rubber and soft murmur of the outboard were the only sounds. A hundred yards off the beach, the two CRRCs were virtually invisible to the naked eye. At fifty yards from the beach, the boats heaved to while A.J. and a SEAL from the Team One squad slipped into the water and swam ashore. Once they crawled onto the beach, they paused to listen and to survey the backshore with their NODs. Then they scurried up the rocky slope and into the sparse veg-etation, pausing once more to look and listen. They could hear distant salsa music coming from the direction of the village, but there was nothing else. They waited for five minutes, then called the boats in. First one, then the other, came through the line of surf, disgorged their black forms, and returned back through the shallow breakers. For the SEALs and the SWCC coxswains, this from-the-sea evolution was a well-practiced maritime skill. It was something SEALs and swicks did again and again during basic training and on every pre-deployment training cycle. Once into the backshore, the SEALs went into a loose security perimeter, the Bandito SEALs rallying on A.J., and the other squad on their scout swimmer. Again they listened and waited. Nolan quietly moved from one Bandito SEAL to another to ensure they were up and ready, and had no equipment issues from the transit or the trip through the surf. The Team One squad chief did the same. At 0540, Engel judged they were fifty minutes from first light. It was time to move; he keyed his tactical radio.

"Tomcat, Blackbeard. Let's do it, over."

"Tomcat here. We're moving, out."

The Team One point man led both squads quietly toward the village. The music grew louder, but there was no one moving about the half dozen or so scattered clapboard and adobe structures. There was enough light spilling from an occasional window for the SEALs, with their NODs, to see at least ten vehicles, mostly pickup trucks, and a potholed, gravel road running through the village. At fifty yards south of the first building, the Bandito squad halted, and the Team One squad continued on patrol. Their job was to set up fire-support stations between the harbor and village along the eastern edge of the village. They moved slowly and carefully as they skirted the village. The lives of their brother Bandito SEALs depended on their finding and establishing effective support-by-fire positions.

The Team One sniper and his spotter found an old semitrailer along the harbor-access road and carefully climbed to the top of the freight box. It was as good as they could do on this flat, rocky terrain. The other SEALs found shallow rises to set in an Mk48 machine-gun emplacement and their Mk46 squad assault weapon. They had a reasonable command of the village, and when the sun came up, it would be at their backs. After the platoon officer was satisfied with his squad's deployment, he keyed his tactical radio.

"Blackbeard, this is Tomcat. We're in position. Let us know when you're moving, and good hunting, over."

"Roger that, Tomcat, stand by, out." Engel nodded to Ray to call in the start of their assault, which he did. On the *Bonhomme Richard*, two Knighthawk helicopters lifted off into the darkness with four SEALs in each helo. Rat Pack was now airborne, heading for an orbiting station ten miles out to sea and five minutes flying time from their village.

"Beacons on and radio check," Engel spoke into his mic.

"A.J. here."

"Ray here."

"Weimy here."

"Sonny here."

"Nolan here." Nolan rose so he could look along the line of SEALs with his NOD to verify that their IR beacons were all active. "We are up and active."

"All right, brothers," Engel replied, "let's go take this town. Tomcat, we're moving, over." With one squad in an overwatch support position and the other standing by as a quick-reaction element, Roark Engel was free to lead the ground assault.

"Tomcat copies you moving, out."

As one, the Bandito squad rose and approached the village on a skirmish line. One at a time, they crossed a rickety bridge that spanned a dry wash running past the village. On the other side, they reconstituted their line and continued on. From the fire-support positions, it was as if six dull, light-green bulbs in a ragged line moved to and into the small village. As they closed on the first structure, three of them, the clearing team, moved to the front entrance while the other three held security.

The first two-room hut was empty, as was the second and third. They took them in sequence—carefully, slowly, and quietly, so as to leave cleared and secure structures at their back. The fourth hut was not empty and the two SEALs who entered slowly backed out.

"Uh, Boss, Weimy here. We got what looks like a mom and a bunch of sleeping kids."

"Understood. Tomcat, mark this hut as unsecured with noncombatants, over."

"Roger that, Blackbeard. Tomcat out."

"Let's keep moving, guys."

"Roger," Weimy whispered, "moving."

There were only two more fixed structures: a small mud-adobe hut and the larger, wooden cantina still playing salsa music. Behind the cantina, the SEALs could now see two single-wide mobile homes. Sonny and A.J., along with Weimy, moved to set up on the adobe. Sonny stepped through the door and found himself standing at the foot of a single bunk with a dirty mattress. There were two children—one sleeping and the other nursing. He put his fingers to his lips to ask for silence, but it didn't work. The mother screamed, and the scream brought a man from behind a curtained area in the rear of the hut. He wore only a soiled white shirt and undershorts, and held an AK-47 loosely at his side by the trigger grip. He moved, giving Sonny no choice. The element of surprise was now over; it was time for violence of action. Sonny took him mid-chest with a five-round burst from his Mk46 SAW. The woman continued to scream.

"One Tango down," Sonny calmly reported on the tactical net, and he backed out the door. "Noncombatants still inside."

On the command net, Ray called in the action. "Rat Pack, Home Plate, we are in contact. I say again, we are in contact, over."

"Rat Pack, roger. We are inbound, out."

"Home Plate, roger, out."

North of Cedros Island, two MH-60S Knighthawk helos dropped to five hundred feet and headed south at best speed. The first signs of dawn were now making their appearance over Baja California, yet the aircrews and SEALs still wore their NODs. West of Cedros, the *Bonhomme Richard* was closing at flank speed.

Moments earlier in the cantina, a rough-looking Hispanic and the leader of the Filipino recruit contingent were carefully laying out explosive vests on a long table. Six other Filipinos sat quietly in a corner of the large single room drinking tea. At another table, three other men, with the sun-hardened look of fishermen, sat around a single bottle of tequila, playing dominos. Two others were drinking at a shabby bar made from low-grade plywood. When the short burst of Sonny's SAW split the night, they all reacted, and within seconds, everyone had a gun. The Mexicans looked wildly around; the Filipinos were more disciplined and carefully moved to the doors and windows. They were Muslim extremists and prepared to die. If it was to be their time, then so be it. One of them quietly slipped on one of the explosive vests.

"On me, Banditos," Engel called over the tac net, and the five SEALs took a position on a line abreast with Engel, facing the cantina. "Tom, you have us?"

"Negative. You must be behind a building."

Engel took a portable laser and pointed it skyward, moving it in small circles. The motion created an IR shaft of light marking his position.

"Now?"

"We got you, Blackbeard. Stay tight there unless you call out your move."

"Roger that, Tom, and you are cleared hot."

At that instant, three of the locals burst from the front door of the cantina and were immediately taken under fire by both the Mk48 and the Mk46. All three went down before they had gotten ten yards from the door, dead or mortally wounded. Then came the Filipinos, and it became an IR shooting gallery. They moved with good tactical discipline, but they were blind and had no cover. The SEALs all had LA-5 IR target lasers on their weapons. Through their NODs, it was just a matter of putting the green dot on the Tango and pressing the trigger. Two squirters bolted from the rear door and were picked up by the sniper on the top of the freight hauler. Then suddenly it became very quiet. That silence was quickly broken by the fast-approaching Knighthawks. They came in fast and low, tail-walking across the beach as they bled off airspeed and altitude. First one, then the other, touched down for but an instant and disgorged their SEAL fire teams. The two fire teams took up positions north and west of the cantina.

"Blackbeard, Tomcat, this is Rat Pack. We are in place, over."

"This is Blackbeard and roger that. Welcome to the party, Rat Pack. We are going in by the front door. Three of us inside, two flankers, and one holding at the door. How copy, over?" Engel was now as much concerned with friendly fire as he was with clearing this last building. He listened as his Team One SEALs acknowledged. One of the Tomcat support-by-fire positions hurriedly moved so as to bring the cantina under a better field of fire.

"Banditos moving," Engel called.

"Banditos moving," the other two squads acknowledged.

Sonny and his SAW flanked left, and Weimy went to the right. A.J. led Nolan, Ray, and Engel to the door. The new dawn continued to grow in the east, but the cantina was now dark, with the front door half open. They were flattened at the front door frame, A.J. and Engel on one side, Ray and Nolan on the other. Engel nodded to Ray and Nolan, and all three pulled a flash-bang grenade from their vests and jerked out the pin.

"Three, two, one," Engel quietly counted, and all three tossed their grenades inside.

BANG! BANG! BANG!

A.J., as always, was first in, crossing right to left—then Nolan, left to right. Engel came straight in. Ray, the radioman, would hold security at the door. From behind the bar, a man with an old M79 40mm grenade launcher popped up. He could hear nothing but ringing in his ears from the flash-bangs and saw almost nothing but spots—almost. He did see enough to catch the outline of a form in the door against the coming dawn. He pointed and fired, and a fraction of a second later, the same man was double-tapped by Chief Nolan. A lone Filipino fled out the rear door. Ray fired twice, hitting him once, but it was a through-and-through shot. The man kept running.

Outside, there were a great number of SEALs looking for a diminishing number of targets. The man carrying Ray's bullet ran like a man with a hot poker in his side, which, in effect, he had. He took but three strides before being cut down by tracers from both the support-by-fire positions and the blocking force.

Atop one of the trailer homes, a man with an RPG raised up and fired. With a loud *WHOOSH*, the rocket sailed over Sonny's head and exploded in a fireball just behind the cantina. The gunner immediately became a magnet for tracer rounds. He was dead before he could take the launcher from his shoulder. Then muzzle flashes appeared from the windows of both trailers, and for ten full seconds, the two mobile homes were shredded by automatic weapons fire and rocked by grenade hits. There was no more fire from the trailers. The silence that followed was cut by Nolan's voice on the tactical net.

"Man down! I got a man down! Get me a medic in here!"

The Team One platoon officer immediately stepped in. "Rat Pack, this is Tomcat. Hold your position. My element will be assaulting the target building from the southeast. Tomcat moving, break, Blackbeard, what is your status, over."

It was Nolan again. "Blackbeard actual is down. Get your medic here A-S-A-P!"

"Roger that, Blackbeard. Tomcat, out."

The eight SEALs of the Team One support squad made their way through the village on a skirmish line, moving quickly. Four converged on the cantina, while the other four moved to clear the two shot-up trailers. The platoon officer and his combat medic made straight for the front door of the cantina. Inside, headlamp beams cut through the smoke to converge on a man lying on his back on the floor. It was Roark Engel. He was breathing shallowly, but he was not moving. With Nolan at his side, the medic began cutting the straps to his combat vest and body armor. Then they began cutting away his clothing, looking for wounds. There were none. The medic shrugged as he took a pencil flashlight and lifted one of Engel's eyelids. This got a reaction. The lieutenant jerked his head away from the offending light and tried to sit up.

"Whoa, easy there, sir," said the medic. "You can talk, but don't move. How are you feeling?"

Engel's voice was scratchy but audible. "Like someone's sitting on my chest." He saw Nolan hovering nearby with more than concern on his face. "Have you been sitting on my chest again, Chief?" Nolan sat back on his heels, the relief visible. "Hey," Engel continued, "I think I can move, okay?"

Nolan and the medic helped him to a sitting position, but he clutched at them as his head began to spin.

"Easy there, sir," said the medic. "Something knocked you on your ass. We're just not sure what it was."

"I think it was this." Dropping to one knee beside them, A.J. was gingerly holding a 40mm grenade round, sans the propellant charge, in his thumb and forefinger.

"Take that fucking thing outside," Nolan ordered. "Now!"

A.J. grinned but left with the grenade, still holding it carefully.

"Who . . . What was it?" Engel asked, still confused.

"That dead Tango behind the bar," Nolan explained, "center-punched you with a forty mike-mike round when you stepped inside. It takes about fifteen feet for that round to arm itself coming out of the tube. You were only about ten feet away."

"Lucky me," Engel managed. Then to the Team One platoon officer, "We secure?"

"We are, and your communicator has called us in secure. My guys are conducting a cordon and search of the area right now. And there are some FBI agents and Homeland Security people inbound from the *Bonnie Dick*. This place will soon be crawling with civilians."

Engel considered this and nodded, still not thinking too clearly. Then he jerked his head around, "Anybody hurt?"

"Just you, Boss," Nolan replied, looking at the bruise that was now beginning to form on Engel's chest. "Just you." He was trying to make light of what had just happened, but when he had turned and found his platoon officer unconscious on the cantina floor, his heart had leapt into his throat. "And sir, don't ever do that to me again."

"Help me up, will you?"

They pulled him to his feet. His gear was still on the floor, and his assault uniform was in rags, but he still clutched his M4. Soon helicopters began to arrive with inspectors, analysts, and intelligence professionals. In the growing light, they inspected, photographed, and tagged the ceramic-ball vests. Explosive ordnance technicians watched as an FBI forensic specialist individually bagged them. Outside in the growing daylight, Roark Engel walked around the cantina flanked by Chief Nolan and A.J. Three steps from the front door, one of the Filipinos was facedown in the rocky soil with a bullet in his brain. He was wearing one of the explosive vests, his hand motionless on the activation lanyard.

"C'mon, Boss. Let's get you to the helo and back aboard the *Bonnie Dick* for a good going-over by the ship's doctor."

With the *Bonhomme Richard* closing on the island, it was but a fifteen-minute Knighthawk ride from the village to the ship. The platoon from SEAL Team One stayed behind to provide security for the investigators, while the Bandito squad was lifted out. Lieutenant Engel said he was fine, but Chief Nolan insisted he first go to sick bay and get himself checked out. He was still in his sliced-and-diced assault uniform when he arrived at the *Bonnie Dick*'s sick bay. He looked like a tramp in a train yard. Ray had radioed ahead that his officer would need some attention, and a doctor and a corpsman were standing by. The medical officer, a full commander, wasn't happy when Nolan declined to leave while the doctor examined Engel.

"Y'know," Nolan said while the doctor checked him, "that was a pretty stupid thing to do, stepping in front of the forty mike-mike grenade just to keep it from traveling the arming distance. Not one of your better moves, Boss."

"I'll keep that in mind."

"Now, if you had just stepped a little to one side, Ray could have taken that round. Course, he was farther away, and it might have had time to arm itself."

"Might have," Engel replied.

"How's he doing, Doc?"

The physician ignored Nolan and kept prodding at Engel. Then he again listened with his stethoscope for several minutes.

"No permanent damage," he finally announced, "but we'll give you a chest X-ray just to be sure. It's like you were in a head-on collision at moderate speed and the air bag deployed. Your vest and body armor sufficiently disbursed the force of the round or it might have cracked your sternum, perhaps with fatal results. But it was the chest plate in your body armor that made the difference— that and the grenade not going off. That bruising on your chest will probably become more pronounced, and you'll have some discomfort, but I think you'll be fine. You're a lucky man, Lieutenant."

"Tell me about it, sir."

"You want something for the pain? Or something to help get you to sleep?"

"I think I'll be okay, sir. We've been up awhile, so I'll have no problem going to sleep."

"Well then," the doctor offered, "I'd tell you to take it easy, but I'd probably just be wasting my breath."

Engel grinned. "I'll do what I can to get some rest, Doctor, and thank you."

When they reached the SEAL compartment below-decks, the Banditos were overhauling their equipment. It was standard SEAL procedure: equipment first. Once they had their gear and weapons cleaned and set up, they would eat, shower, and then maybe get some sleep. Engel quickly pulled on a fresh set of cammies and began to disassemble his M4 to prepare it for cleaning. Out of curiosity, he found his combat vest and took out the chest plate. There was a shallow indentation in the ceramic armor, but it was otherwise intact. It was advised that a plate be replaced after it received a strike, but he pushed it back into its carrier on his armor. It was a lucky plate.

After cleaning his rifle and reloading his magazines, he took his radio from his vest and set it on the charging bank. Then he laid down on his bunk for just a minute to rest before finishing up with his gear. He was looking forward to a shower and some hot chow. And that's the last thing he remembered until Chief Nolan shook him awake.

"Wha—what is it, Chief?" He came awake quickly and would have bolted upright but for the pain in his chest. It was excruciating.

"Easy, sir. Maybe you ought to sit up slowly." And he did.

With his feet on the deck, he managed to take a full breath. The pain was still there but manageable. Engel looked around and saw that his boots were off and that his combat gear was set up and staged on a folding chair at the foot of his bunk. He frowned at his own inattention; a SEAL was supposed to take care of his own gear. Nolan again, he suspected, although it could have been any one of them.

"How long have I been down?"

"About six hours. They want us up in the TOC. Something's come up."

He stood and found the pain in his chest a little more bearable. "I got time for a shower?"

"I think they want us now, Boss. The master chief from the intel shop just left. Seems there may be a follow-on operation in the offing."

"The fun never stops, does it?" With some discomfort, he sat back on his bunk and began to lace on his boots. Then he noticed a donut and a steaming cup of black coffee on a chair beside his bunk.

"Pretend you're in the Navy and have some coffee, Boss. It'll do you good."

He did, and as the warm liquid surged down into his chest and stomach, it did indeed feel good.

The little TOC off the *Bonhomme Richard*'s large CIC was once again crowded. There was the ship's intelligence officer; the man from the NSA, who seemed very nervous; and Lieutenant Susan Lyons. She greeted Roark Engel and Dave Nolan warmly.

"Thanks for coming up here so quickly, and I never did get the chance to thank you for getting Dr. Lisa Morales out of that hellhole in Costa Rica. And she asked me to again thank you."

"How is she doing?" Engel asked.

"Quite well, actually. She's come a long way, but as you know, there was a lot of physical and psychological damage. She's getting help with both. I'll tell her you were asking about her. Now, the reason for this meeting is a follow-up to the operation on Cedros Island. There's good news and there's bad news."

Engel noticed that the intel commander and the NSA man deferred to her, so she was definitely something more than a Navy lieutenant or a Navy intelligence officer. Engel guessed CIA or Homeland Security, with strong liaison connections to one or the other. Both Engel and Nolan assumed the lieutenant cover was just a means to allow her to blend in with the ship's company and move about a little easier.

"The good news is that we now have a dozen of those explosive vests and at least eight of those who were slated to enter the U.S. on a mission of terror. There were five men and three women that we've positively IDed. The bad news is that we can't account for the other vests or the terrorists. Or Shabal for that matter. And since all of those on Cedros were killed in the fighting, we have no one to interrogate. One of the women was still alive after the shooting, but she's since died of her wounds." She unintentionally made it sound like an accusation.

"Well, between all the grenades and the rockets and the automatic-weapons fire coming our way," Nolan said evenly, "I guess we just got carried away."

If she perceived some censure in Nolan's comment, she didn't let on, and continued. "The follow-on search teams did find a few cell phones, a satellite phone, and an iPad computer. Isaac here," indicating the NSA man, "and his people are examining them for anything that might give us a clue to where the other vests and the terrorists might be."

For his part, the National Security Agency man appeared restless. He seemed fixated on his Apple laptop while absentmindedly twirling a pencil in a rolling manner across his fingers, pointer to pinkie and back again.

"We're working on it," he mumbled, "but what they brought us from the island was pretty beat up. The computer had a bullet hole in it and most of the cell phones had been drenched in blood. Do you know just how corrosive human blood is?"

Nolan started to say something, but Engel placed a hand on his shoulder. "So where does that leave us?"

"We've confirmed that the Tupolev landed at the airport at Isla de Cedros Aeropuerto," Lyons continued, "which was no small thing to get that plane onto a five-thousand-foot strip. The 'passengers' were taken away in open pickup trucks, and the plane immediately left. There is daily air service to Guerrero Negro, and we're checking their bookings as we speak. And there are small craft that routinely cross the channel between Cedros and Baja. It's safe to say that the other vests and the other terrorists, and probably Shabal as well, have made the crossing. We can only assume that they are headed north for the border. So the *Bonhomme Richard* is now steaming north to the Baja-U.S. border. But this will do us no good unless we can pinpoint where they are and where they plan to cross."

"So," Nolan said, "we stand by to stand by and wait for something to break."

Lyons shrugged. "Unless you have a better idea. We've alerted all our border contacts to be on the lookout for anything out of the ordinary, but we've stopped just short of a terrorist alert. At this time, it would serve no purpose. We have, however, let the Mexican authorities know that there may be terrorists attempting a border crossing, but we've given no details on just how serious this threat is. They've moved one of their tier-one special-operations units to the border where *they* are on standby. If it comes to mounting another operation on Mexican soil, either they will be working with you or you will be working with them. The State Department and Homeland Security are working out the liaison details."

"You mean," Engel said evenly, "that we might be working side-by-side with, or even under the tactical control of, these Mexican SPECOPs types?"

"That's right, the Grupo Aeromóvil de Fuerzas Especiales, or GAFE—Mexican special forces. I've been led to believe they're very good. Maybe not as good as you SEALs, but we're south of the border here. It's their turf, so it's their game. The Cedros Island venture was a one-time, offshore thing. Maybe if you hadn't, well . . ."

"Yeah, we know," Nolan interjected, "if we hadn't killed so many people and broken so much stuff."

"Look," Lyons replied, with a measure of anger in her voice, "it is what it is. They are cooperating, but there are limits to that cooperation. And we're the beggars here; the terrorists are targeting us, not them. It took a lot of log rolling to allow you to go onto Cedros. Now we want to put an armed military unit on their mainland—even a small team, which is what you will have to go in with. So we have boundaries. Their special-operations people are supposed to have good capabilities. They operate against cartel security, which is every bit as nasty as the Taliban. So there it is; we do it this way or sit back on our side of the border and wait for them. If Isaac and his people can find them, then we have a target. If not, then we'll have to wait for a break and watch the border smuggling routes.

"We've already received some help from the GAFE. They operate almost exclusively against the drug smugglers, and they say that the most numerous routes and most porous border points along the southwest border regions are in and around Mexicali. We understand that these crossing points are also the most closely guarded and defended by the cartels. They feel that if the terrorists and the smugglers are indeed in bed with each other, then they will try to cross in the Mexicali area. But that still takes in a lot of border. Meanwhile, I recommend that your team get ready to marry up with the Mexican GAFE team. They're already set up at a small airstrip just outside of Mexicali. We can fly you off as soon as you're ready." She paused and seemed to soften a little. "And, I understand that you, Lieutenant, were hurt on the island raid. Are you up to this?"

"I'm up to it," he answered, then paused to frame his words. "We can be ready to go in two hours, three at the outside. It'll take that long to set up a communications plan and get our radios encrypted. We also have to put together a small support package. I'll take my squad, all six of us, as the primary assault element, and I'll want a sniper and a communicator from the Team One platoon, if their platoon officer approves."

Nolan started to say something, but Engel again put his hand on his shoulder. "We need to get to our SEALs and start getting them ready. We'll keep you advised on the progress of our preparations. You don't have anything, do you, Chief?"

"Well, since you put it that way, Boss, I guess I don't." He rose and walked out of the TOC with Engel on his heels.

When they were out of earshot, Nolan turned to face him. "Look, sir, this is fucked. We don't even know . . ." Engel raised his hands in an act of surrender and to interrupt.

"I know, and I hear you, Chief. We have no intelligence, and we know nothing about these Mexican special operators. But I think we have no choice but to go along, at least for now. We need to get ashore and in a position to react if we do get better intelligence. And I've got some ideas on how we can work around this. Now I want you to go and get the guys turning and burning. And talk to the Team One platoon chief; see if we can borrow a sniper and a backup SEAL communicator. I'm going to have a private little chat with Ms. Lyons to see if I can get some ground rules in place as well as a little more detail." Engel paused and looked at his chief, who waited, arms folded, to hear him out. "I know this is not how we like to do business, but this could be a crucial operation, Chief—one that could prevent a lot of Americans from getting killed. So I, we, have to bend a little and go with the flow. As always, none of us steps out into the deep linguini unless both of us say it's a go. Fair enough?"

Nolan smiled, relenting. "Fair enough, sir. But this Mexican SPECOPs unit bothers me. What do we know about them? How do they operate? Hell, we don't even know what kind of radios they have."

"Again, I hear you, Chief. Seems a bit strange, doesn't it? We've worked with the Iraqi SOF and the Afghans and the Canadians and just about every NATO SPECOPs component in the world, but never with the Mexicans. And now, to have a shot at some really bad guys who are about to attack our country, we may have to. So?"

Nolan shrugged. "So we go with the flow, I guess. I'll go and get the boys cracking, and I don't think there'll be an issue with the two guys from Team One. Hell, they'll all want to go."

Engel started to head back to the TOC, thought better of it, and headed up to the flight deck, where his Iridium sat phone worked best. He hit number one on the speed dialer. It took a few moments for the encryption to click in and the call to go through.

"Extension 3725," came the sleepy voice on the other end.

"Good afternoon, Senior Chief, or I guess it's good morning there."

"It's morning all right, very early morning. What can I do for you, sir?"

"You still have our friend there, right?"

"We do. He's no longer on his yacht but doing nicely in a guarded stateroom here on the *Makin Island*. He's in isolation and, so far, very cooperative. I'm just not sure that operationally, he knows all that much."

"Here's where we are, Senior," and he gave him a brief breakdown of the Cedros Island operation and of the missing terrorists and explosive vests. "We don't know where they are, and we don't know where Shabal is. If there's *anything* you can get from him that might lead us to where they are or where they might cross the border, it might be our only shot. Otherwise, they could slip into the country, and we'll never know where they are until they strike."

"Understood, sir. Give me a few hours. No promises, as he just may not know, but I'll do what I can from this end."

"Thanks, Senior. That's all we can ask."

"And, sir, you take care of yourself. I understand that you've been confronting large-caliber objects at close range. Most unwise, sir."

"I'll keep that in mind, Senior," he said and cut the connection.

As he headed for the TOC, he wondered how Miller had heard about his close call with the 40mm grenade. On further consideration, he realized there were Navy communication channels and Navy chief-to-chief communication channels. And the latter were the faster of the two.

When he reached the TOC, one of the ship's communicators handed him a message. It was a set of orders—and a notice of his promotion to lieutenant commander. The orders were to the White House for a two-year tour as a junior military aide-de-camp. He smiled. For the first time since he was a high school running back, he would carry "the football." He couldn't wait to tell Jackie—two full years and he'd be home most every night. This would please her to no end. Then he frowned as he thought about telling Dave Nolan and the others that he was leaving. He'd wait until after this operation was over. And, he reflected, it would probably be his last one as leader of the Bandito SEALs. Promotion to lieutenant commander meant that he would be leaving the operational platoons.

He tucked the message into his shirt pocket and set off to find Lieutenant Susan Lyons.

"You say that they are all dead? All dead! And the vests gone as well?" Shabal paced as he shouted into the cell phone. "How could this have happened? . . . Very well . . . There is nothing to be done. Immediately destroy your cell phone and stay out of sight!"

Shabal threw his own phone to the floor and crushed it underfoot. He continued to pace while several swarthy Mexican smugglers sat at a nearby table and watched him. These were hard, fierce men, but this violent and mercurial Chechen scared them. They watched as Shabal paced, the rage etched on his features. How could they have found the other contingent of recruits on Cedros, he wondered? And what bad luck. In another few hours, they, too, would have been on the mainland and moving to their border-crossing point. *So be it,* he reasoned, *we will make do with what we have left.*

For his part, he had done everything he needed to do, and done it to perfection. He shook his head. Was it ego, or was it just a fact of life? If he left it to others, they made a mess of it. And Christo wanted him to deal with his intermediaries. What a crock! This was too important to leave to intermediaries. Perhaps too important to leave to those who did not believe as he believed.

They had made it to Cedros Island and made the channel crossing to Baja. Now they were in a safe house in Mexicali. He didn't trust these Mexicans, but they were useful to him—at least for the moment. He pulled aside the dirty window shade on the second floor bedroom and looked down on the dusty Mexicali street below. A hairless dog wandered down the street, looking for food scraps. Soon they would be at this place they called the milk factory and their border-crossing point, and nothing could stop them from there.

Long ago Christo had explained the vast tunnel system running from Mexican border towns north into the United States. It was one of the things he liked about Christo. He didn't describe them as a clandestine or an illegal network for smuggling drugs and people into the United States—a network that had made Christo wealthy beyond imagination. These details were simply a part of his business empire. They were but a means of transportation as normal to Christo as the U.S. Interstate Highway system was to truck drivers.

But now that Shabal was here, the tunnels were no longer an abstraction. They were part of the tactical plan he needed to execute to consummate his assault on America. With half of his recruits dead and half of his vests gone, he needed to ensure the remaining vests produced maximum carnage. He must now carefully prioritize the targets. *Even so,* he thought, *with eight targets and thousands dead, it will still make 9/11 pale by comparison.*

He now sat with the one Mexican he could communicate with—but never fully trust. Christo had already transferred a considerable sum of money to the man's offshore account. The man knew that once Shabal told Christo this part of the mission was complete, and Shabal and his eight martyrs were safely across the U.S. border, another great sum of money would be sent to that same offshore account. The man needed no further motivation. Money, Shabal knew, was all these Mexicans wanted.

"So tell me again why you picked this tunnel system here," Shabal said as he stabbed his finger at a hand-drawn map.

"Yes, well, you can see, my friend, it is close to this safe house," the man who called himself Sanchez began. He was a younger man, handsome in a vaguely exotic way, and urbane compared to the thugs who guarded the safe house. "And even more importantly, the entrance to the tunnels is as well guarded as anything in this country."

"How do you mean?" Shabal asked.

"Look, it is vastly more complicated than just going down into the tunnels and crossing the border. Moving drugs and people into the United States isn't a side business for us, it is our *only* business. You looked around this town as the bus brought you here, no?"

"Yes," Shabal replied. He wanted information, not a lecture, and Sanchez was starting to irritate him.

"Yes, just so. Forget about the drugs for a minute, something that made our friend Christo a wealthy man. Think about people. Think about how many millions of poor Mexicans want to enter the United States. If we just let anyone into these tunnels, they would be clogged with many thousands wanting to go north. No, we control who enters, eh?"

"All right, I see that."

"I'm not sure you do, or if you realize how lucrative it is for us, and important for us to control this access."

Sanchez nodded toward one of the big men sitting on a battered sofa.

"See Antonio over there. He has two sons. One is at Duke, the other is at Colgate. Most Americans can't afford to send their children to private colleges, let alone Ivy League schools. Antonio has three more kids, younger ones, and they'll all attend university in the United States. So, you see, we control it. We control the access, and so we control the profits."

"I see," Shabal replied.

"So, here, here is where we will insert you," Sanchez

said, drawing his finger to a point on the map. "It is our most well-protected location. It is a compound that is as closely guarded as the homes of some of our richest citizens. No residents of this city dare come within a hundred meters of it. You are paying us well, so we will take you to our best and most secure route to the north."

"How will we get there?"

"Not by the bus that brought you here. That would attract too much attention. No, we move in thirty minutes. This is the time of day when the delivery trucks make their deliveries to the restaurants and cantinas. We can fit all nine of you in the back of one of them. In the compound they know we are coming, and they know what our truck looks like. It is as simple as that, my friend."

"It is never simple," Shabal snarled.

The two MH-60S Knighthawks set down on a hardstand near the small airport's single strip. The reinforced Bandito squad and their gear were quickly unloaded, and the Knighthawks lifted off. They would await any call to action from a military airfield twenty miles to the south. There was little to be gained by the conspicuous presence of two American military helicopters sitting on a civilian airstrip near Mexicali. After the helos lifted off, the SEALs surveyed their surroundings. Just off the airstrip were a series of heavily locked self-storage units and a few light aircraft tied down nearby. Most were old taildraggers. The complex was surrounded by an eight-foot chain-link fence with coils of razor-wire running along the top. Captured plastic shopping bags dotted the rusty chain link. But most noticeable and pervasive was the smell. Nearby and, unfortunately, upwind, a large column of birds circled over a garbage dump. A parade of open dump trucks were making their pilgrimage to the waste site, dumping loads of refuse, and heading back into Mexicali for more.

Parked near the hardstand, well back and off to one side, were four battered Ford Explorers. As the SEALs moved toward the vehicles, a single figure in a tailored black combat uniform stepped out from a group dressed in a variety of shabby, civilian attire. Except for the lone figure in black, they looked like an undercover narcotics squad. Given their area of operations, this was not surprising.

"Well, well, what have we here?" Nolan said quietly.

"I'll talk to the jefe," Engel replied under his breath. "Why don't you and the others mingle with their troops and get a feel for them. I'll want to know what you, A.J., and Ray think of these guys." Nolan could understand more Spanish than he could speak. A.J. and Ray were fluent. As the other Banditos peeled off to one side, Engel made straight for the tall man in black. He dropped his gear, came to attention, and saluted.

"Good afternoon, or *buenos dias*, sir. I'm Lieutenant Engel, SEAL Team Seven."

The man was tall and slim with fine Castellón features. He wore only the oak leaves of a lieutenant colonel on his buttoned-down cloth epaulettes and a badge on his left breast that read *Todo por México*—"all for Mexico." Stopping in front of Engel, he, too, came to rigid attention and rendered a parade-ground salute. He had high cheekbones and a pencil-thin mustache. Yet for all his bearing and formality, Engel thought he detected a twinkle in his eye.

"Welcome to *México, Teniente*. I am *Commandante* Juan de Rio de la Ribandeo. Or," an easy smile now accompanied the twinkle as he extended a hand, "until we finish this unpleasant business, please call me Juan. And your Christian name is?" His English was precise and impeccable.

"Uh, it's Roark, sir."

"Please, Roark, it's Juan—I insist. And before we get started, let me say it is a privilege to be working with the Navy SEALs. We are honored—all of us." He paused to regard his men, who were now mingling with the Banditos. "They may not look like much, but they are good boys, and brave. You *Norte Americanos* have your overseas ventures that keep you quite busy. We here in Mexico don't have to go far to confront evil. Our war is right here. Our enemies are well financed, well armed, and committed to their enterprise. So our operations, like yours in Afghanistan and Iraq, are deadly and ongoing. Like you, I've lost some good men, and as with you and your wars, there seems to be no end to it." He paused a moment, "But then, we are not here today to talk about the burdens we warriors must bear. We have our duty. More to the point, I understand we have a job to do. I look forward to hearing all about it." And Roark Engel brought him up to speed with what he knew so far.

Dave Nolan spoke just enough Spanish and *Sargent Primero* Lopez just enough English for them to get a feel for not only each other but the capabilities of their special operators. Senior enlisted leaders the world over are very good at getting to the point, and when it comes to the issues that relate to risking their men in battle, brutally honest. Nolan could have this same conversation with an Israeli *Rav Samal Rishon* or a German *Hauptfeldwebe,* and with the same results. There is something about the prospect of mortal combat that causes men who must lead other men into danger to be candid and truthful. Up the chain of command, politics might enter into the equation, but not at the troop level. In the U.S. and other armies, they call it ground truth, and that was what was taking place between Chief Nolan and Sergeant Lopez.

"So what do you think of these guys?" Engel asked after they were off by themselves. He watched as Sergeant Lopez and De la Ribandeo, over by their vehicles, seemed to be having the same conversation.

"They've seen a lot of combat and probably have more trigger time than our guys do. Tactically, I doubt they are as good as we are, but they've been in a fight, and it seems they know how to fight. I don't think there's anything to be gained by integrating our guys with theirs unless we're dealing with local noncombatants. But if it comes to a fight, I believe they'll stand tall. How about their jefe?"

"I'm not sure, but I think he's okay. More to the point, what do his troops think about him?"

"They seem to like him. He's obviously a dandy and a blue blood, but they call him *El Lobo,* "the wolf." It seems he's been known to show up before a raid and jump into the assault element. He's a fighter. He's also the number two guy in the GAFE. I guess the commander is a regular-army colonel who no one ever sees. But the operational teams see a lot of this guy."

While the other SEALs continued to mingle with the GAFE soldiers, Nolan and Engel were joined by A.J. and Ray.

"What's your take?" Nolan immediately asked them.

"I think they're all right," Ray said. "They seem to have both a respect and a hatred for the druggies. For them it's personal. It's like if the Taliban or al-Qaeda controlled some of our neighborhoods in San Diego, and we had to fight them here, not over there."

"And speaking of neighborhoods," A.J. offered. "I talked to a couple of them who grew up right here in Mexicali. They say that the border-crossing routes are drug turf, and there's no way to get to the actual crossing points without being detected. I guess half the kids on the streets have cell phones, and they'll know we're coming long before we get there. He says they probably already know we're here, and they'll know when we leave."

Engel digested all this. "What about helicopters, coming in low and fast?"

"They don't like helos," A.J. continued. "The bad guys have RPGs and heavy-caliber machine guns in those areas they want to protect. When they do have a solid tip and have to go in, they go in their Explorers, drive like maniacs, and hope it's not a setup, like with a big roadblock and snipers on the roof. These guys take fire on almost every raid, even when their intel is good and they have total surprise."

"So Cedros Island was a cakewalk?" Nolan asked.

"We're up against the varsity here, Chief," Ray said. "The druggies have good weapons, they're not afraid to die, and there's lots of them. So it could be anything but a cakewalk. I don't know what they pay these GAFE guys, but it's not enough."

"So what we're talking about here," Engel summarized, "is opposition that's every bit as dangerous as anything we go up against in Kandahar or al-Anbar." Both Ray and A.J. nodded.

"And without the support we have over in the sandbox," Nolan added.

Engel looked over to where Juan, Sergeant Lopez, and the other members of the GAFE were gathered. They were all smoking and laughing. De la Ribandeo seemed to move easily among his men. Then his satellite phone began to vibrate. He stepped away to answer it.

"Engel here."

"Sir, its Senior Chief Miller. I understand you're now on border patrol."

"Border patrol standby, Senior. We have a target but no target location. Any luck on your end?"

"I'm not sure. I again took our friend through his conversations with Shabal, and it seems Shabal purposely kept a lot from him. He did overhear him while he was on a coded cell phone, talking about a milk factory. Something about getting them all to the milk factory. It's not much, but it may be something. If I get anything more, I'll let you know."

"Thanks, Senior. Keep me posted."

Nolan was at his elbow. "Anything?"

"I doubt it, but we'll see."

They made their way over to where De la Ribandeo and his sergeant were talking. The tall GAFE leader took out a gold cigarette case and offered one to Engel, then to Chief Nolan, but both politely declined. It seemed as if all the GAFE smoked, while none of the SEALs did. Lopez gratefully accepted and De la Ribandeo made a show of tapping his cigarette on the case before lighting it.

"Sir, I mean, Juan," Engel began. "I just received a call from one of our intelligence people. He had little for us except for the mention of a place called 'the milk factory.' Does that mean anything to you?"

Engel and Nolan watched this register. Lopez, in spite of his dark complexion, seemed to grow a shade lighter. De la Ribandeo drew heavily and thoughtfully on his cigarette and exhaled slowly.

"It means," the GAFE commander said easily, "everything. We know the place, and your 'intelligence people,' as you call them, could not have given us a more difficult objective. It's an abandoned milk-processing and packaging complex. And it is indeed a border crossing, the location of a border-cross tunnel complex. Your terrorist friends could not have chosen a better location from their perspective, nor a more difficult one from ours. It's in an area totally in their control. We seldom go there, and the local police never do. And there's no way to get there undetected. There are concentric rings of well-armed security retainers around the milk factory. The element of surprise, which I know you are so fond of, is not an option here. We'll have to fight our way in."

Engel considered this. Maybe, he thought to himself, and maybe not. He had an idea how they might go about this. Normally, he would have liked to have gone over this with Chief Nolan in private, but there simply wasn't time.

"Do you have a map of the city?"

Sergeant Lopez pulled a dog-eared, laminated map

from his jacket and spread it on the ground. The four of them squatted around it.

"We are here," De la Ribandeo pointed, "and the milk factory is here, just south of the border. And the whole area underneath it is a warren of tunnels. There's a good chance that while we are fighting our way to this place, those whom you wish to capture will be filtering out the other side and on their way north."

"How would you go in?" Engel asked.

"In those," indicating the battered Explorers. "We do not have up-armored Humvees, and if we did, it would only announce our presence that much sooner."

"How about if we went in two or three of those," he said as he pointed toward the dump.

It took a moment, then a broad smile began to crease De la Ribandeo's handsome features. "And I thought you were only about your expensive equipment and the huge salaries they pay you. I see now that you SEALs are clever as well."

"Juan, do you understand what a blocking element is?"

De la Ribandeo drew himself up formally, but there was still a twinkle in his eye. "I am a graduate of your Infantry Officer Basic School at Fort Bragg *and* I have earned my Ranger Tab."

"That is good to know," Engel replied. "Now, here is what I propose . . ."

Deep inside the underground warren beneath the heavily guarded compound above, Shabal and his recruits worked feverishly to complete the last assembly of their vests and make preparations to deploy through the tunnels and into the United States on the final leg of their journey to inflict jihad on the hated Americans.

Shabal alternated between urging his recruits to hurry and make the vests ready for wearing—due to their destructive power, they didn't dare travel with them fully assembled—and reviewing the map with Sanchez.

The recruits were bent over some old wooden tables Shabal had Sanchez bring down. The tables were positioned under the few fluorescent lights hung from the concrete ceiling. The lights cast a cool, white glow as the recruits used several tables to assemble their vests, treating them with the same care a parachutist might pack his chute. Every time Shabal urged them on they just grew more and more nervous, and it actually slowed their assembly.

On another nearby table, Shabal and Sanchez reviewed the hand-drawn map of the tunnel maze.

"Here, Shabal," Sanchez said, alternately pointing at the map and to a darkened passageway to their right, "Here is the passageway you must all travel down. It is a little more than 150 meters long."

"I see," Shabal replied.

"Then, you must break up into smaller groups. There are three smaller tunnels that go deeper and then actually cross the border, here, here, and here," he offered, pointing to the primary smuggling routes on his maps.

"Then these are the ones you use most? Are they secure?"

"As I told you at the safe house, this is our business, and we are good at it. No one we have sent through these tunnels has been stopped at the U.S. side of the border—absent some gross stupidity, like hitchhiking on a major highway. But you must decide who goes through which one, though I do advise you to use all three—as a precaution."

"Yes, I will decide that when I give each of them their final assignment," Shabal replied, waving a number of envelopes at Sanchez, envelopes that contained the name of an American city and an exact location where each martyr was to detonate his or her vest, as well as ample American currency to travel and fake identification for each one. Each envelope also carried a precise time that they were to make their attacks—the same time in each case. Above all else, Shabal had told them time and again that this must all be done simultaneously.

As the first recruit finished the final vest assembly and donned her deadly vest, Shabal walked over to her and handed her an envelope.

"Open it, please."

The woman opened the envelope and gasped at the amount of money it contained. Then she pulled out the postcard. It read: WELCOME TO LAS VEGAS!

"You will be there by tomorrow night, my dear."

"But . . . but . . . how will I get there?" she began to protest.

"It's all in your envelope. A taxicab stop is close to where you will emerge on the U.S. side of the border. Follow the map and the instructions in there. The taxi will take you to a bus terminal. It will be a long bus journey, but you will get there safely. The MGM Grand—the picture of that hotel complex is also in your envelope—is your target. Look at it carefully once you are on the bus. There is a major convention at the hotel. You will be on the convention floor at the time indicated. Now, I must go check the others."

Shabal checked each of his recruits in turn, wanting to hurry but also knowing that once they passed through that first long tunnel and branched out into separate ones, his ability to give them instructions was over. He had trained them all for almost a year, and now it came down to this . . . hurried instructions just before the last leg of their journey.

"I urge you to hurry," Sanchez shouted as Shabal was checking one of the last of his recruits. "We can't linger here too long."

Forty minutes later, they were in two dump trucks and charging through the residential districts of Mexicali. De la Ribandeo drove the lead truck, with Ray riding shotgun. Both wore old work coats over their body armor and combat vests. Some thirty yards behind them, the second dump truck followed, with Lopez driving and A.J. riding in the passenger's seat. The GAFE squad, less three of their number, rode in the dump bucket of the lead truck. With them were Sonny and the two Team One SEALs. The other Banditos and three of the GAFE were in the second truck. The trucks were equipped with canvas roll-top appliances that helped to keep refuse from flying out from a loaded bucket on the way to the dump. It provided concealment while allowing the SEALs and GAFE to peer out from underneath the canvas covering. As they approached the abandoned milk factory, they began to see idle teenagers on the streets, then teens with guns. Finally, there were armed men on rooftops with guns and bandoliers of ammunition.

Ray, riding with De la Ribandeo in the lead truck, had an old stocking cap pulled over his ears to hide his earphones and partially cover his lip mic. "Boss, you copy?"

"Right here, Ray."

"We are entering an armed enemy base camp. I've never seen so much security, at least not out in the open."

"I hear you. How much farther?"

There was a pause, then, "The GAFE leader says about three more blocks, unless we get stopped. Get ready."

"Okay, guys," it was Nolan coming on the net, "let's get our game face on and stay sharp. This is probably going to be a dick-dragger."

The security gunmen gave them puzzled looks as they rolled past, but no more than that. De la Ribandeo, with a cigarette dangling from his lips and an Uzi in his lap, smiled and waved to everyone. This guy, Ray thought, is a gamer. As they approached the main entrance to the milk factory complex, an old stretch Mercedes rolled out to block their path. De la Ribandeo slowed as if he were going to stop, then slipped the transmission into low range and mashed the gas. He hit the Mercedes on the nearside quarter panel and spun it off to one side. Two guards were taken out along with the car. As he drove past, De la Ribandeo killed another with his Uzi. The dump truck was through the gate before Ray could get his M4 up and into action. As they roared past, the guard who dove to the right of the gate to avoid the oncoming truck rose and began shooting at the rear of the fleeing truck. But he only got off a few rounds. A.J., coming in the second truck, saw it all. He leaned from the window and put two rounds in the guard's back.

The two trucks stopped ten yards from each other and began to disgorge SEALs and GAFE. In the lead truck, Sonny and the Team One sniper rose through a hole they had cut in the canvas shroud and began to look for targets. Per their plan, De la Ribandeo, Sonny with his SAW and a heavy ammo load, and the two Team One SEALs were to hold the entrance to the main building and, if possible, get the sniper and a GAFE rifleman or two up to a perch, where they could command as many building entrances as possible. Their job as the blocking element was containment and isolation. They would shoot any hostiles who came out of the building and shoot any hostiles who approached the building. For now, all was quiet. They had taken out the inner circle of security and the gate guards. But those gunmen on the outer rings of security would soon be collapsing back in on the milk factory, so there would be no shortage of bad guys inbound to their position.

The Team One communicator was to stay with De la Ribandeo and serve as a relay between the GAFE commander and his men outside and the assault team inside. He was also on both his sat and cell phones, letting anyone and everyone know they were in contact, in Mexicali, and within sight of the border. Sonny found a good shooting position, where he could command both the gate and the main entrance to the building.

De la Ribandeo stepped to where Engel and Nolan were preparing to enter the building. "I think Sergeant

Lopez and his men can stand with your men here," he said in a conversational tone. "If you don't mind, I think I'll join you inside."

Engel started to protest but knew he hadn't the time nor, he rightly guessed, the authority to overrule him. Aside from that, the twinkle was no longer there; the slim Castellón was all business. Engel nodded, and the assault team moved to the building.

Sergeant Lopez and three of his men ran to the sandbagged guard shack by the gate and dragged the dead sentries aside. When the first of the cartel gunmen cautiously approached, they casually waved to them. When they got close enough to see that all was not right, Lopez and his men opened fire. From then on it was a gun battle, and the bodies began to collect in the street outside the abandoned milk factory.

Engel, assuming the front door might not be the best entry point, led his team to the loading dock, and a single steel door next to a series of loading-bay doors rolled down. They paused for a moment while Weimy quickly taped a breaching charge to the door. It had a command initiator. After a "Fire in the hole!" the door was hurled inward by the force of the explosion, and the squad filed in through the smoke. A.J., once more, was the first man in and almost tripped over the body of the cartel gunman who had been guarding the door.

Several floors below in the subbasement, Shabal and Sanchez looked at each other when they heard the explosion. They and one of the Filipino recruits were bent over a map of Southern California. On a nearby table, a dozen explosive vests were neatly laid out. The building was concrete, as were the floors, and this was their first warning that they were under attack. Shabal instantly knew it had to be the Americans.

"No," he seethed. "First Cedros and now here! This cannot be happening!" Christo, he reasoned; it had to be Christo. *If I live through this,* he vowed, *I will find him and his precious family, and I will kill them all.*

"How many men do you have down here? How many?" Shabal demanded harshly.

Sanchez hesitated, his eyes wide with fear. "I don't know, not many," he admitted. "They are all up on the street." He was both puzzled and frightened—puzzled that a Mexicali or the federal police force was in the building without his knowing about it. He had paid them all off, and there were dozens of his gunmen for blocks around the abandoned factory. And he was scared not so much from the authorities; they could be reasoned with or bought off. But this Chechen madman was different. He could neither be reasoned with nor bribed.

"We must hurry," Shabal said as he scooped up an armload of vests, about half of them. "Get whatever men you can find and hold them off."

"What if we can't hold them off?"

"You will hold them, or as surely as Allah is Great, I will kill you." Sanchez knew he meant it. He went off to round up whatever men he could find in the basement. There were but a handful. Sanchez gave them their instructions and hurried after Shabal and the safety of the basement tunnel complex. Just ahead of him, Shabal was rallying his Filipino recruits. There was now shouting and gunfire coming from the main basement stairwell.

On the street level, the battle raged, but it was a controlled rage. Initially, there was much bravado in the young cartel bucks who charged at the milk factory. Most were veteran gunmen in that they had ambushed rival gangs and preyed on the families of policemen and *federales*. But they had never been exposed to the disciplined, interlocking fields of fire presented by the SEAL and GAFE defenders. Sonny and the Team One SEALs melded well. They had never before worked together, but they immediately fell into their roles. Sonny with the Mk46 light machine gun suppressed enemy fire and broke the early en masse charges. The SEAL radio man guarded Sonny's exposed flank and took up the slack when Sonny changed ammo drums on his gun. The Team One sniper and his SR25 7.62 semiautomatic sniper rifle found a ladder to the top of the building and took up a position there. Both Sonny and the other SEAL called out targets, and he took them out. Soon the GAFE riflemen were calling out targets. The spotters were needed, as the SEAL sniper had to move after each shot or risk counter-sniper fire. He popped over the shallow roof abutment, took his shot, and ducked back behind cover.

Before taking up their defensive positions at the gate and behind the building, the GAFE soldiers had gathered the weapons and ammunition from the security contingent at the gate. For now, they had plenty of ammo. But the Tangos kept coming. And there was a Darwinian component to the battle. As the defenders killed the younger and more inexperienced fighters, smarter and more seasoned ones took their place.

In the basement of the old factory, Engel, Nolan, and the others began the deadly business of clearing the dark recesses of an unknown building. Had they been able to find the power source and extinguish the lights, they could have moved much more quickly and safely. In the shadows, dimly lit hallways, and bright splotches of bare bulbs, they were constantly going from NODs to naked eyes—IR targeting lasers to visible red-dot lasers.

Without direction or commands, the SEALs and the GAFE fell into a rhythm. The SEALs—Weimy, Ray, and A.J.—cleared one room, while the three GAFE soldiers cleared the next. Engel, Nolan, and De la Ribandeo served as security and led the file down the hall to the next room. As the basement level had multiple hallways and corridors, they had to be prepared for threats ahead of them as well as behind. Nolan, with his NOD, picked up one such Tango following them and shot him dead. In one of the rooms, they found a dozen or more cartel hostages. Most were bloody and showed signs of torture. There was a low, collective moan as the GAFE clearing team kicked in the door. After a quick consultation, De la Ribandeo elected to leave two of his men with the hostages, and the others moved quickly on. On occasion, they could hear footsteps receding down the hall.

At one point they came to the room with the maps and leftover vests. Engel quickly looks at the maps and map notations while Nolan counts vests.

"Boss, we don't have all the vests."

"And the others are headed for L.A. and other points north," Engel replies. "We gotta find these guys."

They hear scrambling down one of the passageways leading away from the room, toward the rear of the factory subbasement. They head down the passageway. Soon the concrete floor gives way to dirt. They're moving quickly now, accepting the risk that comes when forced to do so. From a window, one of the cartel gunmen sprays a short burst into their corridor, before De la Ribandeo turns his Uzi on him and kills him.

Engel, now on point, is rounding a corner bathed in shadows, with the firing now behind him. Suddenly he is shoved against a wall by a small man, one of the Filipino recruits. The man is surprisingly strong. He has only a pistol, but he manages to parry the barrel of Engel's M4 and bring the pistol up. Engel blocks the handgun, but the man begins to fire. The rounds splash against the concrete near his head, and are getting closer. For his part, Engel releases the pistol grip of his M4, slides a sheath knife from his lapel, and inserts it between his attacker's ribs and into his heart. As the Filipino slides to the floor, Engel takes the pistol from the dying man's hand, tosses it aside, and resumes heading down the hall.

"Everyone, okay?" Engel calls back.

"Took a ricochet in the calf," A.J. says, "but drive on. I can keep up."

They move on with A.J. now in trail, but he's watching their back.

"Hey, Boss, you there?"

"Copy, Sonny, but I'm kind of busy. What you got?"

"We're getting low on ammo here, and there's no shortage of Tangos. I have one GAFE down hard and another wounded." Engel pauses and looks back at Nolan.

"Let's send A.J. back with some of our ammo. One way or another, we won't need that many more rounds."

Engel nods. "Hold on Sonny. A.J.'s coming back with some bullets."

"Roger that, Boss."

Nothing more needed to be said. A.J. works his way up the file, collecting magazines. Then he turns and hurries back up the passageway, half limping and half jogging. With the prospect of more ammunition on the way, Sonny and the two Team One SEALs easily repel the next assault. There is no more extra ammo for the sniper on the roof, but every round he has left, he makes count. Like all snipers, he's in a zone—one shot, one kill. Soon, the new milk factory defenders on the ground have a new supply of ammo, and A.J.'s gun is in the fight.

Back underground, one of Shabal's diminishing number of recruits decides that she has had enough. She pulls a pistol from her waistband, turns, and runs back at her pursuers. The team is in yet another room, trying to decide which of the two passageways is the right one. Engel hears her running toward him long before he sees her, and takes a knee. Chief Nolan is checking out the other tunnel, but De la Ribandeo is at Engel's side. Seeing the backlit silhouettes, she begins firing wildly as she runs. The two men at the mouth of the passageway, seeing the muzzle flashes, return fire, killing her instantly.

"Well," Nolan remarks, stepping back from the other passageway, "at least we know which way they went so we can . . . Aw, shit, no!"

On the dirt floor is *Commandante* Juan de Rio de la Ribandeo, lying on his back with a bullet entry in his high, aristocratic forehead. His dark, sightless eyes stare at the ceiling as a pool of dark blood begins to collect around the back of his head like a crimson halo.

Engel sits back on one heel, his M4 pointed up and his head lowered. "Dammit!" he says quietly. Then he rises and sets off at a run, down the passageway where the woman had come from. He is followed by Nolan, Weimy, Ray, and the last remaining GAFE. As the GAFE soldier passes the woman's body, he puts two rounds into her head.

The woman had brought the pursuers hot on their heels, but she had also given Shabal an idea. At the next room opening—a small cavern lit by a single small-wattage bulb—he halts with Sanchez and now only three of his recruits, a woman and two men. He selects the woman. She is anxious, her forehead glistening with sweat.

"Sister," he says in Tagalog, "are you ready to be with your martyred husband in paradise?"

She nods, not trusting herself to speak. He quickly slips one of the vests on her and removes the safety shunt from the initiator. Then he pulls the final safety clip.

"You know what to do. *Allahu Akbar.*"

"Allahu Akbar," she mumbles back, but she does not move.

"Now!" Shabal commands. She turns and begins to walk back up the passageway.

The five pursuers pause at a cross tunnel to listen, unsure if Shabal and the others have continued on or have taken one of the side paths. It's dark in the passageway, and the four SEALs have on their NODs. The woman is walking slowly with only the aid of a small flashlight. Engel sees her first, and in the glow of the small light, he sees what she is wearing.

"Bomb!" he yells, and the SEALs all dive into the side tunnels. The SEALs make it, and the GAFE almost does. His legs don't clear the edge of the tunnel. His

lower torso is shredded by the force of the blast and several of the ceramic balls. The SEALs all have on Peltors,
so they still have their hearing. The GAFE soldier can't
hear or feel anything. Nolan gets to him first and drags
him by the collar into the cross tunnel, not that it will do
much good now.

"No es bueno, eh, Jefe?"

"Su es un Mano, amigo. Es tambien," replied Engel,
but the soldier merely smiles and grips Nolan's hand.

"Anybody else hurt?"

"I took a ricochet under my arm, Boss," Weimy says.
"It went through, but I don't know how bad it is. I don't
think it's a sucker." What Weimy was saying was that he
didn't think it had penetrated his chest cavity, meaning
that he may not be a pneumothorax candidate. But there
was no way to be sure. Engel makes a quick decision.

"Weimy, radio check," he says on his radio, and Weimy
responds, which means his radio and Weimy's are both
still working. Then audibly, "I want you to stay here
with our GAFE brother. Call me if that wound starts
sucking or you collapse a lung." SEALs can talk like that
to each other; they've all either seen it before or experienced it.

"Roger that, Boss. Go get that son of a bitch."

Engel looks at Nolan, then at Ray. "Ready?"

"Ready, Boss."

"Let's do it."

Ray is on the move quickly, beating them both to the
passageway entrance, where he takes off at a run. The
first man is almost always at risk. They keep a ten-yard
interval and move quickly. The next room, or cavern,
presents them with three alternative passageways. Ray

quickly studies each with his NOD and sees a faint glimmer coming from one of them, a glimmer that immediately extinguishes itself.

"They went this way," he says and they're off again.

The tunnel leads them to a small cinder-block enclosure with doors on both ends, one leading into the room and one leading out. As they regroup in the center of the room, a sprinkling of dust drifts down from the ceiling. Too late, Engel looks up and sees one of the Filipinos. He's waiting for them crouched atop a steel I-beam. Engel shoots him twice, but he has already dropped the grenade. It's a standard American-made M67 hand grenade—effective, reliable, and lethal. The cinder-block room was a ready-made killing enclosure. In just a blink of an eye, Roark Engel takes it all in. He sees the grenade that will kill or disable them all. He knows there is no escape for any of them in the small enclosure. And he knows Shabal will then be able to come back and kill those who survive the blast at his leisure. He also knows that Shabal still has several of the vests, and a clear path to continue his journey north into America. All this is clear to Lieutenant Engel—in that moment. There is only one course of action open to him, and he takes it. Had he minutes, even hours, to think about it, there was still only one course of action to take.

Roark Engel dives onto the grenade, cradling it to his chest and the same ceramic plate that had stopped the *other* grenade less than twenty-four hours ago. Only this grenade is much more powerful, and it does not need a distance of travel to arm itself, only time. The explosion lifts Engel eighteen inches into the air and deposits him back onto the hard-packed dirt floor. He absorbs most of the blast and a good portion of the detachable-link, circular shrapnel band that was wrapped around the explosive core. Both Dave Nolan and Ray Diamond absorb some of the shrapnel but little of the blast. They will live, but their lieutenant will not.

Nolan gets to him within seconds of the blast, but he knows it's too late. Already Engel's eyes are beginning to dilate. He exhales once and it's over. In that brief terrifying moment, Roark Engel is gone. He had no other choice. It was how he was raised, trained, and lived: the mission first, next his men, and then himself.

"Stay with him, Ray," Nolan says as he takes up his M4 and heads out the other door. Ray, who has taken only a few more pieces of shrapnel that Nolan, retrieves his rifle and crawls over to his lieutenant. He sits close and presses Engel's cheek close against his thigh with one hand. He holds his rifle at the ready with his other.

"Boss . . . Boss. Why did it have to be you?" He begins to cry, but he never takes his eyes off the door that Nolan just went through.

Dave Nolan grimly moves forward through a tunnel that is now all hard-packed dirt—floor, ceiling, and both walls. Like an old mine shaft, there is knob-and-tube wiring that services an occasional bare lightbulb. Nolan senses danger and advances slowly, the butt of his M4 in his shoulder and looking over the front sight. He comes to the next node in this seemingly endless series of tunnels and rooms, where three forms are pressed up against the walls of a small room, just out of his line of sight. One of the Filipinos comes at him, pistol in hand, and Nolan cuts him down with a short burst. Next, Sanchez steps out to get a better firing angle, and Nolan immediately fires and kills him. He stays with Sanchez a nano-second too long. He's shifting aim to the other side of the room when the bullets begin to strike him. They are rounds from Shabal's AK-47.

The first several rounds tear into his trigger hand and knock his rifle away. The next ones slam into his chest plate, driving him back against the wall. Without con-scious thought, Nolan draws his secondary weapon, a Sig Sauer 9mm, with his good hand. A single Filipino, the last one, darts up the tunnel. Nolan puts three rounds into his back, and he goes down. But there are more rounds slamming into him, into his plates and into his bowels below the plates. He sees the muzzle flashes and takes aim, but a round slices through his remaining good gun hand, severing his thumb. The Sig is slick with his blood and hard to hold, but he keeps firing. Finally the slide locks to the rear—empty.

Nolan slides to the floor and to a sitting position with his back to the dirt wall. Without looking down, he begins to fumble at his ammo pouches for a fresh 9mm mag. Sha-bal hears the slide go back and knows he has this man. He checks his AK quickly to ensure he has at least one more round and moves forward. Nolan's eyes lock on Shabal's as he desperately tries to fit a new magazine into his weapon with his crippled hands. Shabal himself has been hit twice, but he is now focused only on Nolan. This American now represents all his frustrations and his hatreds and his thwarted attempts at retribution. He is now but five feet from the prostrate Nolan; he wants to stand over him when he kills him. Then something like a fist punches into his chest. Then another blow, and another.

Shabal tears his eyes from Nolan and looks down the

dimly lit tunnel. The form of yet another Navy SEAL coalesces around the muzzle flashes. By the time Ray steps into the dimly lit room, Shabal has gone to his knees, his weapon has fallen away. His hatred holds him upright—the hatred and the overwhelming disappointment of what might have been. How did it come to this? Then Ray sends a bullet through his brain, and all is blackness.

Dave Nolan, now a bystander, watches this drama unfold in detached fascination. He's aware of the firing behind him; he sees Shabal drop to his knees and the AK-47 fall from his hands. Yet all is taking place in slow motion. Then it all fades away.

EPILOGUE

It was the final day.

The last week was a blur for Jackie Engel. It began with the SEAL officer in his dress uniform, accompanied by a Navy chaplain, knocking at her door. Then there was the shock and disbelief that Roark had been killed in action. There was the ongoing and continuous support of the entire SEAL family. Julia Nolan was there for her, just as she herself had been there for other SEAL wives who suddenly found themselves widowed. Her parents, then Roark's, flew in from the Midwest. The Navy CACO, or Casualty Assistance Calls Officer, had called on her. He gently and compassionately walked her through the myriad of details involved when a service member dies. It seemed so surreal, yet it *was* happening— and happening to her. But any dreamy denial that this *did* happen ended when the Navy C-130 Hercules aircraft landed at NAS North Island with Roark's body.

There followed the wake at Pinkham-Mitchell Mortuary in Imperial Beach, California, just a short drive from Coronado. And there were the condolence calls from senior SEAL flag officers she had never met. It was a conveyor belt of grief that seemed to never stop. The days seemed to drag by, as did the sleepless nights.

As much as anyone can be prepared for the sudden death of a spouse, Jackie Engel was prepared. More than fifty Navy SEALs had died in action since September 11, 2001, and Jackie had been to many wakes, funerals, and burial services. Several of the men whose wives and families she had consoled had served with Roark in his previous tours. One young wife was only nineteen years old when she became a Team widow. She had been completely inconsolable, and Jackie had taken it upon herself to help the woman deal with her grief. To this day, she considered Jackie to be the big sister she'd never had. Only now did Jackie have some insight into what that young woman had endured, and she understood now how the pain had made her numb.

But as prepared as she was, nothing had readied her for this day. Today she would bury her husband—her Roark. She had steeled herself for this day, or thought she had. She had watched other SEAL widows perform this ritual, but could she? She would have to, she told herself; if nothing else, it was her duty—to her husband and what he had died for. The SEAL family was with her every step of the way. At one point during Roark's wake at Pinkham-Mitchell, she had to console Julia and Dave Nolan's second youngest, three-year-old Maggie, who presented her with a picture she had drawn of Jackie and Roark surfing. As she presented it to her, Maggie had completely broken down, and Jackie had hugged and rocked her for what seemed like an eternity until the girl had fallen asleep in her arms. A wise Julia Nolan did not intervene and let Jackie comfort her daughter for as long as it took.

Now she walked out of the door of their local church in Coronado, Christ Episcopal Church, flanked by her mother and father, and moved toward the car waiting at the curb on the Ninth Street side of Christ Church. Father Geisen's words had been uplifting, and the overflowing crowd of friends, neighbors, and SEAL families listened in respectful silence. Jackie, too, had listened but had heard little.

Just outside the door, the Naval Special Warfare Command commander, Rear Admiral Frank O'Connor, approached her.

"Mrs. Engel, I'll accompany you and your parents in my staff car if that's all right."

"Yes, Admiral, that will be fine. Thank you. You've met my mom and dad earlier this week."

"Sir, ma'am. Your son was one of our finest."

Jackie's parents were only able to utter a quiet, "Thank you."

Admiral O'Connor helped Jackie and her parents into the backseat of the car. The six SEAL pallbearers had already placed Roark's casket in the hearse that would lead the procession. Their destination was Rosecrans National Cemetery, but instead of driving straight to the Coronado Bridge that would take them to San Diego, the hearse turned onto Orange Avenue, Coronado's main boulevard.

Coronado, California, is where every Navy SEAL

begins his training and where many Navy SEALs are stationed. While the San Diego metropolitan area has a large Navy presence of aviation, surface, and subsurface commands, for the small city of Coronado, the bond with the SEALs is an especially close one. This became clear as the procession made its way down Orange Avenue.

Flanked by her mother and father in the back of the staff car, Jackie Engel saw hundreds of Coronado's citizens lining both sides of the avenue. They stood in quiet reverence as a tribute to her fallen husband. Every hundred feet there was a large American flag. At the first intersection, at Orange and Eighth Street, Coronado Police Department cars blocked the intersections on both sides. Jackie quickly realized that they were there to ensure that no other traffic was allowed on Orange Avenue. The city had shut down this morning to honor Lieutenant Roark Engel.

Admiral O'Connor turned around to Jackie and simply said, "They're here to honor Roark and to share in your grief."

When the long line of cars finally did cross the bridge and into San Diego, the admiral again directed the procession onto a local route. The details of the operation Roark had led were still classified. But that didn't prevent the Naval Special Warfare Command and the City of Coronado from telling their neighboring communities of the death of a hero. The funeral procession passed through Barrio Logan, National City, Downtown San Diego, Liberty Station, and Point Loma on its way to Rosecrans National Cemetery. It was said, unofficially, that this SEAL officer had helped to foil a terrorist plot that would have killed thousands of Americans.

The flanking American flags continued all the way down Harbor Drive, past the San Diego International Airport, and into Point Loma. There were American flags along Rosecrans Street, up Canon Street, all along Catalina Boulevard, and all the way to the cemetery. Jackie and her parents were stunned by how this large metropolitan city had turned out to honor a fallen hero—their fallen hero.

The procession of cars, more than eighty of them, arrived at Rosecrans to a scene all-too-familiar to Jackie and to everyone in the SEAL community. The rolling hilltops of Rosecrans National Cemetery were covered with the white sentinels of the dead—wars past and wars ongoing. The gravesite was prepared. The seven SEALs in the honor guard were standing by with their rifles, ready to salute their fallen comrade. A senior Navy chaplain was standing by, ready to render more consoling words. Jackie had seen this so many times before. Yet none of that could make her immune to the crushing and all-but-overwhelming grief she felt at this very moment.

Admiral O'Connor took her arm as he escorted her to her seat while the six SEAL pallbearers carried Roark's coffin from the hearse to the gravesite. The admiral did not flinch as, halfway to her seat, Jackie's knees buckled and she almost lost her footing. He held her up in such a way that no one, not even her parents walking a few steps behind, noticed her unsteadiness. But then, Jackie Engel was not the first SEAL widow this admiral had helped to a graveside service. Inside her, their baby stirred uneasily, as if he somehow knew the father he would never meet was to be lowered into the earth. James Roark

Engel—Roark had requested that if it was a boy, he be named James for his grandfather, whom Roark so admired. And Roark had never known that he was to have a son. Or did he?

Jackie took her seat and sat stoically in the front row of chairs. Her parents, and Roark's, were there to lend support as well as deal with their own deeply personal grief.

"Friends," the chaplain began, "John 15:13 tells us, 'Greater love hath no man than this, that a man lay down his life for his friend' . . ." He spoke loudly, to be heard by the hundreds assembled on the hillside on this bright, crystal-clear, San Diego day. Christ Episcopal Church in Coronado was small, and the many mourners were unable to attend that service. They were all here now.

While the chaplain droned on, Jackie let her eyes survey the scene. There were the military men and women standing ramrod straight. There was Roark's casket, draped with the forty-eight-star American flag that Roark and his grandfather had carried into battle. There were his men from the Bandito Platoon—Weimy, Sonny, Ray, A.J., and, of course, Mikey, with a black patch covering one eye. Standing with them was Senior Chief Otto Miller. And there was Dave Nolan, wheelchair-bound from his injuries but sitting tall. She knew he was there against his doctor's orders, and yet she knew he could not stay away. Nolan, like the other Banditos, was in dress blue uniform.

She heard the chaplain's words, but they were lost on her. She was already planning—planning how to do what she knew Roark wanted and needed her to do. She knew that for the rest of her life, no matter what direction it took, she would somehow bear the full responsibility of ensuring that James grew into a man both she and Roark would be proud of. That was *her* SEAL mission.

She knew she would be up to the task, but she also knew it wouldn't be easy. Yet Roark's teammates would be there to help her. Their wives and their children would be there for her as well. She could also count on Roark's strength and their too-few years together to give her the determination she needed to complete her mission.

Her reverie was broken by the first of three volleys fired by the seven-man honor guard. Then the next, and the next. Jackie, along with many of Roark's brother SEALs, flinched slightly at each of the three volleys. It was impossible not to; it was an emotional reaction, not an auditory one. She was still holding it together, though just barely. And she knew it was almost over.

But as the bugler played taps, slow and sad, Jackie felt a week's worth of emotions welling up inside, almost choking her. She began to tremble involuntarily, no longer sure that she could maintain her composure through the end of the ceremony.

The honor guard approached the casket. In one of the most well-rehearsed and solemn of all military rituals, they folded Roark's flag with care and precision. The senior man in the honor guard took the flag, executed a perfect ninety-degree facing movement, handed the flag to Admiral O'Connor, and saluted. Prior to accepting the flag, the Naval Special Warfare Command commander also saluted. Then with the flag, he walked slowly toward Jackie and dropped to one knee. One hand atop the folded flag, the other on the bottom, he held it out to her.

"On behalf of the president of the United States and the chief of naval operations, please accept this flag as a symbol of our appreciation for your loved one's service to this country and a grateful Navy."

Jackie took the flag and cradled it next to her stomach—forcing it as close to their baby as she could. Tears now streamed down her face. No response was necessary, yet as the admiral stood and again saluted, she met his eyes for a moment before lowering her head. Now, her shaking was becoming visible. Her father on one side and her mother on the other put their arms around her. Roark's parents, sitting behind her, rested their hands on her shoulders.

Jackie Engel somehow reached deep within herself and found a reserve of strength. She sat up straight, looking directly at the casket. She had been to enough of these burial services to know that the next moments were not about her, or her unborn son, or Roark's parents, relatives, and friends, or anyone else. The next several minutes were for the brotherhood. She had been to many SEAL graveside services and knew that what was about to take place didn't happen every time SEALs buried one of their own. Yet, somehow, she knew it would happen today.

Ray wheeled Dave Nolan to the casket of their fallen leader, followed by Sonny, A.J., Weimy, and Mikey. Each in turn, with a swift blow of their hand, hammered their Trident pin into the top of the polished wood of the casket. Then the honor guard of pallbearers did the same.

Then more and more SEALs walked up to the casket and, each in turn, tendered his Trident. Finally, Otto Miller returned to the casket and delivered nine more Tridents—his own and eight others for the Bandito SEALs still on deployment. When the last SEAL pin was rammed into the casket lid, the SEALs all turned, faced the casket a final time, and saluted.

The funeral party began to break up. Some passed close to the casket, others didn't. Those in uniform who did came to attention and saluted. Finally, Jackie stepped to the head of the casket for one last moment with her husband. She touched the wood. Julia Nolan had handed her a single rose, which she laid atop the sea of gold Trident pins. Another quiet moment, then she allowed Admiral O'Connor to escort her back to the staff car. It was over—the service, but not the grieving.

As the crowd began to thin, Chief Dave Nolan asked his wife to wheel him closer to the casket so he could be alone with his officer. She knew her husband well enough to understand that he needed time alone with the man he so greatly admired. She took their two oldest children, the two old enough to attend the service, off to another section of the hillside.

After several moments of silence, he began in a quiet voice. "Boss, you know I wanted to take that grenade instead of you. How did you get there so quickly? You always did run my ass because I was so damn slow, and now it played out in the worst possible way. But then again, you always were a step ahead of all of us; that's what made you the best officer, the best man, I've ever known. As long as I live, I'll never be able to get over feeling that I let you down. All I can do now is to try and make up for it. I'll do what I can for Jackie and James. I'll take care of our men—our brothers by different mothers. You have my word on it. And I'll think of you every day of my life."

He wiped away a tear with his one good hand. Dave Nolan, the doctors at Balboa Naval Hospital all agreed, was something of a living medical miracle. In addition to a load of shrapnel from the grenade, he had taken twenty-seven bullets. Luckily, none to the head, and those to his torso, the ones that would have been kill shots, had been absorbed by his body armor. But he had still taken a lot of bullets.

"Safe journey my friend." Nolan paused, then continued in a softer voice. "Before you died, you gave me this reading by Tecumseh for your kid—just in case. At the time I told you that I'd make it into a paper airplane, that you'd be there to say these words yourself." Nolan then chuckled to himself as he recalled their talking about it, even though it hurt to do so. "That's not all I said I'd do with it, but that was then. Now I'll complete the mission and do as you asked. I'll give it to Jackie, but I'm going to keep a copy. In a few years, James and I will sit down and read it together. We'll have a talk about old Tecumseh, and we'll have a talk about you as well."

The last of the mourners drifted away. Most sensed that Dave Nolan and Roark Engel needed to be alone and gave them a wide berth. Yet one man walked quietly up to the casket and the man in the wheelchair.

"Admiral," Nolan said, as Admiral Burt Jackson approached. Jackson had been their operational commander and had sent the Bandito Platoon into action. There is a special sense of loss known only to those who must give the orders that send other men off to die. Unfortunately, Jackson was no stranger to this sense of loss and grief.

"Chief. We lost a true hero, and I know you lost a friend. Thank you for all you did for him, and all you've done for the Teams. I understand you want to return to duty as soon as you're fit. We'll be blessed to have you back."

"Thank you, Admiral."

They were silent for several minutes until Jackson again spoke. "Tell me something, Chief. He had an honored place waiting for him in Arlington. Why here?"

"He wanted to be near Jackie and the Teams."

Jackson nodded, and the two waited in silence for a few moments longer. Then the admiral moved down the hill, leaving Nolan alone with his SEAL brother.

Ten months after Roark's death, Jackie was having a light breakfast while Jimmy was scattering his Cheerios about his high chair and onto the kitchen floor. It had soon become clear to everyone that James was much too confining for this boy; he was now called Jimmy. She was thinking about making a change, perhaps a move to a bigger city where there was a demand for her professional skills. Maybe to New York or L.A. She wondered what it might be like to be just another single mother. But at the end of the day, she knew she would do none of those things. For now, she knew she would stay here, to be near Roark and those who had been a part of their lives back when he was alive. The SEALs, the SEAL wives, and the command had all been so good to her.

Yet she often wondered what it would be like to be away from it all and to not be a SEAL widow—one of the SEAL widows.

She stood up, hesitated, then walked into their small living room. There she reached up to their fireplace mantel and unfolded the last letter Roark had written, the one to his unborn son. It was the letter Dave Nolan had folded into the shape of a paper airplane almost a year ago. She unfolded it gingerly, carefully, just as she had so many times before. And each time she unfolded it, she read it to Jimmy. Each time she did, she somehow sensed that he understood the words. At least she wanted to think he did. She cleared her throat, looked into his blue eyes, and read what Tecumseh had said over two centuries ago and what Jimmy's father had written to him—to the both of them.

Live your life that the fear of death never enters your heart. Trouble no one about his religion. Respect others in their views and demand they respect yours. Love your life, perfect your life, and beautify all things in your life. Seek to make your life long and of service to your people. When your time comes to die, be not like those whose hearts are filled with fear of death, so that when their time comes they weep and pray for a little more time to live their lives over again in a different way. Sing your death song, and die like a hero going home.

Jackie paused a moment and looked at Jimmy. He smiled, spit up a few Cheerios, and smiled again. And she knew that Roark's words were reaching his son.

Jackie Engel carefully folded the letter and returned it to the mantel. There she placed it atop a folded American flag. The flag was flanked by a shadow box displaying Roark's military medals and decorations. There on the other side of the flag was a similar display of his grandfather's military achievements. Somehow she knew that the warrior legacy would not skip a generation this time.

DICK COUCH served as a surface warfare officer aboard a Navy destroyer and as a platoon officer with Underwater Demolition Team 22 and SEAL Team One. While with Team One, he led one of the only successful POW rescue operations of the Vietnam War. He has served as a maritime case officer with the CIA, has been an adjunct professor of ethics at the U.S. Naval Academy, and has been an ethics advisor with U.S. Special Operations Command. Dick began his professional writing career in 1990. His novels include *SEAL Team One*, *Pressure Point*, *Silent Descent*, *Rising Wind*, *The Mercenary Option*, and *Covert Action*. His nonfiction works include *The Warrior Elite*, *The Finishing School*, *Down Range*, *Chosen Soldier*, *The Sheriff of Ramadi*, and *A Tactical Ethic*. Scheduled for release in June 2012 is his latest work of nonfiction: *Sua Sponte: The Forging of a Modern American Ranger*. Dick and his wife, Julia, live in Central Idaho.

CAPTAIN GEORGE GALDORISI, U.S. NAVY (RETIRED), spent a thirty-year career as a naval aviator, including commanding officer tours of two helicopter squadrons (HSL-41 and HSL-43), the USS *Cleveland* (LPD-7), and Amphibious Squadron Seven. His last operational assignment spanned five years as chief of staff for

Cruiser-Destroyer Group Three, where he made combat deployments to the Western Pacific and Arabian Gulf, embarked in the USS *Carl Vinson* and the USS *Abraham Lincoln*. Subsequent to his Navy career, he was a senior advisor with the Center for Security Strategy and Operations in Washington, D.C., where he was involved in Navy and Marine Corps strategy and policy formulation. He has written two previous novels; four works of nonfiction, including a definitive study of the history of combat search and rescue entitled *Leave No Man Behind*; and more than two hundred articles in professional journals, newspapers, and conference proceedings. He and his wife, Becky, live in Coronado, California (home of the Naval Special Warfare Command). He works as a senior analyst for the Department of the Navy.